DATE DUE

920
F

Faber, Doris.

American government

GREAT LIVES
American Government

American Government
GREAT LIVES

Doris and Harold Faber

Atheneum Books for Young Readers

Atheneum Books for Young Readers
An imprint of Simon & Schuster Children's Publishing Division
1230 Avenue of the Americas, New York, New York 10020

Printed in the United States of America

10   9   8   7   6   5

Library of Congress Cataloging-in-Publication Data

Faber, Doris, date.
    Great lives: American government/Doris and Harold Faber.
        p.   cm.   Bibliography: p. 265   Includes index.
        Summary: Relates the life stories of thirty-six significant individuals who held important
public offices and contributed to the development of the United States from the Declaration
of Independence to the nuclear age, including presidents, judges, leaders of the national
legislature, and female and minority leaders.   ISBN 0-684-18521-0
        1. Statesmen—United States—Biography—Juvenile literature.
        2. Presidents—United States—Biography—Juvenile literature.
        3. United States—Biography—Juvenile literature.
        4. United States—Politics and government—Juvenile literature.
        [1. Statesmen. 2. Presidents. 3. United States—Politics and government.]
        I. Faber, Harold. II. Title.   E176.F17 1988   973'.09'92—dc 19
        [B] [920] 88-4968 CIP AC

Contents

Foreword

Any reader glancing at our table of contents may wonder how we selected
the thirty-six men and women whose life stories are related in this book.
It was not an easy process. To start with, we decided that only individuals who
had actually held an important public office would be included. Yet even though
this restriction simplified our selection task to some extent, it also raised a major
problem concerning Presidents of the United States.

Without question, any list of outstanding figures in American government since
the nation's founding would have to include such names as George Washington
and Abraham Lincoln and Franklin D. Roosevelt. Indeed, a good case could be
made for including every chief executive. After all, just forty men have so far
been elected to the country's highest office, which surely raises even the least of
them far above the common herd of officeholders.

Still, our purpose was not to write a book solely about Presidents. Given the
limited space available to us, we felt that the best policy would be to choose only
the most notable of the chief executives, leaving room for a variety of other major
figures down through the years.

So we set out to pick three dozen names from among hundreds of possibilities—
an absorbing game we played during weeks of preliminary research. Several factors
influenced us as we kept jotting down or crossing out potential subjects for our
chapters.

First, we wanted to cover the whole sweep of American history from the Declaration of Independence to the nuclear age of today. But there were giants among the Founding Fathers, and the stature of many leaders in other periods seems minimized when they must be measured against Benjamin Franklin or Thomas Jefferson. Thus, to avoid unfair comparisons as much as we could, we divided the two centuries into four separate time frames; for each period we chose about the same number of significant figures.

Besides seeking a balance between past and present, we aimed for a balance between various kinds of contributions. Because so many of our Presidents have been exceptional in one way or another, many of our subjects—sixteen, to be precise—held the nation's top office. Yet we have included outstanding judges, too, along with leaders from both branches of the national legislature.

But we certainly tried not to give undue weight to the upholders of any particular political outlook. Nor did we automatically omit some controversial figures who may strike many readers as less than heroic. We selected Jefferson Davis and Richard Nixon, to name two in this category, because we believed their negative impact on the nation could not be ignored.

Although we had to recognize the preeminence of white males in governmental positions of importance, we tried to show the emergence of female and minority leadership during the last half century. Toward that end, we perhaps stretched our rules by including Eleanor Roosevelt, whose renown rests on her twelve years in the unofficial post of First Lady. Yet her influence over public affairs during this period was so extraordinary that we felt justified in making an exception in her case, particularly since she did cap her career by serving as a member of the United States delegation to the United Nations.

Similarly, our inclusion of some lesser-known figures, such as Albert Gallatin, George Norris, Jeannette Rankin, and Margaret Chase Smith, may be open to question. Even if their contributions have not won them lasting renown, however, it seems to us that their impact on their own day makes them fitting subjects for contemporary notice.

Sometimes, in fact, the nearly forgotten have had more of an effect on the nation's course than more celebrated figures. Justin Morrill, for instance, by sponsoring legislation to establish land-grant colleges, has affected the life of anyone who ever attended a state university founded under the provisions of that legislation. It would be impossible to measure the enormous debt this country owes him for his educational leadership.

Many readers may dispute the validity of some of our selections or wish we had not overlooked other figures they admire. Quarrel with our selections, by all means; we invite you to do so and to draw up your own list. We think you'll find this an exhilarating exercise in the study of American history.

D. F. and H. F.

PART I

The Founding Fathers

John Adams

1735–1826   Second President of the United States.

After John Adams graduated from Harvard College in 1755, the only work he could find was that of a schoolteacher in Worcester, Massachusetts, about fifty miles from his home near Boston. He hated the job.

Fifty boys ranging in age from five to fifteen came to his one-room schoolhouse every day. They sensed that he knew nothing about teaching and made his life miserable. He wanted desperately to escape from them, but what else could he do?

On a warm day in May, he noticed unusual activity around the local courthouse. Refreshment booths sprang up on the village green. Saddled horses stood tied up in rows before the tavern. Lawyers from all over the state had crowded into Worcester for the opening of the law courts. A school holiday was declared, leaving Adams free to go to court and listen to the lawyers arguing before the judge. Sitting there, he felt himself taking part in the arguments. He made up his mind: He would become a lawyer.

It was a big step up for the son of a farmer. He had been born in Braintree, Massachusetts, on October 30, 1735. As a boy, he liked the hard work on the farm, but his family was determined that he would have a college education, so he mastered Latin to pass the entrance exam for Harvard.

In those days there were no schools for studying law. After deciding on this profession, Adams became an apprentice to a man who already was a lawyer. He copied legal papers, read law books,

John Adams was President when he sat for this portrait by Gilbert Stuart, the most famous American painter of his day. *Courtesy of the National Gallery of Art, Washington; gift of Mrs. Robert Homans*.

attended court sessions, and talked about cases. He learned enough so that he was admitted to the bar as a lawyer in Boston in 1758.

At the age of twenty-three, Adams was impatient and ambitious. He was blunt in speech and serious in his belief that laws were made to protect people. He argued cases about boundary lines and wandering horses that ate grass in a neighbor's field. More and more people came to seek his help.

As his career progressed, he began to think of marriage. He fell in and out of love frequently as he courted the young women of the area, but his wandering stopped when he met Abigail Smith, the daughter of a local minister. She was seventeen years old, he was twenty-six.

One day when he came to call, he noticed her reading a book. "A big book for such a little head," he said. "You think so," she replied. And then she went on. "Girls are not to know anything, I am told, beyond kitchen and parlor. Yet girls, too, may have their curiosity. And even a little head, Mr. Adams, may possess a longing for knowledge, or at least for understanding."

They were married on October 25, 1764. Their marriage became one of the most remarkable in American history. Not only did Abigail Adams' hus-

Abigail Adams was the wife of one President and the mother of another. Portrait by Gilbert Stuart. *Courtesy of the National Gallery of Art, Washington; gift of Mrs. Robert Homans.*

band become President of the United States, but so did one of their sons. Moreover, Mrs. Adams was a keen observer of events and her letters give a vivid picture of the political life of her times.

They were exciting times: the days of the American Revolution, then the founding of the United States. And the Adams family was right in the middle of the excitement as the new nation grew out of the thirteen English colonies on the Atlantic coast.

Adams became involved in the struggle when the British passed the Stamp Act of 1765. This law required Americans to buy stamps to affix to all sorts of items—newspapers, wills, legal documents, and even playing cards. The American colonists protested that this was taxation without representation. They blocked the customs house in Boston to prevent distribution of the stamps.

But Adams had a different and more powerful weapon—British law itself. He wrote a long series of articles for a local newspaper to show that the Stamp Act was illegal. In those and other articles over a period of years, he set out legal arguments that led to a logical conclusion—independence.

Adams' belief that the law was a protection for all people was tested in an unusual way in 1770 when British soldiers fired on a mob throwing rocks and shouting insults at them. Even

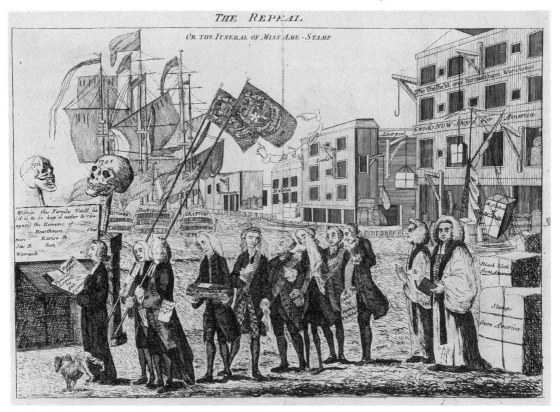

Colonial outrage forced Britain to repeal the Stamp Act—the subject of this contemporary woodcut. *Courtesy of the Library of Congress.*

though only five people were killed, this action became known as the Boston Massacre.

The British commander, Captain Thomas Preston, could not find a lawyer to defend him against a charge of murder. One of his supporters came to Adams and pleaded for help. Adams did not hesitate. "If Captain Preston thinks he cannot have a fair trial without help, he shall have it," he said.

Adams pleaded self-defense for Preston and won his acquittal. He was surprised to find that the people of Boston, who were so angry with the British, did not hold that victory against him. They admired his courage in fighting for the rights of an enemy and elected Adams to the colonial assembly.

As the conflict between the British and the colonies grew, Adams was also elected to the first Continental Congress meeting in Philadelphia. "You will ruin your career," one of his friends warned.

Adams replied, "Sink or swim, survive or perish, I am with my country from this day forward." In later years, many people called him Old Sink or Swim because of that statement.

At the Continental Congress in 1774 and 1775, Adams was one of the strongest supporters of independence. He nominated George Washington to command a new American army. This was

to show that the thirteen colonies could act as one and that Massachusetts would fight under a leader from Virginia.

During the early days of the Revolutionary War, Adams served on so many committees of Congress that he was, in effect, the Secretary of War. Then Congress decided that he could be more valuable abroad, seeking friends, arms, and money from foreign countries.

At first, in 1778, he was minister to France. Then he served in Holland, raising a large loan of money from that country. Later he went back to France and, together with Benjamin Franklin and John Jay, negotiated the treaty of peace with England in 1783 that ended the Revolutionary War.

Through those lonely years, John Adams had kept in touch with his wife and children by letter. But now he wrote to his wife, "I cannot be happy or tolerable without you." She joined him in London when he became the first United States minister there.

While the Adamses were in London, one of their closest friends, Thomas Jefferson, was minister to France. Adams and Jefferson wrote to each other and helped each other in many ways. Mrs. Adams ordered shirts in London for Jefferson, whose wife had died many years earlier. He bought shoes for her in Paris. She asked Jefferson to buy figurines for her London dining room. He

In 1770, Paul Revere made this engraving of the Boston Massacre. *Courtesy of the Library of Congress, Batchelder Collection.*

asked her to send tablecloths for his home in Paris.

The Adamses returned to Boston in 1788. In the new government that was formed the following year, Washington became the nation's first President as had been expected. Because Adams had received the next highest total of electoral votes, he became the first Vice-President. He took the oath of office in New York on April 21, 1789.

Being Vice-President was a disappointment to the outspoken, ambitious Adams. He wrote to his wife that the vice-presidency was "the most insignificant office that ever the invention of man contrived or his imagination conceived."

In office, Adams was not easy to get along with. He was now in his fifties, medium-sized, slightly plump, and pompous in speech. Behind his back, some of the Senators made fun of him, calling him His Rotundity, a reference to his stoutness and his habit of lecturing them.

When Washington was reelected in 1792, so was Adams. His chance to become President came in 1796, the year of the first partisan election for the nation's highest office. In this contest, two old friends who disagreed politically ran against each other.

As Washington's heir, Adams was the nominee of the Federalist party. His opponent was Jefferson, the candidate of the Democratic-Republican party. Adams won a close election, with seventy-one electoral votes to Jefferson's sixty-eight.

Adams was sworn into office as the second President on March 4, 1797, in Philadelphia. Most of the crowd's cheers were for the departing Washington, however. Adams wrote to his wife, "Me thought I heard him say, 'Ay, I am fairly out and you fairly in! See which one of us will be the happier!'"

From the beginning, Adams' term of office was marked by trouble. The most serious threat came from abroad, when a war with France seemed to be at hand. Adams asked Washington to return to duty to command a new army, if needed. A Department of the Navy was organized and new warships were built.

In fact, American and French ships did fight at sea. Some historians have called that period "the quasi war," because battles were fought even though war was not declared. Many of Adams' own party, led by Alexander Hamilton, wanted a full-scale war, but the Jeffersonians opposed it.

The divisions at home were made worse by two new laws, the Alien and Sedition Acts. Under the Alien Act, the President could expel any foreigner he considered dangerous. The Sedition

Act provided fines or jail sentences for any false or critical writing about the President or Congress. The Jeffersonians were furious at what they saw as unconstitutional laws aimed at them.

Despite those strong measures, Adams was determined to make peace with France. Over the objections of Hamilton and his own party, he sent a series of ambassadors to France to work out an agreement. They finally brought back a treaty of friendship in 1800. Adams considered that keeping the peace was his greatest achievement in office, even though his support of the controversial treaty cost him reelection to the presidency.

In that same year of 1800, the national capital moved to the new city of Washington. Adams became the first President to occupy the executive mansion later known as the White House, moving in on November 1, 1800. In a letter to his wife, he wrote, "I pray heaven to bestow the best blessings on this House and all that shall hereafter inhabit it. May none but honest and wise men ever rule under this roof."

Adams was defeated for reelection later that year, losing to Jefferson. Bitter at his defeat, he left Washington without attending the inauguration of his former friend. He returned to his farm in Quincy, Massachusetts.

After Jefferson's retirement from the presidency, the two men resumed their old friendship, writing each other letters. Jefferson was sympathetic when Abigail Adams died in 1818, and he shared in Adams' pride when his son, John Quincy Adams, became President in 1825.

Adams died at the age of ninety-one in Quincy on July 4, 1826, the fiftieth anniversary of the adoption of the Declaration of Independence. By an amazing coincidence, Jefferson, his associate in adopting the Declaration, died on the same day.

Benjamin Franklin

1706–1790   Diplomat; participant in drafting of the Declaration of Independence and the U.S. Constitution.

It's possible that Benjamin Franklin never did his country a greater service than just being himself over in Europe. Good-humored and shrewd, with an amazing range of talents, he made even the King of France feel a certain amount of awe. If America could produce a man like this—why, the new United States must be taken seriously.

To sum up Franklin's career is not easy. Journalist, scientist, inventor, he also gave his best efforts to an almost unbelievable variety of public service. As a young man, he founded Philadelphia's first fire company. In his old age, he helped to negotiate the peace treaty that ended the Revolutionary War.

In between, Franklin never stopped amusing and inspiring his fellow citizens. Many of his sayings are still repeated; for instance:

> Early to bed and early to rise,
> Makes a man healthy, wealthy,
> and wise.

Still, it was Ben Franklin's personal example that probably did the most to make him famous. Well before thirteen separate colonies became the United States, he had already proved there was no limit to what a poor boy could accomplish in the New World. In effect, his own life was the first American success story.

Born in Boston, on January 17, 1706, he was the youngest son of Josiah Franklin, a candlemaker. About twenty-five years earlier, Josiah had left England hoping for a better life across the ocean. As far as anybody could remember, his family had been hardworking folk who barely managed to pay their cottage rent.

But Ben's mother gave her son at least a slightly literary background. Abiah Folger had grown up on the island of Nantucket, the daughter of an early settler who wrote verses besides being a teacher, surveyor, and town clerk. She raised five children left motherless by the death of Josiah's first wife, in addition to bearing ten more children herself.

So the little house on Milk Street, where the Franklins lived above their candle shop, could hardly have been busier and more crowded. Yet Ben's loving parents noticed very soon that their last son seemed extremely bright.

During his schooldays, he was full of ideas. One summer afternoon when a group of boys went swimming in a pond, Ben brought along a kite—and tried a trick that made him especially fond of kites from then on.

As he lay floating on his back, the notion of using the kite as a sail popped into his head. After getting the string, he carried it with him into the water, lay on his back and, as he recalled long afterward, "I was drawn along the surface of the water in a very agreeable manner." The pond was a mile wide and Ben sailed the whole distance, landing on the other side in great high spirits.

His father thought that a boy with such a lively mind would make a good minister, but he could not afford to keep him at school. When Ben was only ten, he had to give up school and learn how to mold candles.

The work bored him terribly. Soon he began talking about running off to be a sailor, as one of his older brothers had done. Then his father worried enough to arrange a different future for him.

At the age of twelve, Ben went to work for his older brother James as a printer's helper. Throughout his long life, nothing else that happened to him was as important as his start in the printing trade. It suited him perfectly.

He thoroughly enjoyed the task of placing in trays the tiny metal letters that would be inked to produce pages of printed words. And now he could do plenty of reading. By the time he was fifteen, Ben also began doing some writing.

Franklin's employer published one of Boston's early newspapers. Ben suspected that anything written by someone as young as he would simply be ignored, so he slipped his first compositions under the door as if a stranger had left them there. He signed these essays Silence Do-Good, pretending he was an old widow living quietly in the country.

No matter that these early works

were rather wordy; they had a humorous tone and people liked reading them. Ben was delighted, except for a big problem. He found it increasingly difficult to get along with his brother James, who had quite a hot temper. One day when Ben was seventeen, he made up his mind to run away and find work in another city.

Much later, when the mature Franklin got around to writing his *Autobiography,* he cheerfully described how he arrived, nearly penniless, in Philadelphia. It was 1723, and the Quaker settlement had only about 10,000 residents. In fewer than ten years the runaway youth became a leading citizen.

Before settling down there, however, Franklin sailed to England and spent eighteen happy months as a printer in the great city of London. On returning to Philadelphia, he married his landlady's daughter, a good-hearted girl named Deborah Read. With his gift for making friends, he soon found a well-off backer who lent him money to set up his own printing house.

Then Franklin not only began putting out his own newspaper, the Pennsylvania *Gazette.* In the autumn of 1732, he published the first issue of *Poor Richard's Almanack*—and *Poor Richard* made his creator rich.

Throughout the colonies, most families had hardly any reading material in their homes. Even before Franklin launched his publication, some printers had thought of selling a yearly calendar, with facts about the moon and tides, along with guesses about what the weather might be. But Franklin added a new ingredient.

Cannily, he made up the character he called Poor Richard to give his *Almanack* a special flavor. This imaginary fellow had a mind filled with all sorts of sayings that fit neatly into little gaps on the *Almanack's* pages. "It is hard for an empty sack to stand upright," Poor Richard said. Or, in a lighter mood, "Fish and visitors smell in three days."

Published once a year for twenty-five years, Franklin's almanac earned him a comfortable fortune. Of course, it was widely understood that Poor Richard was none other than Ben Franklin himself. But even while he was so busily involved with his printing and writing, he still found time for other activities that brought him fame in other directions.

Since Franklin was tremendously curious about everything, he taught himself French, Italian, and Spanish in order to study books in these languages. Then he began concentrating on scientific subjects. In 1742, at the age of thirty-six, he worked out detailed plans for an improved heating stove that could warm a room with only one-fourth of the wood used by a conventional fire-place.

The same interest in solving scientific puzzles led to Franklin's experiments with electricity. Around 1750, the idea that flashes of lightning during a thunderstorm were really electricity occurred to several men. But it was Franklin who proved it—by his celebrated experiment of flying a kite one stormy afternoon in the summer of 1752.

Raising his kite right into a storm cloud, Franklin observed the loose wisps of the kite's string suddenly standing out like a line of tiny soldiers, drawn by the electrical charge above them. Such a simple experiment may not sound very important two centuries later, but at the time it fascinated everyone who heard about it.

After Franklin wrote to some foreign friends about his successful test, he was

In 1876, the famous American lithographers Currier and Ives published this work commemorating Benjamin Franklin's experimental use of a kite to test lightning for electricity. *Courtesy of the Library of Congress*.

made a member of Britain's Royal Academy, a group of outstanding scientists. Later he received diplomas from several universities, honoring him as a doctor of science. That was why he was often referred to from then on as Dr. Franklin.

A few years before Franklin's kite-flying attracted such attention, he had retired from his printing business, intending to spend the rest of his life on scientific studies. Soon, though, the call to public service made him put everything else aside.

Even during his busiest years as a journalist, Franklin had always been starting a library or a hospital. He had personally designed better streetlights and worked on improving the delivery of mail between his own colony and its neighbors.

In 1754 the French and Indian War made defense of the colonies an urgent issue. Franklin was appointed one of Pennsylvania's representatives to a meeting in Albany, New York, attended by delegates from New England to Georgia. This marked Benjamin Franklin's debut on a wider stage.

At Albany, he proposed a plan for a loose sort of union of all thirteen colonies so they could deal more effectively with common problems like fighting hostile Indians. "Join or Die" was the message on a cartoon he drew to support his idea. But the British saw danger to their own rule if such a scheme were adopted, and nothing came of it.

From then on, though, one issue after another brought the colonies further along the path to independence. During the next thirty years, Franklin played a major role in many of the great events that led to the birth of the United States.

While he was in London as the "agent" of Pennsylvania's colonial legislature, American protests against the Stamp Act began alarming the British government. Thus it happened that for two days in February of 1766 Franklin stood up in the British Parliament and answered 174 questions about why the Stamp Act was so hated. His skillful defense of American rights made a strong impression on both sides of the ocean.

Home again in 1775, Franklin was elected to the Continental Congress. The following year, he served on the committee that drafted the Declaration of Independence. At the ceremony signing the Declaration, he came out with one of his most notable quips: "We must all hang together, or assuredly we shall all hang separately."

Although Franklin was seventy years old in 1776, he served the next seven years as America's minister to France. He was so popular there that some his-

BENJAMIN FRANKLIN
Né à Boston, dans la nouvelle Angleterre, le 17 Janv. 1706.

Honneur du nouveau monde et de l'humanité,
Ce Sage aimable et vrai les guide et les éclaire;
Comme un autre Mentor, il cache à l'œil vulgaire,
Sous les traits d'un mortel, une divinité. Par M. Feutry.

Justus Cevillet engraved this portrait of Benjamin Franklin sometime between 1778 and 1784. *Courtesy of the National Portrait Gallery, Smithsonian Institution.*

torians say he deserves much of the credit for the French decision to help the American cause.

After remaining abroad to help John Adams and John Jay negotiate the peace treaty that officially ended the Revolution in 1783, Franklin was welcomed home with pealing church bells. Loved by his fellow citizens even more than he was admired, Franklin was not permitted to retire. For three years, he was president of Pennsylvania's governing council. As a grand old man of eighty-one, he calmed many tempers at the convention that wrote the American Constitution in 1787.

A few months after his eighty-fourth birthday, on April 17, 1790, Franklin died.

He was survived by several grandchildren, his married daughter, and a son who had caused him much sorrow. William Franklin, having risen to be the last royal governor of New Jersey, then turned Tory and spent the Revolution behind bars as a traitor. Franklin forgave him but did not attempt to dissuade him from settling permanently in England after his release from prison.

Albert Gallatin

1761–1849   U.S. Congressman; Secretary of the Treasury.

During George Washington's second term as President a tax was imposed on the making of whiskey in order to help pay the expenses of the new federal government. That brought about an uprising in the mountains of western Pennsylvania—and people were soon calling this the Whiskey Rebellion.

Parties of armed men rode about, threatening law and order. Faced with a growing revolt, Washington decided he must send troops to the area. Before they arrived, the tide had already been turned at a tense meeting of local citizens.

A leader of the rebels, seeking support for the cause, boldly admitted that a barn owned by a farmer not in favor of the resistance had been burned.

"It was well done!" one of his friends called out.

"No," said a man who looked as if he might be more at home in Europe than on the western frontier, "it was *not* well done."

Albert Gallatin proceeded then to speak up forcefully against any further violence. Even though he spoke English with a foreign accent, he spoke so convincingly that, in the words of one historian, "he saved western Pennsylvania from a civil war."

Over a period of forty years, Gallatin contributed in many other ways to strengthening the government of the young United States. If not for his birth across the Atlantic—which, by the terms of the American Constitution, barred him from the highest office in

18

his adopted land—he might have been one of the country's most notable Presidents. As it was, he became the first of a long line of European newcomers who had a major impact on the conduct of public affairs in their adopted land.

Abraham Alfonse Albert Gallatin had been born on January 29, 1761, in the city of Geneva, later part of Switzerland. At that time, it was an independent city-state with an unusual standing. Very close to France, which was ruled by powerful kings, Geneva used the French language but was a self-governing republic that had developed a high-minded culture of its own.

A few old families in Geneva held a special status—and none were prouder than the Gallatins. They claimed they could trace their ancestors back to the top public officials in ancient Rome, more than 1500 years earlier. Fortunate as he was in some ways, though, young Albert did not have an easy childhood.

When he was only four, his father died. At the age of nine, he lost his mother, too. From then on, his mother's closest friend and his strong-willed grandparents took charge of his upbringing. Geneva was known for its excellent schools, and Albert was given every educational advantage.

A good student, thoughtful and well-mannered, he seemed set on the right path toward becoming a respected mer-

chant like his father. Yet the boy was not really as contented as he appeared to be. At the Geneva Academy, a fine college, he gave the first signs of how he felt.

He distressed his strictly proper grandparents by joining a group of students inspired by a famous French writer, Jean Jacques Rousseau, whose ideas struck many solid citizens as nonsense. Rousseau insisted that people would be much happier if they gave up the complications of busy towns and returned to the "natural" life of earlier times.

Young Gallatin and his friends had a particular reason for taking Rousseau seriously. While they were at the academy, a grand drama was being enacted across the ocean in the New World. There Great Britain's American colonies had issued a stirring Declaration of Independence and then begun fighting a war to gain their freedom.

With only the haziest notion of what the American wilderness was like, Gallatin felt sure he would prefer America to Geneva. In 1779, when he graduated, his grandmother decided he would change his mind if he saw what hardships were involved.

One of her friends was the head of a German kingdom, who had hired out his own troops to help the British defeat the rebels. She arranged for Albert to receive an offer to join the Hessians as a lieutenant colonel.

The idealistic young man refused—he had no wish to fight—but his grandmother's plan made him realize that he certainly did want to try his luck in the wilderness. With one of his former classmates, he set out bravely during the spring of 1780, when he was barely nineteen.

They landed near Boston with very little money and hardly any knowledge of the English language. In the next several years, Gallatin's friend got sick and faded out of the picture—but Gallatin himself proved amazingly resourceful.

He managed to get a post teaching French at Harvard College and soon met a Frenchman who had acquired a large tract of land in western Virginia and Pennsylvania. When Gallatin was offered one-fourth of the property in exchange for personally surveying it and taking charge of selling plots to people eager to move westward, he jumped at the opportunity.

That was how he happened to be in western Pennsylvania when the Whiskey Rebellion erupted in the summer of 1794. By then he was thirty-three, and he had crammed quite a variety of experience into the fourteen years since his arrival in America.

One tragedy had almost made him give up and go back to Geneva. When he was twenty-three, his land business had obliged him to spend some time in Virginia's capital city of Richmond. There he fell in love with the daughter of the woman who kept the boarding-house where he was staying. His beautiful Sophia married him but, a few months after they went west together, she caught a fever and died.

Instead of returning to Europe, as the sorrowing young widower first vowed he would, he got caught up in local politics. A few years later he was elected to Pennsylvania's legislature, and his obvious talent quickly made him stand out. As he himself said, "I enjoyed an extraordinary influence. . . . I was put on thirty-five committees, prepared all their reports and drew all their bills."

His success as a lawmaker in Philadelphia was especially marked because Gallatin strongly supported the political party that was favored by only a minority of the state's voters. The majority backed President Washington's Federalists, who stood for a strong central government. But Gallatin's personal convictions, and his position as a representative of liberty-loving Westerners, made him a warm partisan of the Democratic-Republicans led by Thomas Jefferson.

While serving in the Pennsylvania legislature, Gallatin met a young

Albert Gallatin might have been President had he been born in the United States. Portrait by Thomas Worthington Whittredge. *Courtesy of the National Portrait Gallery, Smithsonian Institution.*

woman whose family had many important political connections. Hannah
Nicholson's father and uncles had risen
to high ranks in the American Navy
during the Revolution, and three of her
sisters were married to members of the
national Congress.

After Gallatin married her—and after
he attracted wide attention for his
peacemaking efforts in the Whiskey Rebellion—he, too, was elected to the
national House of Representatives.
During three terms there, his exceptional mind and his willingness to work
hard won him the position of leader
of the Jeffersonians.

Gallatin's special interest lay in the
field of finance. When Jefferson became
President in 1801, nobody was surprised by his announcement that Gallatin would be his Secretary of the
Treasury. Still, many people were surprised to see what an important part
Gallatin played during Jefferson's two
terms and then in the same post under
Jefferson's successor, President Madison.

Even in those days, the size of the
national debt was a major political issue.
By extremely careful management, Gallatin reduced the debt from $80 million
to only $45 million in ten years. Experts
agree that if not for the heavy expenses
arising from the War of 1812, he almost
surely would have succeeded in his

aim of completely paying off the debt.

Still, it was by proposing to spend a
substantial amount of money that Gallatin won even more popularity. Although a basic principle of Jeffersonian
democracy was that the less a government did, the better off its citizens
would be, Jefferson's Secretary of the
Treasury worked out a bold new plan
for "internal improvements" that hardly
any voters found fault with.

Gallatin suggested that by using
funds gained from selling government-
owned western land to would-be settlers, a network of new roads and canals
could be built, linking remote areas
with more populated parts of the country. Besides being a great convenience,
better routes would stimulate trade between distant sections.

This ambitious program began with
the construction of the so-called National Road from Maryland westward
through the Cumberland Gap of the
Allegheny Mountains. Again, the War
of 1812 interfered, so the rest of Gallatin's plan had to be abandoned, but his
popularity among people in outlying
districts resulted in a number of new
townships or counties being named after him.

Despite his disappointment, Gallatin
used the war to embark on a whole
new phase of public service. President
Madison appointed him, at his own re-

quest, to the commission charged with making peace terms with the British. These difficult negotiations ended on Christmas Eve, 1814, with the signing of the Treaty of Ghent, named for the Belgian seaport where British and American negotiating teams finally reached an agreement.

The other members of the American commission agreed that Gallatin's patience and grasp of complicated issues were the main factors leading to a comparatively favorable outcome for the United States. When he returned home, Gallatin was rewarded with another foreign assignment: minister to France.

Gallatin spent seven happy years representing American interests in Paris, then another year conducting delicate trade negotiations in London. But as much as he enjoyed life in these cities that reminded him of his youth, the pull of the wilderness drew him back to western Pennsylvania in 1823. On his property there, he built a fine stone house he called Friendship Hill.

However, the area was still too remote to suit his wife. She longed to be closer to their three children and grandchildren. After a year, Gallatin pleased her by moving to New York City.

Although retired from public service, he kept very busy. For a time he was president of a bank, and he wrote several books about money matters. He also helped to found the University of the City of New York.

Gallatin's main interest in his vigorous old age was the study of the languages of American Indian tribes. One of the first to delve into this subject, he founded a group of specialists called the American Ethnological Society and won acclaim as "the father of American ethnology," the science dealing with the culture of native American peoples.

Until Gallatin passed his eighty-sixth birthday, he remained active and in sturdy good health, but after the death of his wife he began failing, too. At the age of eighty-eight, in the New York home of his married daughter, he died on August 12, 1849.

Alexander Hamilton

1757–1804   Secretary of the Treasury.

A crowd gathered on the town green in New York City on July 6, 1774, to listen to arguments about the major topic of the day: Should New York send representatives to the new Continental Congress called to meet in Philadelphia?

Toward the back of the crowd stood a seventeen-year-old college student. He was not impressed by the orators. Impatiently he pushed his way forward and began to speak himself, explaining why sound-thinking men in the thirteen American colonies should oppose British taxes decided upon in faraway London.

It was the public debut of Alexander Hamilton. A slender young man, only five feet seven inches tall, he had red-brown hair and deep blue eyes. Despite

his youth, the crowd paid attention to him. There is no record to show that he convinced anybody, but his earnest talk impressed an editor standing in the crowd. He asked Hamilton to write something for the New York *Journal*.

When the Continental Congress did meet, Hamilton wrote a long article. He called it "A Full Vindication of the Measures of Congress from the Calumnies of Their Enemies." Soon after, he wrote an even longer article with an even longer title.

Many of his readers were impressed by this ambitious newcomer to New York. Hamilton had been born on January 11, 1757, on the Caribbean island of Nevis, a small British colony. His father was a Scottish merchant, Andrew Hamilton, who fell in love with but did

William Rollinson produced this stipple engraving of Alexander Hamilton in 1804. *Courtesy of The Henry Francis du Pont Winterthur Museum*.

not marry a local woman named Rachel Fawcett Levine.

As young Hamilton grew up, he showed a remarkable ability to learn quickly. Soon after his mother died he had to go to work, however, even though he was only twelve years old. He became an apprentice in a trading company and displayed unusual talent in the world of business.

Still, he set his mind on getting a proper education. Thanks to some money from an aunt, he sailed off to school in New York. In 1773, he entered Kings College, which later became Columbia University. He was a good student but eager to get out into the real world.

The times were right for an able, ambitious young man. When George Washington passed through New York in 1775 to take command of the new army of the united colonies, Hamilton gave up his books. Even at eighteen, though, Hamilton was not willing to become an ordinary soldier. He organized a volunteer student company called Hearts of Oak, with himself in command.

The following year, at the age of nineteen, he received a formal commission as a captain, commanding sixty-three men and four officers, all of them older than he was. Studying from a book, he drilled, marched, and trained them.

When Washington arrived back in New York with the Continental Army, Hamilton's company joined him. Their first experience in battle was a defeat. They retreated with Washington into New Jersey, but Hamilton's well-trained company stood out. "It was a model of discipline," one observer wrote.

Soon he was promoted, but not because of his military ability. He owed his advancement to the fact that he could write and handle figures easily. In 1777, at the age of twenty, he became a lieutenant colonel, stationed at Washington's headquarters as an aide to the general himself.

The assignment gave Hamilton a good opportunity to learn how government works. From the field, where soldiers were often without pay or sufficient supplies, he saw at first hand the results of a weak government. He came to the conclusion that the new nation he was fighting for could survive only under strong leadership.

After the Battle of Saratoga in 1777, Washington sent Hamilton to Albany. There the young aide stayed at the home of General Philip Schuyler, an old friend of Washington's. Hamilton fell in love with Elizabeth Schuyler, one of the general's daughters. Their marriage in 1780 made him a member of one of the most aristocratic families in New York.

When the war ended, Hamilton turned to the study of law. Instead of the normal three years of apprenticeship that most would-be lawyers required, Hamilton finished his preparations in five months. For the next several years, he conducted a private law practice in New York City.

He also got involved in helping to organize a new government for the United States. At the Constitutional Convention in Philadelphia, he was one of three New York representatives. When the document was finished, he was the only representative of New York to sign it.

Yet it was after the convention that Hamilton made his major contribution. No one was more persuasive than he in arguing for adoption of the Constitution, which had to be ratified by two-thirds of the states before it went into effect. He spoke wherever he could find listeners, but his most powerful weapon was his pen.

On his way home from a trip to Albany, he began to write the first in a series of eighty-five articles that became known as The Federalist Papers. He wrote fifty-one himself and three more with James Madison. The others were written by Madison and John Jay.

The papers presented clear and forceful arguments why the Constitution, with its system of checks and balances, should be adopted. "I am persuaded

Elizabeth Schuyler Hamilton, a daughter of one of the richest and most powerful families in New York, was deeply cherished by her husband. *Courtesy of the Library of Congress.*

that it is the best which our political situation, habits and opinions will admit," he wrote.

Hamilton's second major contribution came at a New York State convention that began meeting in June of 1788. Only nineteen delegates seemed to be for the new Constitution, with forty-six opposed, on the grounds that the new federal government would be too strong.

Leading the fight from the floor, Hamilton was on his feet day after day, defending the Constitution. One by one, some of the anti-Federalists became convinced. On July 26, New York approved the Constitution by a vote of thirty to twenty-seven. It was a personal triumph for Hamilton.

When Washington became the first President in 1789, he called upon his former aide to become Secretary of the Treasury. Hamilton was ready. He presented a plan for the new government to take over all the debts of the Continental Congress and of the states. The total was $70 million, an enormous sum for those days.

By taking over the debts, Hamilton believed he could create support for the new government among merchants, bankers, and other important people who would benefit from a strong economy. His followers became known as Federalists. His opponents, led by Thomas Jefferson, the Secretary of State, were called Anti-Federalists, or Democratic-Republicans.

The key question was: Should the United States assume the debts of the thirteen states? At last, a compromise was worked out. Jefferson consented to the debt plan, but Hamilton agreed to move the nation's capital south to a new city to be built on the Potomac River.

In five years as Secretary of the Treasury, Hamilton—with Washington's support—established the credit of the United States on a firm basis. In 1795, at the age of thirty-eight, he retired from public office, but he remained the leader of the Federalist party. He tried to control the presidential election of 1800, opposing a second term for President John Adams and supporting C.C. Pinckney of South Carolina instead. The plan backfired. Adams was defeated, not by Pinckney, but by Jefferson, Hamilton's major political opponent.

There was a complication, however, since both Jefferson and the man running with him as vice-presidential candidate, Aaron Burr, received seventy-three electoral votes. Under the original terms of the Constitution, the candidate receiving the largest number of electoral votes became President and the runner-up Vice-President. As a result of the tie, the election was thrown into the House of Representatives.

This created a dilemma for Hamilton. Much as he opposed Jefferson, he thought Burr was not fit to be President. Finally, Hamilton urged his supporters not to vote at all. After thirty-six ballots in the House of Representatives, Jefferson was declared elected. Burr became the Vice-President.

Once more, Hamilton returned to his law practice, his wife, and his family of seven children, but the Hamiltons'

On July 11, 1804, Aaron Burr fatally wounded Alexander Hamilton in the first round of a duel.

happy family life was shattered in 1801 when their oldest son, Philip, was killed in a duel.

Although dueling was illegal, it was a method that men of the time used to settle questions of honor. It was considered manly to challenge an opponent to stand a test of courage in which each party to the dispute would fire a pistol at his opponent. No matter that death could be the outcome, tradition decreed that no gentleman could refuse such a challenge.

In 1804, Aaron Burr challenged Hamilton himself to a duel. The chal-

lenge arose because of a political feud between Burr and Hamilton. Still the Vice-President of the United States, Burr was running that year for another post—governor of New York. Hamilton organized the opposition to Burr, who lost the election.

Burr's defeat left him eager for revenge. He found an opportunity in a statement in which Hamilton had described him as a "dangerous" man. To Burr, that was an insult calling for action to defend his honor.

Although Hamilton opposed dueling, he felt he had no alternative but to accept the challenge. At dawn on a summer morning, both men were ferried from New York City across the Hudson River to a field in Weehawken, New Jersey. The two opponents stood, ten paces apart, each holding a pistol. The signal to fire was given by one of the men accompanying the duelists.

A shot roared out. Then another. Hamilton had satisfied his honor by firing into the air, but his opponent showed no such restraint. Burr's bullet did not miss its target, and Hamilton fell to the ground. It was clear to the men with him that his wound would be fatal. His last words were, "Let Mrs. Hamilton be immediately sent for, let the event be broken to her, but give her hope."

Yet there was no hope. Hamilton died on July 12, 1804, at the age of forty-seven.

Thomas Jefferson

1743–1826   Author of the Declaration of Independence; Secretary of State; third President of the United States.

Carved in granite on a tomb near Charlottesville, Virginia, are these words:

> Here was buried
> Thomas Jefferson
> author of the Declaration
> of American Independence,
> of the Statute of Virginia
> for religious freedom,
> & Father of the
> University of Virginia.

Written by Jefferson himself, that memorial does not mention his accomplishments as Secretary of State, Vice-President, and President of the United States. For Jefferson, the high offices he held were less important than his contributions to freedom—political freedom in the Declaration of Independence, religious freedom in Virginia, and freedom through education.

The major weapon in his struggle against tyranny was his pen. More than two hundred years ago, he wrote these words: "We hold these truths to be self-evident, that all men are created equal, that they are endowed by their Creator with certain inalienable rights, that among these are Life, Liberty and the Pursuit of Happiness."

Those words made the American Declaration of Independence one of the most influential documents the world has ever known. It is still a beacon of hope for oppressed people around the world.

What is most remarkable about those words is that they were written by a young man of thirty-three, the youngest man at the Continental Congress in Philadelphia in 1776. He was only one

A Declaration by the Representatives of the UNITED STATES
OF AMERICA, in General Congress assembled.

When in the course of human events it becomes necessary for one people to
dissolve the political bands which have connected them with another, and to
assume among the powers of the earth the separate and equal station to
which the laws of nature & of nature's god entitle them, a decent respect
to the opinions of mankind requires that they should declare the causes
which impel them to the separation.

We hold these truths to be self-evident; that all men are
created equal, that they are endowed by their creator with
inherent & inalienable rights; that among these are the
life, & liberty, & the pursuit of happiness; that to secure these rights, go-
-vernments are instituted among men, deriving their just powers from
the consent of the governed; that whenever any form of government
becomes destructive of these ends, it is the right of the people to alter
or to abolish it, & to institute new government, laying it's foundation on
such principles & organising it's powers in such form, as to them shall
seem most likely to effect their safety & happiness. prudence indeed
will dictate that governments long established should not be changed for
light & transient causes: and accordingly all experience hath shewn that
mankind are more disposed to suffer while evils are sufferable, than to
right themselves by abolishing the forms to which they are accustomed. but
when a long train of abuses & usurpations [begun at a distinguished period,
&] pursuing invariably the same object, evinces a design to reduce
them under absolute Despotism, it is their right, it is their duty, to throw off such
government, & to provide new guards for their future security. such has
been the patient sufferance of these colonies; & such is now the necessity
which constrains them to expunge their former systems of government.
the history of the present king of Great Britain is a history of unremitting injuries and
usurpations, among which appears no solitary fact to contra-
-dict the uniform tenor of the rest, all of which have in direct object the
establishment of an absolute tyranny over these states. to prove this, let facts be
submitted to a candid world, for the truth of which we pledge a faith
yet unsullied by falsehood.

Thomas Jefferson drafted the Declaration of Independence. *Courtesy of the Library of Congress.*

of a committee of five; John Adams, Benjamin Franklin, Roger Sherman, and Robert Livingston were the others. They left it to Jefferson to write down the reasons why the American colonies were declaring their independence from England.

Jefferson already had made a name for himself as a skilled writer in his native Virginia. He had been born there on April 13, 1743, the son of a prosperous planter, Peter Jefferson, and his wife, Jane Randolph Jefferson.

His mother was a member of one of the first families of Virginia and, through her, Jefferson himself was connected with the colony's wealthiest landowners. His father died in 1757, when Jefferson was fourteen years old, but the family was well enough off so that he could continue his studies at a school near home.

By the time he was sixteen, he could read Latin and Greek and had studied science and geology. After graduating from the College of William and Mary in Williamsburg in 1762, he began to study law in the office of George Wythe, one of Virginia's leading lawyers. Admitted to the bar in 1767, Jefferson did well as a lawyer, numbering among his clients some of the colony's best-known families, including the Randolphs.

Over six feet tall, Jefferson was lanky and broad-shouldered. He had hazel eyes, reddish hair, and a ruddy, freckled face. Like other young Virginia gentlemen of his time, he hunted and competed in shooting matches. But there was something different about him.

He played the violin and taught himself French and Italian so that he could read books in those languages. Wherever he went, he could not resist buying and collecting books. He was interested in everything around him—turkeys, fossils, Indians, plants, art, architecture, languages, science, and above all, his farm.

Jefferson designed a home for himself near Charlottesville that he called Monticello, an Italian word meaning little hill. It was there in 1772 that he brought his bride, Martha Wayles Skelton, a wealthy young widow. They had six children, but only two survived to adulthood.

Jefferson was governor of Virginia during the Revolutionary War, from 1779 to 1781. His greatest accomplishment as governor was his fight for religious freedom. Until then, the Church of England had been the official church of Virginia. All citizens were required to pay taxes to support the church, whether or not they were members. Jefferson believed very strongly that religion should be a private matter. After years of effort on his part, Virginia finally passed a law by which "all men shall be free . . . to maintain their opinions in matters of religion." That law later became the basis for the First Amendment to the Constitution of the United States.

Two years after the death of his wife in 1782, Jefferson sailed to Europe as minister to France. There he delighted in French food and thoroughly enjoyed meeting French people of every rank from aristocrats to peasants. He also spent many happy hours conferring with scientists. But he disapproved of the French king's arrogance, so he sympathized with the aims of the French Revolution in 1789.

That year, he returned to the United States to become the nation's first Secretary of State under President Washington. He soon came into conflict with Alexander Hamilton, the Secretary of the Treasury, about money matters.

Hamilton had proposed a plan for taking over all the debts of the thirteen colonies as one means of establishing a strong central government. Jefferson opposed the plan. They finally came to a compromise, Jefferson agreeing to Hamilton's money plan and Hamilton agreeing to Jefferson's proposal to move the nation's capital south to the Potomac River.

But that did not end their political disputes. "Hamilton and myself were daily pitted in the Cabinet like two cocks," Jefferson said. The result of these disputes was the formation of political parties representing differing viewpoints about how the United States should be governed.

When Washington's second term neared an end, Vice-President Adams became the candidate of the Federalist party. Jefferson was the candidate of the Anti-Federalists, or Democratic-Republicans. In 1796, Jefferson lost a close election, receiving sixty-eight electoral votes to seventy-one for Adams. Under the election rules at that time, Jefferson became the Vice-President.

Four years later, in 1800, Jefferson reversed the results, defeating Adams by seventy-three electoral votes to sixty-five. But a peculiar thing happened. Aaron Burr, of New York, who was Jefferson's running mate and a candidate for Vice-President, also got seventy-three votes. As a result, the decision about who was to become President was thrown into the House of Representatives.

An ambitious man, Burr refused to stand aside and let Jefferson win. He thought he had a chance to become President himself because of the opposition of the Federalists to Jefferson. Even though he himself opposed Jefferson, however, Alexander Hamilton

This portrait of Thomas Jefferson may have been sketched by Benjamin Latrobe, the architect who rebuilt the Capitol after the burning of Washington. *Courtesy of the Maryland Historical Society, Baltimore.*

thought Burr was not fit to become President. He advised his Federalist supporters to refrain from voting, and on the thirty-sixth ballot Jefferson was elected.

Jefferson was sworn into office as the third President of the United States on March 4, 1801, in Washington, D.C., the first President to take the oath of office in that new city.

From the beginning, Jefferson was a more informal chief executive than Washington or Adams. He shook hands with visitors instead of bowing formally. He used round tables instead of rectangular ones at dinners so that talk could flow more easily. His visitors were amused at his pet mockingbird, which sat on his shoulders and sometimes took food from his mouth.

The major event of his first term was the 1803 purchase of Louisiana from the French. The United States paid $15 million for the vast territory, which brought the borders of the nation to the Rocky Mountains and more than doubled its size.

Soon Jefferson dispatched Meriwether Lewis and William Clark on their famous expedition to explore the Missouri River and the West. They left in May of 1804 and arrived on the shores of the Pacific Ocean in December of 1805. Their exploration paved the way for settlers to follow and established an American claim to the Oregon territory.

After his reelection in 1804, Jefferson's main problem was with England. Trouble arose because British warships stood off New York harbor, stopping and searching United States vessels for goods that might be going to its enemy, France. Even worse, they took some seamen off American ships, claiming they might be Englishmen, and forced them into the British Navy.

In an effort to keep out of war, Jefferson supported a law that barred American ships from sailing to foreign ports. That caused much hardship for merchants, but it did prevent a war with England at that time.

When his second term neared an end, Jefferson wrote to a friend, "Never did a prisoner released from his chains feel such relief as I shall on shaking off the shackles of power. Nature intended me for the tranquil pursuits of science." So he was very happy when he returned to Monticello and began conducting experiments on various methods of growing crops.

Up at dawn every day, Jefferson wrote and read until breakfast. He rode out daily to supervise his farm with its gristmill, nail factory, and furniture shop. He kept a full house of family and friends. Once there were as many as seventy overnight guests visiting Jefferson.

Hardly a day passed when travelers did not drop in to consult "the sage of Monticello." He relished their news and conversation. But Jefferson entertained so much that he ran into financial troubles. Friends had to come to his aid with contributions to help him maintain his home.

As he grew older, Jefferson forgot the heated political disputes of his earlier days. He and his former adversary, John Adams, renewed their old friendship. Their letters to each other, containing recollections of the days of the Declaration of Independence and the Revolutionary War, provide exciting reading for historians today.

During his retirement, Jefferson made two major contributions to the intellectual life of his country. After the British burned many government buildings during the War of 1812, he sold his library of more than six thousand books to the government. These formed the basis for the huge collection of the Library of Congress in Washington.

Closest to Jefferson's heart was the establishment of the University of Virginia. Over the years, he fought hard to convince the state legislature to set up this institution and to locate it near his home in Charlottesville. When his plan was finally adopted, he designed the buildings, supervised the curriculum, and chose the faculty. The university opened its doors for its first class in 1825.

Jefferson died at Monticello at the age of eighty-three—on July 4, 1826, the fiftieth anniversary of the Declaration of Independence that he had written. It happened, amazingly, that his old friend and foe, John Adams, died in Massachusetts on the same day.

James Madison

1751–1836   Secretary of State; fourth President of the United States.

At five o'clock in the morning, before the sun rose, a bell rang out in Nassau Hall, awakening Jemmy Madison and the other students at the College of New Jersey in Princeton. An hour later, the faculty and students gathered for prayer and Bible readings. At seven o'clock, the students went to their books for an hour of studying before sitting down to a breakfast of porridge and coffee or tea.

It was the beginning of a normal day at the college. The day did not end until nine o'clock at night. Rigid as the schedule was, Jemmy Madison made it even tougher. He combined his junior and senior years, doubling his work load. As a result, for weeks on end he had but five hours of sleep a night. It was no wonder that he got sick.

Although he passed his final examinations in 1771, he was too sick to attend his own graduation. Madison was a small man, about five feet six in height, weighing just about a hundred pounds. His hair was hay-colored, his eyes slate blue, and he usually had a serious expression on his face.

Nearing the age of twenty-one, Madison left Princeton to return to his native Virginia to help tutor his younger brothers and sisters. The oldest of twelve children, he had been born in Port Conway on March 16, 1751. His mother was Nelly Conway Madison, daughter of a tobacco warehouse operator. His father was James Madison, Sr., a planter of tobacco and an important man in the community.

Madison arrived home in the midst

38

of troubled days for his father, who was justice of the peace and head of the king's militia, with the rank of colonel. When news of the Boston Tea Party reached Virginia, Colonel Madison faced a problem. Did he, as an official appointed by the King of England, support the English? Or did he stand with his fellow colonists?

There was no question in young Madison's mind. He admired the men of Boston who had acted on their convictions by protesting unjust taxation. His father agreed. Colonel Madison organized a county Committee of Public Safety, which gathered arms and ammunition in case they were needed. In October of 1776, James Madison, Jr. was named colonel of the militia.

But his public career really began when he was named a delegate to an important political convention. In Williamsburg, then the capital of Virginia, Madison and other delegates gathered to write a new constitution for the state. In the convention hall he met Thomas Jefferson, who became his close political ally for the rest of his life.

During the Revolutionary War, Madison served as a representative to the Continental Congress in Philadelphia. Even though he started out as a strong believer in states' rights, in the Congress he found himself becoming more and more convinced of the need for a strong central government.

After the war, when Jefferson went off as minister to France, Madison remained in Virginia to carry on his friend's crusade for religious freedom. In 1785, he succeeded in getting the Virginia legislature to pass a law guaranteeing freedom of religion for all.

Madison's primary political concern was the future of the new nation. Like many others, he thought that the Articles of Confederation, under which the thirteen former colonies cooperated in government, were not working well. With Alexander Hamilton, at a meeting in Annapolis, he persuaded other delegates to vote for a new convention in which the main business would be writing a new Constitution.

Despite his small size, Madison was a giant at the Constitutional Convention in Philadelphia in 1787. He drafted a plan for a new national government that included checks and balances among the executive, legislative, and judicial branches. As a member of the committee on style, he helped to write the final version of the document, which was adopted on September 17, 1787.

Even to his contemporaries, his contributions were so great that he became known as the father of the Constitution. But that did not end his services. Before the Constitution could go into effect, it had to be ratified by two-thirds, or nine, of the thirteen states.

Madison went to work. In cooperation with Hamilton and John Jay, he wrote a series of eighty-five articles, called The Federalist Papers, that were circulated in all thirteen states. They explained in detail the reasons for establishing the new form of government.

That was only half the job. The other half was to convince a divided Virginia to ratify the Constitution. Many Virginians were distressed because they thought too much power was going to the new central government. Madison answered by pointing out the inefficiencies of the Articles of Confederation. When it came to the crucial vote, Virginia approved the Constitution by a narrow margin, eighty-nine to seventy-nine.

After the new government came into being in 1789, Madison was elected to the House of Representatives, where he became the majority leader. His most distinguished service came in proposing ten amendments to the Constitution—the Bill of Rights—which guaranteed freedom of speech, worship, the press, and assembly for all the people and also protected the rights of states.

While serving in Congress, Madison met a charming young woman, Dolley Payne Todd, a widow with a small son. He was forty-three years old, she was twenty-six. He was a reserved man, she was a lively woman who loved colorful clothes. Despite the differences, they seemed to get along very well. They were married on September 15, 1794.

After serving four terms in Congress, Madison brought his new wife to live at his home, Montpelier, in Virginia. He watched the development of political events from a distance until his friend Jefferson was elected President in 1800. Jefferson summoned Madison to Washington to become Secretary of State.

Eight years later, on March 4, 1809, Madison became President himself. It was a splendid day for the Madisons, especially for Dolley Madison. At the Inauguration Ball that evening, one observer wrote, "She looked like a queen." Her dress was elegant, with a long train, but her hat was even more stunning—a white creation of velvet and satin, adorned by two huge feathers from a bird of paradise.

The ball set the social pattern for the rest of Madison's administration, with the colorful Mrs. Madison acting as hostess at the White House. She overshadowed her plainspoken and plain-looking husband, who always wore black clothes. But he loved the excitement that she caused. She was "the greatest blessing of my life," he said.

At that period of American history,

James and Dolley Madison. Pencil drawings on ivory by T. C. Lübbers. *Courtesy of The New-York Historical Society, New York City.*

he certainly needed some comfort. In office, he was faced with a war crisis. France and England were fighting once more, each of them high-handedly stopping American trading ships sailing across the Atlantic Ocean.

In the United States, opinion was sharply divided about the conflict, but there was unanimous anger over England's policy of searching American ships and taking off sailors who might be English. Madison tried to keep the United States neutral, but a party of "war hawks" in Congress pushed the nation into the War of 1812 against England.

Much of the war was fought at sea, with American ships holding their own against the more experienced British Navy. The public was delighted when the *Constitution* forced a British vessel to surrender. On Lake Erie, a small American fleet under the command of Commodore Oliver Hazard Perry won a victory, too. "We have met the enemy and they are ours," Perry wrote back to Washington.

On land, though, it was a different story. When the French Emperor Napoleon was defeated in Europe, the British sent a large force to the United States. British troops landed in the

The British officer ordered to set fire to the White House and the Capitol in 1814 declared it a pity to destroy anything so beautiful. *Courtesy of the Library of Congress.*

Chesapeake Bay area and marched toward Washington. Madison rode out of the city on horseback to inspect the American defensive positions a few miles east of Washington. There he came under enemy fire, becoming the first and only American President ever fired upon in wartime.

He returned to Washington briefly, but on August 24, 1814, he fled on horseback into Virginia, just before the British captured the city. Dolley Madison was the last to leave the White House, carrying with her a famous portrait of Washington cut from its frame.

When the British entered the White House, they sat down to a hot meal that had been prepared for the Madisons. Then they burned the White House, the Capitol, and many other buildings in the city—in retaliation, they said, for American soldiers' burning of buildings in Canada when they attempted to invade that British colony.

With Washington in flames, the British left for Baltimore where they were to meet a British fleet. As they sailed up Chesapeake Bay, they were attacked by American guns at Fort McHenry. Throughout the night of September 13, 1814, the British ships returned the fire in an attempt to batter the fort into silence.

Despite the heavy bombardment, the next morning Francis Scott Key—aboard an American ship in the harbor—saw that the American flag still flew above the fort. The sight of the flag flying by dawn's early light inspired him to write the words for "The Star-Spangled Banner."

American resistance in Baltimore and another naval victory at Plattsburgh on Lake Champlain gave added strength to an American team of peace negotiators in Ghent, Belgium. Britain and the United States agreed to end the war by signing the Treaty of Ghent on De-

The bombardment of Fort McHenry in 1814 moved Francis Scott Key to write "The Star-Spangled Banner" and inspired this aquatint by John Bower. *Courtesy of the Maryland Historical Society, Baltimore.*

cember 24, 1814, with neither side the winner. Since in those days ships were the only means of carrying news across the Atlantic, word of the peace treaty did not reach America for weeks.

Meanwhile, the British advanced on New Orleans but were defeated by a force of western sharpshooters, led by General Andrew Jackson, on January 8, 1815. Although the peace treaty had already been signed, this American victory raised the spirits of all.

When Madison's term of office ended, he returned to Virginia. There he completed his "Notes on the Convention," the only complete record of the deliberations of the delegates to the Constitutional Convention. It is today the best record of how the Constitution was adopted.

Back at Montpelier, Madison took an active role in state affairs. He succeeded Jefferson as the head of the University of Virginia and was a delegate to the convention that wrote a new constitution for the state. He also became president of the American Colonization Society, which favored the ending of slavery in the United States by purchasing slaves and sending them back to Africa.

Madison died on June 28, 1836, at the age of eighty-five. Dolley Madison lived on, remaining an important figure on the Washington social scene until her death in 1849 at the age of eighty-one.

John Marshall

1755–1835   Secretary of State; Chief Justice of the United States.

Early in 1801, the second President of the United States was feeling hurt and angry. He had just been defeated for a second term—by a political enemy he very much distrusted—so John Adams wanted to do whatever he could to prevent Thomas Jefferson from harming the country.

When Adams heard the news that the Chief Justice of the Supreme Court wished to resign, an idea struck him. Instead of letting Jefferson pick the next Chief Justice, Adams would do it himself. But whom should he choose?

He put the question to one of the few men whose opinion he valued. John Marshall, a Virginia lawyer, had been serving Adams as his Secretary of State. At the White House toward the end of January, Adams asked him to recommend a likely candidate.

Marshall did not hesitate. He proposed the promising young Mr. Paterson, already a member of the high court's panel of Associate Justices.

No, Adams objected. This would cause trouble because other, older Associate Justices would resent being passed over in favor of a younger man. Besides, was the fellow really a sound Federalist? The President looked thoughtful then, and there was a long silence.

At last, he peered directly at Marshall. "I believe I must nominate you," Adams pronounced.

Many years later, Marshall wrote his own account of this scene. He said that until President Adams spoke those words, he himself had never even thought of becoming Chief Justice. He added: "I was pleased as well as surprised, and bowed in silence."

John Adams also remembered the scene. As a very old man, he told a visitor about it. He said that his gift of John Marshall to the people of the United States was the proudest act of his life.

During the next thirty-four years Marshall proved to be such an outstanding Chief Justice that his place in American history is something like George Washington's. In much the same way that Washington set the pattern followed by every future President, Marshall provided a model for every future Chief Justice.

Even though three other men had briefly headed the Supreme Court before Marshall took over, hardly anybody can remember their names. But nearly two hundred years after John Marshall began issuing Supreme Court rulings, law students still study many cases he decided. Legal experts differ in their verdicts about some of his opinions, depending on their own political outlook. No matter whether they are liberals or conservatives, however, almost all agree that he was a legal genius.

Marshall was forty-six when he was appointed, and he had already shown assorted talents, yet many people underestimated him. A tall, skinny man,

he wore clothes that never seemed quite to fit him, and he had the sort of plain, good-humored face that made him appear more like a country storekeeper than an important public figure.

Once a friend of Marshall's was asked to describe him. After trying for several minutes, he finally came out with a simple sentence. "I love his laugh," he said.

This lack of stuffy formality was at least partly owing to Marshall's frontier upbringing. Born on September 24, 1755, in a log cabin in the western part of Virginia, he spent his childhood far from any fancy influences. His lifelong fondness for games like pitching horseshoes certainly could be traced to these early days.

But even if he lived on the edge of the wilderness—in a roadside village called Germantown—he by no means missed some of the advantages of civilized society. Both of his parents were connected, either by blood or friendship, with several of Virginia's most prominent families, and his father took a leading part in the colony's public affairs.

It was his mother who had the highest-ranking ancestors. One of Mary Keith Marshall's grandfathers had been the same William Randolph from whom Thomas Jefferson was descended. Thus John Marshall and the third President of the United States, whose policies dis-

John Marshall, painted by Chester Harding in 1830, served thirty-four years as Chief Justice of the Supreme Court. *Courtesy of the Boston Athenaeum.*

tressed him deeply, were actually not-very-distant cousins.

John's father came of a less aristo-cratic background, but Thomas Marshall, in his own youth, had lived near the farm where George Washington was born. They were classmates at the same private academy, and later they fought together in the French and Indian War. Then Colonel Marshall moved west to supervise selling some land he had ac-quired, and soon he was elected to represent the Germantown area in Vir-ginia's colonial legislature.

Since John was his first son—in fact, the first in a family that eventually in-cluded fifteen living children—the colonel felt a special fondness for him. John grew up hearing from his father about what a fine man the famous Gen-eral Washington was. These stories made Washington the boy's great hero.

In addition, Colonel Marshall taught John to be a careful reader. By the age of twelve, the boy had memorized large portions from the books that filled a few shelves in their rude but comfort-able home. Around this time, the colonel's land business brought another move—eastward, into less primitive surroundings. Here the colonel ar-ranged for a young man from Scotland to live with them, teaching his sons more than he could teach them himself. Although John never attended any

school, he was studying law at home when he was nineteen. Then stirring news from Massachusetts began arriv-ing in Virginia. It appeared that the colonies might soon be fighting for their independence.

John and his father both started rounding up volunteer soldiers. Wear-ing rough, homespun hunting shirts, they and their troops practiced military drilling. Then, in 1775, at the age of twenty, John went off to war.

He fought in several major battles during the Revolution, and he was pro-moted twice, ending as a captain. Al-though he never spoke much about his war experiences, the years he spent away from Virginia, serving in the army of the Continental Congress, had a last-ing effect on his thinking.

Instead of considering himself a Vir-ginian, he formed the habit—as he him-self put it—"of considering America as my country." Moreover, he saw first-hand how inefficient the loose associa-tion of separate states was, so he became thoroughly convinced of the need for a strong central government.

Toward the end of the war, while Marshall was waiting in Virginia's old capital of Williamsburg for new orders, he attended some lectures on law at the College of William and Mary. These qualified him to receive a license as a lawyer.

In 1782, at the age of twenty-seven, he was elected to the state legislature. By that time, the capital had moved to Richmond. Settling there, he married Mary Ambler, a young woman he had fallen in love with during his army days. He also put out a sign announcing he was available to any client who needed a lawyer.

Marshall's far-from-stylish appearance at first worried some people intending to hire him. Although they heard he had a keen mind, they could not believe it when they saw his rumpled appearance. Over the next ten years, though, the force of Marshall's legal arguments brought him plenty of business.

What's more, his intense belief in the importance of a strong national government made him the leading spokesman for the Federalist party in Virginia. He turned down several offers of jobs in the new federal government while it was still located in New York and then in Philadelphia because he hated the idea of leaving his wife and their six children at home.

Finally, in 1798, George Washington himself warmly urged Marshall to help his successor, President Adams. Marshall ran for Congress, then agreed to assist Adams further by going on a special mission to France. That was how he happened to be Secretary of State when Adams was mulling over the matter of appointing a new Chief Justice.

A good part of the reason why Marshall accepted the post was the fact that the federal government had moved by this time to the new city of Washington, not far from his home in Richmond. But if Marshall was ready to serve now, that certainly did not mean that everybody welcomed his appointment. Jeffersonians were furious because their standard-bearer was being deprived of the opportunity to put his own man into this high office. Even Federalists wondered whether such an odd-looking Virginia gentleman could be trusted.

Over the next thirty-four years, Marshall did not become universally popular. It is mainly from the vantage point of history that Marshall's greatness stands out clearly.

Like a pioneer going into a wilderness, he blazed a path that gave the young United States a firm legal system. Using only the resources of his own acute mind, Marshall developed the vital ideas that still are the underlying philosophy of American justice.

In brief, he held that the Constitution must always be considered the supreme law of the land. But what if there were differing opinions about what the Constitution meant on a particular issue? Then, Marshall insisted, it was up to the Supreme Court—and only the Supreme Court—to give the final ruling about what the writers of the Constitution had intended.

All of the famous cases Marshall decided as the Chief of the Supreme Court dealt with interpreting one or another clause in the Constitution, according to his own reading of the document. *Marbury v. Madison* and *McCullough v. Maryland* were two of the most widely studied, because they asserted the Supreme Court's superior status over two other possible competitors.

In the first of these cases, a man named Marbury had been appointed to a minor office by President Adams on his last night before leaving the White House, but Adams forgot to hand over the paper making the appointment official. Marbury sued James Madison, the new Secretary of State, claiming that an act of Congress setting the procedure for filling such posts entitled him to the document and the job.

Chief Justice Marshall used this seemingly not very significant dispute to bring forth a legal principle of immense importance. He found that the act of Congress cited by Marbury violated a clause in the Constitution—and

was, therefore, not valid. Thus he established that the Supreme Court could set aside any law it considered unconstitutional.

In the complicated *McCullough v. Maryland*, Marshall established that a state law violating the Constitution could also be declared void. Not surprisingly, many people protested that he was assuming too much power on behalf of the Supreme Court. Yet several efforts to curb his court's influence failed.

Over the years, even opponents of Marshall's conservative viewpoint have mostly come to agree that his very strong leadership on legal matters gave the young government of the United States a stability it might otherwise have lacked.

Personally, too, Marshall proved exceptionally strong. Until he was seventy-five, he never knew a day of illness. After undergoing surgery then for a diseased gallbladder, he seemed perfectly healthy again.

But a few years later, after the death of his beloved wife, he began failing. Two months before his eightieth birthday, on July 6, 1835, Chief Justice Marshall died.

James Monroe

1758–1831   Minister to France; Secretary of State; Secretary of War; fifth President of the United States.

The quiet campus of the College of William and Mary was changing rapidly in the spring of 1776. Instead of going to class, students marched in military drill. Without proper uniforms, some of them wore hunting shirts and carried tomahawks.

In those opening days of the American Revolution, there was no division on that Virginia campus. Others might question the wisdom of taking up arms against the English, but the students were stirred by the idea of independence for the thirteen colonies. They were willing to fight to bring about the birth of a new nation.

One of the students was James Monroe, then eighteen years old. He had been born in Westmoreland County, Virginia, on April 28, 1758, the oldest

of five children of a hardworking farmer, Spence Monroe, and his wife, Elizabeth Jones Monroe. He was brought up in a household where politics was a major topic of conversation.

By the time Monroe was ready for college, talk of independence for the United States was in the air. He arrived at William and Mary in the fall of 1774, just as the first Continental Congress was starting its historic meeting in Philadelphia.

Two years later, the new Lieutenant Monroe marched north with the Third Virginia Regiment to join General Washington's army in New York. He was of medium build, awkward and shy, but he proved to be a good soldier.

When Washington retreated from New York City, Monroe was wounded in the Battle of Harlem Heights in 1776. Following his recovery, he joined the fighting again at the Battle of Trenton. He did so well that he was promoted to the rank of captain.

After the American troops crossed the ice-filled Delaware River on Christmas Eve, Monroe led an advance guard into the enemy camp. The Hessian troops there—part of a force hired by the British to fight for them—were completely surprised, but some tried to resist. Monroe was wounded in the shoulder, and yet he kept command of his company until the enemy surrendered.

After the Revolution ended, Monroe decided to study law. He was accepted as a beginner in Thomas Jefferson's law office. In 1783, when the young apprentice completed his studies, his public career began. Instead of going into practice, he was elected to Congress, along with Jefferson and James Madison. This trio from Virginia would remain close friends and political allies throughout the early days of the new nation.

Monroe's service in Congress also changed his personal life. In the North, he met Elizabeth Kortwright, the daughter of a New York merchant. They were married in 1786, just as his service in Congress was ending.

Monroe brought his wife back to Virginia, where he opened a law office in Fredericksburg, but the life of a country lawyer did not appeal to him. Although he was a quiet and retiring man, he preferred the active life of politics and government.

Only two years later, in 1788, he was elected a delegate to a Virginia convention called to ratify the new Constitution of the United States. There, even though he was a political ally of Madison, he found himself opposing his friend, "the father of the Constitution."

Monroe was against the new Constitution because it did not contain a Bill of Rights for the protection of private citizens. When the Virginia delegates approved the Constitution by a narrow vote, Monroe gracefully accepted his defeat and began to take part in the formation of the new government.

He ran for election to the new House of Representatives but lost to Madison. The following year, in 1790, he was appointed one of the first Senators from Virginia. Later he was elected governor of Virginia.

His major contribution to his country in those early days, however, came not at home but abroad. His friend Jefferson, who had become President in 1801, appointed Monroe as the United States minister to France. In Paris, in 1803, Monroe and Robert R. Livingston negotiated the purchase of the Louisiana Territory. This doubled the size of the United States.

From Paris, Monroe went to London to try to end a dispute between England and France about freedom of the seas. Americans were angry because of the British policy of stopping ships at sea and taking off sailors who might have been deserters from the Royal Navy. But the British, who were at war with the French, refused to change their policy.

Back in the United States, Monroe returned to Virginia, where he was elected to the governorship again in 1811. He served only three months before President Madison called him to Washington to become Secretary of State.

It was a time of crisis, when the President needed a loyal and capable ally at his side. The War of 1812 had begun, on the issue of freedom of the seas that Monroe had sought to settle peacefully. But now angry "war hawks" in Congress thought the issue could be settled only by force of arms.

Even though he was Secretary of State and a civilian, Monroe made two major contributions during the war. One was on the field of battle, the other was in preparing defense forces to fight.

When a British force landed in Chesapeake Bay and started to march on Washington in 1814, the American troops fled. Monroe stepped in and organized a defense for the capital. It failed. The British captured Washington, burning both the Capitol building and the White House. But Monroe at least had tried to defend the city.

Madison then named Monroe Secretary of War. It was the first and only time in American history that one man had served in two Cabinet positions at the same time. As Secretary of War, Monroe made his second great contribution. He dispatched General Andrew Jackson to New Orleans to meet a British threat there. And he sent this message to the governors of the western states: "Hasten your militia to New Orleans! Let every man bring his own rifle."

As a result, Jackson commanded a force of American sharpshooters who mowed down the British redcoats as they advanced toward New Orleans. It was a great American victory, which came just as the war was ending. It made Jackson into a national hero, but some observers in Washington gave Monroe equal credit.

It was no surprise at the next presidential election in 1816 that the nation turned to James Monroe, the candidate of the Democratic-Republican party. He won an overwhelming victory. Nearing the age of fifty-nine, he was inaugurated as the fifth President of the United States on March 4, 1817. The third in a line of Presidents from Virginia, Monroe followed his friends Jefferson and Madison into office.

At least from a distance, Monroe bore a striking resemblance to George Washington, perhaps partly because Monroe was a conservative man in the matter of clothing. He still wore old-fashioned knee breeches, white stockings, and shoes with buckles, even though younger men of fashion had taken to wearing long pants, and he still powdered his hair in the style of the eighteenth century.

At his inauguration Monroe said, "Never did a government commence under auspices so favorable." And it was true. The nation was at peace, both abroad and at home. Things were so calm that his years in office were called, even in his own time, "the era of good feeling."

Shortly after he took office, Monroe discovered this for himself. In May of 1817, he left Washington for a tour of the country. Even though an appearance by any President, then as now, brought out cheering spectators, Monroe was surprised by the warmth with which he was greeted.

Even when he visited states in New England, which he had not carried in the election, he found himself popular with people of all parties. It was a time of peace and prosperity for the United States, and the nation was growing, both economically and geographically.

After his tour, Monroe and his wife settled into the White House, rebuilt after the British had burned it. A stately and reserved woman, Mrs. Monroe restored formality to the White House, after the lively Dolley Madison. The Monroes brought elegant furniture they had purchased in Europe to give the executive mansion a fitting grandeur.

Monroe's growing popularity was not the result of a colorful personality or of strong leadership. Rather, it came about because of the weakness of his opponents. In the "era of good feeling," there was little opposition to him—so little that the opposition party, the Federalists, collapsed.

Monroe's opponent in the 1816 election had been Rufus King of New York, who turned out to be the last presidential candidate of the Federalist party. He said that Monroe "had the zealous support of nobody, and he was exempt from the hostility of everybody."

By the time Monroe ran for reelection in 1820, there was no opposition at all. He received all but one of the votes of the electoral college. That one vote was cast by an elector who thought that Washington should remain as the only President to be elected unanimously.

Monroe was a competent administra-

James Monroe was President when Charles Goodman and Robert Piggot executed this stipple engraving of him in 1817. *Courtesy of the National Portrait Gallery, Smithsonian Institution.*

tor. One of his cabinet officers described him as "a plain and modest gentleman." Another observer said that he performed every duty that fell to him with fairness and care.

With the help of John Quincy Adams, his Secretary of State, Monroe made three major contributions in foreign relations.

First, a treaty was negotiated with England in 1817 that eliminated defense forces along the United States–Canadian border. Today, that undefended border is a major sign of the friendship between the two largest nations in North America.

Second, in 1819, Adams completed lengthy negotiations with Spain; as a result, Florida, until then a Spanish colony, became part of the United States.

Third, he issued a message to the world that became known as the Monroe Doctrine. This warned that the Americas were no longer open to become colonies of any European power.

The United States, Monroe said, would stand firm in the defense of freedom in the Western Hemisphere.

Monroe felt the message was necessary to protect the newly won independence of former Spanish colonies in South America. Following the example of the United States, they had just fought in revolutions to gain their freedom.

After completing his second term, Monroe retired to a new home, Oak Hill, that he built near Leesburg, Virginia. There he continued his close personal relationships with his old friends, Jefferson and Madison, and served as a trustee of the University of Virginia.

In his later years, in the days before Presidents received pensions, Monroe suffered financial losses. He was forced to sell Oak Hill and went north to live with a married daughter in New York City. He died there on July 4, 1831, at the age of seventy-three.

George Washington

1732–1799   First President of the United States.

When George Washington was four-teen years old, he was offered a chance to become a midshipman in the British Navy. If he accepted, he would be taking the first step on a ladder that would lead to a career serving the King of England.

The year was 1746, and Virginia was one of England's thirteen colonies in North America. Washington, who had been born in Virginia on February 22, 1732, lived on a farm there with his mother and five younger brothers and sisters. His father, a planter of tobacco, had died three years earlier.

With his education completed, Washington was unhappy under his mother's rule, but his older half brother Lawrence saw a way out for George. Lawrence had married into the family of the Fairfaxes, who owned a large amount of land. When the captain of a Royal Navy vessel told the rich Fair-faxes that he had a vacancy, they thought of George.

The offer resulted in tearful scenes at the farm. At one point Mrs. Washing-ton consented, and George packed his bags. Then she changed her mind. No, he could not go, she said, and he un-packed.

Historians have wondered what would have happened if Washington had accepted service under the British flag. Who, if anybody, could have re-placed him as commander of the Conti-nental Army in the Revolutionary War? Who would have become the first Presi-dent of the United States?

At the time, Washington was disappointed, but the Fairfax connection soon gave him another opportunity. When he was sixteen, he went with a party into the wilderness of the Shenandoah Valley to map Fairfax properties there. This experience taught him enough about making maps so he could set himself up in business as a surveyor.

As he was starting to make his way in the world, his brother Lawrence died. Tragic as the death was, it presented another opportunity for Washington. Lawrence left his estate, called Mount Vernon, to his younger brother. He also left vacant a position as an officer in the Virginia militia.

Washington applied for the job. Despite his youth and his lack of experience, he got an appointment as a major because he had influential friends. And so, in 1753, at the age of twenty-one, his long military career began. It was an exciting time for him, with the English and French fighting for control of the Ohio Valley.

"I heard the bullets whistle and believe me, there is something charming in the sound," he wrote home. But even though he liked the soldier's trade, his first adventures in the field were a disaster. He commanded a small force that had to surrender to the French, mainly because he had shown ignorance of military tactics in the face of a superior enemy. But he learned from his mistakes, as he later demonstrated.

When a new British force under the command of Major General Edward Braddock arrived in 1755, Washington joined him in a fresh campaign to recapture the disputed area. It turned out to be another disaster. An invisible enemy hiding behind trees poured shots into the advancing British, wounding Braddock and killing most of his officers. Washington had two horses shot out from under him and four bullets tore through his coat, but he was not wounded. He took command of the battered force and retreated.

Despite his demonstrated skill, Washington was unable to get the commission that he wanted as a regular officer in the British army. As a result, his attention turned back to his farm and domestic affairs. On January 6, 1759, he married Martha Dandridge Custis, a rich widow with two children. They settled down to life at Mount Vernon.

He loved the land, never tiring of the chores of a working farm. An imposing-looking man, he was six feet two inches in height. He liked to hunt foxes, bet on racehorses, flirt with attractive women, play cards, and fish. He was, according to Thomas Jefferson, "the best horseman of his age."

Washington's peaceful life changed in 1775 after the first shots of the Revolutionary War were fired at Lexington and Concord in Massachusetts. It was clear that war was at hand. By unanimous vote on June 15, 1775, the Continental Congress turned to Washington, America's most experienced soldier. Then forty-three years old, he was appointed commander-in-chief of the new American army.

He took up his command outside Boston a few days after the Battle of Bunker Hill. The British occupied Boston, but the Americans camped around the city. It was months before his new troops were trained and ready for action.

Silently in the night, on March 4, 1776, Washington concentrated his men overlooking Boston harbor. Faced with a threat to their fleet from American cannon, the British withdrew from Boston. It was an American victory even though not a shot had been fired. That action took place even before the Declaration of Independence was adopted on July 4, 1776.

But the military situation looked bad for the Americans because they faced an experienced British army. After leaving Boston, the British captured New York by defeating Washington on Long Island, in Manhattan, and at White Plains. Washington retreated into New Jersey and then across the Delaware River into Pennsylvania.

He realized that the only military choice open to him was to conduct hit-and-run raids, avoiding a major battle with the superior British force. On Christmas night of 1776, he ferried his troops across the ice-filled Delaware River into Trenton. There, he surprised the Hessian troops that the British had hired to fight for them. They surrendered.

The biggest American success, however, came in 1777 when its forces defeated the British at Saratoga in upstate New York. This victory had major international consequences. The French recognized the independence of the former colonies and declared war on England.

With the coming of winter, Washington's soldiers settled down at Valley Forge in Pennsylvania. Many of them lacked shoes or heavy clothing. In addition, Washington faced a threat from a group of ambitious generals who wanted his job as commander-in-chief. Dignified as usual, he remained calmly firm until his loyal officers and men rallied behind him.

Soon the focus of the war shifted to the South, where Lord Cornwallis led a British army. Now a new element was added to the battle scene—the French. In the summer of 1780, Washington was joined by a French army. By the following summer they were marching together to Yorktown in Vir-

An engraving by H. B. Hall shows Washington with the Marquis de Lafayette at Valley Forge. *Courtesy of The New-York Historical Society, New York City.*

ginia, where Cornwallis was fortifying a base. When the French fleet arrived in Chesapeake Bay, Cornwallis was trapped.

The surrender of Cornwallis on October 19, 1781, effectively ended the fighting in the American Revolution, but two years were to drag on before a peace treaty was signed. During that time Washington had to keep his army together, a difficult task because Congress, always short of money, had cut funds for the troops.

The lack of support from Congress led to a major crisis. In May of 1782, some of his officers urged Washington to become king of the United States as a means of providing an effective government. He rejected the idea immediately.

But that did not end the discontent. The unpaid officers proposed to march on Philadelphia to take over the government. To stop this new threat, Washington spoke to them at his headquarters in Newburgh, New York, in

March of 1783. He told them he thought Congress would act justly, but he did not seem to be making an impression on them.

He remembered a letter he had in his pocket to read. He took it out but, apparently confused, did not read it. Finally, he reached into another pocket and pulled out a pair of eyeglasses.

"Gentlemen," he said, "you will permit me to put on my spectacles, for I have grown not only gray but almost blind in the service of my country." That simple statement made many of the soldiers weep. As one historian wrote, by that one sentence "Washington had saved the United States from tyranny and civil discord."

After the treaty of peace was signed in 1783, Washington returned to Mount Vernon. At the age of fifty-one, he was ready to spend his remaining years with his wife and family. They had no children of their own, but Mrs. Washing-

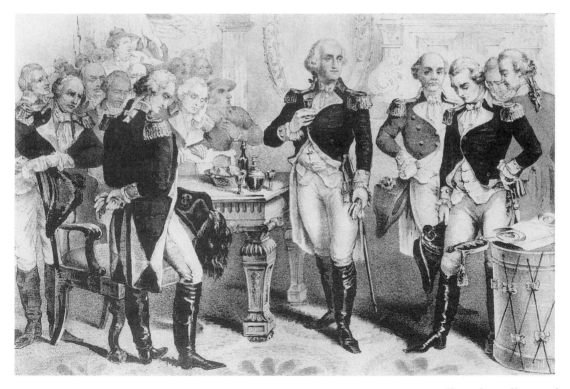

In 1876, Currier and Ives published the lithograph *Washington's Farewell to the Officers of His Army. Courtesy of the Museum of the City of New York, Harry T. Peters Collection.*

ton's son from her previous marriage and his children visited them frequently.

Political developments called Washington out of retirement when the new Constitution of the United States was adopted in 1787. There was no question about who the first President would be, and the electoral college voted for Washington unanimously. He took the oath of office on April 30, 1789, in a ceremony on Wall Street in New York City, then the nation's capital.

The major problem facing the new nation was money. A detailed plan was proposed by Alexander Hamilton, appointed by Washington as Secretary of the Treasury. Hamilton proposed to take over the debts of the former colonies, raising the necessary funds by sell-

Edward Savage painted *The Washington Family* in about 1796, at the end of George Washington's second term as President. *Courtesy of the National Gallery of Art, Washington; Andrew W. Mellon Collection.*

ing bonds. He thought this would show the strength of the new government. But Thomas Jefferson, the Secretary of State, opposed the scheme.

With Washington's approval, a compromise was reached. Jefferson agreed to Hamilton's plan, and Hamilton agreed to move the nation's capital south. As a result, the capital moved temporarily to Philadelphia in 1790, while the new capital city was being built on the Potomac River, not far from Mount Vernon.

The split in Washington's Cabinet did not end. The party backing Hamilton became known as Federalists, supporting a strong central government. The Jeffersonians were called Anti-Federalists, or Democratic-Republicans. Washington belonged to neither faction, but he generally supported Hamilton's policies.

When election day in 1792 arrived, it was clear that Washington was still needed. Once again the electoral college voted for him unanimously, and he was inaugurated in Philadelphia on March 4, 1793. His second term was marked by a crisis at home and war abroad.

The domestic problem arose because of a tax on whiskey, imposed to raise funds for the new nation. When some backwoodsmen refused to pay the tax, Washington sent a small army into western Pennsylvania. The show of force had its effect; the Whiskey Rebellion ended.

Things were not so easy in foreign affairs. When England and France went to war again, Washington issued a neutrality proclamation in an attempt to keep America at peace. Then he sent John Jay to London to settle some problems with England, which resulted in Jay's Treaty of 1794. In the following year, he sent Thomas Pinckney to reach an agreement with Spain on the borders of her colonies in America.

Weary of the presidency, Washington put his thoughts about the nation's future into a Farewell Address in 1796. He criticized the growth of political factions at home, but his most important point was a warning against entangling alliances with any foreign power.

In 1797, at the age of sixty-five, Washington left office and went home to Mount Vernon, content, as he said, "to make and sell a little flour . . . to repair houses going to ruin . . . to amuse myself in rural pursuits."

He died at Mount Vernon on December 14, 1799, at the age of sixty-seven. One of his colleagues said, in a funeral oration, that Washington was "first in war, first in peace, and first in the hearts of his countrymen." Today, almost two hundred years later, the words are still true.

PART II

The Early Days of the Republic

John Quincy Adams

1767–1848   U.S. Senator; Secretary of State; diplomat; sixth President of the United States; U.S. Congressman.

Ten-year-old John Quincy Adams and his father, John Adams, were aboard a sailing ship, the *Boston*, crossing the Atlantic Ocean in the winter of 1777. The small ship tossed and rolled for days in a gale, with winds so strong that they cracked the mainmast holding the sails. After six weeks on the high seas, the *Boston* finally made shore in Bordeaux, France.

But the rough trip was not yet done. Adams and his son climbed into a horse-drawn carriage for a five-day ride over the rutted country roads of France to Paris. There, the elder Adams joined Benjamin Franklin as an American minister to France. Their job was to gain more French aid for the former colonies, struggling in the Revolutionary War against the British.

For young John Quincy, however, it was back to school. Born in Massachusetts on July 11, 1767, he had gone to school there before his parents agreed that a trip abroad would be good for him. And so he was in Paris, attending a French school by day, then quietly listening at night to his father and Franklin talk about foreign affairs.

In the next several years, John Quincy traveled across the stormy Atlantic often with his father on various diplomatic missions. He went to school in England and Holland as well as in France. A good student, he learned to speak Dutch, French, and German as well as Latin and Greek.

By the time he was fourteen, he was well educated in the art of diplomacy. As a result, he was appointed secretary to the new American minister to Russia, Francis Dana. He traveled to St. Petersburg, the capital of Russia, as a junior diplomat.

Soon, though, Adams had to make a major decision. Should he stay in Europe with his parents or go home to get a college education? He chose to return and attend Harvard, earning advanced standing in most of his classes. He did so well in his studies that on graduation in 1787 he was elected a member of Phi Beta Kappa, the scholastic honor fraternity.

Then he began to study law but somehow found time for young women, too. "The art of making love muffled in furs in the open air, with the thermometer at zero, is a Yankee invention," he recalled later.

When Adams completed his law studies, he opened an office in Boston, but the law did not interest him as much as politics and national affairs. Like his father, who was now Vice-President of the United States, he was a Federalist and a strong supporter of President Washington.

He began to write a series of articles defending the Washington administration against its critics. Soon after they appeared, Washington appointed him to his first diplomatic mission on his own, as minister to the Netherlands. He was then twenty-seven years old.

During his three years of service there, from 1794 to 1797, Adams made frequent trips to London to help the American minister. In London, he fell in love with Louisa Catherine Johnson, daughter of an American diplomat. They were married on July 26, 1797, a few months after Adams' father became the second President.

In that same month, his father appointed young Adams minister to Prussia. The President did so only after consulting Washington, because he did not want to seem to be favoring his son. Washington replied that he hoped Adams would not withhold a promotion for John Quincy because he was "the most valuable public character we have abroad."

John Quincy returned home in 1801, reopening his law office in Boston. Once again he found that public service interested him more than the law. He was elected to the United States Senate in 1803 as a Federalist but soon showed his independence of party labels by voting for the Louisiana Purchase, which his party opposed.

The leaders of the Federalist party struck back by electing another man to the Senate six months before Adams' term expired. At the age of forty-one, he found himself without a party and without a job. He returned to Harvard, where he became a professor.

Adams was already showing the traits that made him admired by some but hated by others. He was dignified, intelligent, hardworking. But he was also irritable, impatient with others, and unable to make the quick friends and allies that a successful politician needs.

Still, there was no question that he was an experienced diplomat. In 1809, President Madison called him back into public service. He was appointed minister to Russia, returning to St. Petersburg, the city he had known as a boy. Adams was pleased at the appointment, but he wondered if that was all he could expect.

In his diary, in 1812, he wrote, "I am forty-five years old. Two-thirds of a long life have passed and I have done nothing to distinguish it by usefulness to my country and to mankind."

He wrote too soon. His important contributions to American life were about to begin. They started in 1814, when he went to Ghent in Belgium as part of an American team that negotiated an end to the War of 1812. Then he served as minister to England.

From there, President Monroe summoned Adams home in 1817 as Secretary of State. Under Adams' direction, an agreement was reached with England setting out the boundary line between the United States and Canada, which had remained a British colony.

He negotiated another treaty, this one with Spain, by which Florida became part of the United States in 1819.

Behind the scenes, Adams had an important role in setting forth the Monroe Doctrine. In 1823, President Monroe warned the powers of Europe that North and South America were no longer subjects for future colonization by them. The words were Monroe's, but the idea came from Adams.

A hardworking man, Adams began his day at four-thirty in the morning and seldom ended it before midnight. He managed an efficient and effective department. As a statesman, he was superb, according to historians, but as a politician he was not very good. He thought himself as above partisan politics, refusing to make appointments— and friends—based on what party a person belonged to.

The year 1824 was an important one in American politics. The two major parties, the Federalists and the Democratic-Republicans, had more or less faded away. When the presidential campaign began, four candidates appeared, not representing political parties but sections of the country.

From the West there were General Andrew Jackson of Tennessee, the hero of the Battle of New Orleans, and Henry Clay of Kentucky, the Speaker of the House of Representatives. From the

Thomas Gimbrede engraved this likeness of John Quincy Adams in 1826, two years after Adams's election to the presidency. *Courtesy of the National Portrait Gallery, Smithsonian Institution.*

South, there was William H. Crawford of Georgia, the Secretary of the Treasury, and from the North, John Quincy Adams of Massachusetts, the Secretary of State.

In 1824, for the first time in American history, many of the presidential electors were chosen by a vote of the people. Before then, electors had been chosen by state legislatures. Jackson received more popular and electoral votes than any other candidate, but not a majority. As a result, the election was thrown into the House of Representatives, as provided for in the Constitution.

Because Clay had the fewest electoral votes, he was out of the race, but he and his supporters were able to determine the winner by casting their ballots for Adams, who became the sixth President. He was the only son of a President to become President himself.

The inauguration of Adams on March 4, 1825, was notable because he was the first President to wear long pants at the ceremonies. Every previous President had worn knee-length breeches with white stockings and black shoes, usually with silver buckles, but styles began to change in the 1820s, and Adams adopted the new look.

In office, one of his first acts was to appoint Henry Clay as Secretary of State. Immediately, the Jackson supporters cried, "corrupt bargain." They felt that Clay had been appointed in return for casting his votes for Adams as President in the House of Representatives. But Adams had made the choice because he believed that Clay was the best man for the job.

In his first message to Congress, Adams proposed federal spending for a wide range of internal improvements. He called for an interstate network of roads and canals, a Department of the Interior to regulate the use of natural resources, aid to education, and the creation of a naval academy. All of those things were eventually done, but not in the Adams administration. His political opponents criticized his proposals for two reasons. They were still angry about the way in which Jackson had been defeated in 1824, and they thought that Adams' proposals would place too much power in the hands of the President.

With his policies in trouble, Adams kept busy reading the Bible and his favorite Greek and Latin writers. He took long walks and went swimming often. Getting up before sunrise on summer mornings, he would walk down to the Potomac River, peel off his clothing, and swim, wearing only goggles over his eyes and a cap on his head.

A realist, Adams knew he had no chance for reelection to a second term.

John Quincy Adams' fatal stroke in the House of Representatives is the subject of this lithograph by Kellogg and Comstock. *Courtesy of the National Portrait Gallery, Smithsonian Institution.*

In 1828, Jackson won an overwhelming victory. Bitter because Jackson did not pay him a courtesy call, Adams left Washington without attending Jackson's inauguration. "The sun of my political life sets in the deepest gloom," he wrote to a friend.

And then a family tragedy also struck. His oldest son, George, who had been sick, either jumped or fell to his death from a steamship bound for New York. At the age of sixty-two, Adams was overcome by grief. He tried to keep busy in his garden and in reading and swimming in the cold seawater. But he was not ready for retirement.

In less than a year, the call to public duty sounded once more. Adams was asked to run for Congress and was elected to the House of Representatives. "My election as President of the United States was not half so gratifying to my inmost soul," he wrote. He became the only President ever to serve as a member of the House of Representatives after leaving the White House.

For seventeen years, Adams was a notable figure in the House. He helped to establish the first astronomical laboratory in the United States in 1843 near Cincinnati on a peak named for him, Mount Adams. He was chairman of the committee that created the Smithsonian Institution in 1846.

But his most important work came as an opponent of slavery. In 1836, some Southern Congressmen had tried to stop debate on the issue. Over the objections of Adams, the House passed a resolution barring antislavery speeches.

It did not silence him. Year after year, he kept rising to protest "the gag rule." He spoke so often and so well that even his opponents called him Old Man Eloquent. It took almost ten years, but he finally won his fight. The gag rule was repealed in 1844.

Still active at the age of eighty, Adams collapsed one day on the floor of the House of Representatives. He died in Washington shortly afterward, on February 23, 1848.

John Calhoun

1782–1850 U.S. Congressman; Secretary of War; U.S. Senator.

Tall, with striking dark eyes and an eager manner, he immediately stood out at college. In one of his classes, he even dared to argue about politics with the professor—Dr. Timothy Dwight, a famous figure of the early 1800s, who was also the president of Yale.

But Dr. Dwight listened carefully. He disagreed with everything this bold student from the backwoods of South Carolina was saying, but the fellow certainly had a gift for making his own opinions sound convincing. Dr. Dwight remarked to a friend a few hours later that he wouldn't be surprised if young Calhoun someday became the President of the United States.

At least for the time being, the young man himself had a lesser goal. One day during his senior year, he was being teased for sticking so strictly to his books. He replied that he had to study hard in order to be a success when he was elected to Congress.

"I would leave college this very day," he added, "if I doubted my ability to reach Congress within three years." He spoke the words in 1804—and it turned out he was a little too optimistic. Not till 1810, when he was twenty-eight, did he become a Congressman.

John Caldwell Calhoun had always been full of self-confidence. It came in part from growing up on the edge of the wilderness, where only the strong could survive. Calhoun was born on March 18, 1782, on a farm outside the frontier town of Abbeville, near South Carolina's western border.

He had received a harsh sort of training from his stern, religious father. Patrick Calhoun, a county judge of Scotch-Irish descent, had fought against Indians during his own youth. Later he had fought in the South Carolina legislature, too, demanding a fair allotment of seats for the newly settled upcountry he represented.

It was Patrick Calhoun's third wife, Martha Caldwell, who became John Calhoun's mother. A beautiful woman, she gave her son his exceptional, darkly handsome appearance. Although he was next to the youngest of her five children, she relied on him the most when her husband died of a sudden fever in 1796.

John was fourteen then, and he had just finished a year at an academy in Georgia run by a minister his sister had married. Apart from learning to read at a log-cabin school not far from home, this had been his only opportunity to get acquainted with the world of books.

But now his mother needed him, so John stayed home to help her manage the family's property. Judge Calhoun had left his widow and sons several hundred acres—along with thirty-one slaves, who planted and tended the cotton that was their main crop. For the next several years, John never spoke of what he might be missing. Once he came upon a copy of a newspaper from the city of Charleston, and he studied it at night, underlining the reports about a debate in Congress. During the day, he worked in the fields with the family slaves.

He must have longed for a different life. One morning a friend of his father's from Abbeville found John out plowing—with a book tied to the handle of the plow. This man told John's mother it was wrong to make the boy spend the rest of his days farming.

Mrs. Calhoun sent letters to her two older sons, who were working as clerks in Charleston. Wouldn't they come home to help her, so that John could go back to the academy in Georgia? John's brothers obeyed their mother's summons, but John himself made a surprising statement. Unless he could be promised the best possible schooling—at Yale, in New England—he would rather stay where he was.

As a result, after cramming years of basic lessons into just two years away in Georgia, John Calhoun turned up as a member of Yale's class of 1804. There, his ambition flowered. There, too, he met some distant cousins (they spelled their last name Colhoun) who had a great effect on his future.

Mrs. Floride Colhoun was a rich widow from the Charleston area. Since she spent her summers by the sea in Rhode Island, she invited her young relative to visit there. A woman wise in the ways of the world, she suggested he should go to law school.

By the time Calhoun finished law school, he had fallen in love with Mrs. Colhoun's charming daughter, also named Floride. She was still too young to marry, so Calhoun went back to Abbeville, where he opened a law office and let it be known that he was very interested in politics. Soon he won a seat in South Carolina's legislature.

Finally, on January 11, 1811, an elegant wedding was held at the Colhoun plantation. A few months later, the bridegroom left his wife with her mother and boarded a ship for Washington, where he took his oath as a newly elected member of Congress.

It was a crucial time in the only partly built capital of the young United States. There was a strong possibility that another war with England might be coming soon. Also, an amazing number of talented young lawmakers had begun turning up, determined to make their mark.

Among them were Henry Clay of Kentucky and Daniel Webster of New Hampshire. In the eyes of Southerners, the most promising of all seemed to be John Calhoun from South Carolina. After Calhoun's first speech to the House of Representatives, a leading newspaper in Virginia gave him high praise. The Richmond *Enquirer* called

him "one of the master-spirits, who stamp their names upon the age in which they live."

Calhoun attracted this widespread attention as a leader of the young "war hawks" pushing the country toward involvement in the War of 1812. In the South and West, the idea of fighting England again was popular because it might lead to the taking over of new territory beyond the Mississippi or even of Canada.

In the North, however, there were bitter protests because Northern prosperity depended on trade with England. During the two years the war lasted—distressing years for all patriots, during which the British even burned the White House—some oldtime Federalists in Massachusetts threatened to quit the Union, but a great victory by Tennessee's General Andrew Jackson at the Battle of New Orleans came just as the war ended. It gave America the heady feeling of being a really important power, and sectional differences seemed almost forgotten.

During this early period of Calhoun's career, he obviously thought of himself as a national leader. He belonged to the party originally founded by Thomas Jefferson, still known as the Democratic-Republicans. So did President Monroe, who took office in 1817.

Monroe nominated Calhoun to the

post of Secretary of War. Only thirty-five when he entered the Cabinet, Calhoun clearly began thinking of becoming President himself. He rented a Washington mansion where his wife, in gorgeous satin gowns, gave frequent dinner parties.

Even though half a dozen leading members of his party vied for the White House in 1824, Calhoun believed he would surely be nominated. He was mistaken. John Quincy Adams won the top place. At the age of forty-two, Calhoun accepted the vice-presidency.

It seemed sure that he would succeed the not-very-popular Adams in just four years, but political feelings around the country had begun changing remarkably. In 1828, General Andrew Jackson was the winner and once again Calhoun settled for being Vice-President.

A good part of the reason why Calhoun had already failed twice was a fact that he could not, and would not, ignore. He was intensely proud to be a Southerner. It was becoming very difficult, however, to stand up for the special interests of the South without losing support in other parts of the country.

Nobody could deny that the South and the North were developing along very different lines. The North, with more factories every year, depended increasingly on selling its products all over the world. Meanwhile, the South

not only remained primarily agricultural, its whole way of life depended on slave labor.

The first flare-up of trouble between the two sections of the country had nothing to do with slavery. A kind of tax called a tariff was the cause. In 1828, Congress passed a bill setting a high tariff on various items imported into the United States from foreign countries. This greatly pleased Northern areas where similar products were manufactured, for it meant they would be able to sell more of their own output.

In the South, however, the new tariff aroused fury. It would raise prices there, without any benefit to the region at all. Although Calhoun felt he could not speak out openly because of his vice-presidential office, he wrote a protest message issued by the South Carolina legislature.

This advanced the idea that a single state could refuse to obey a federal law—or nullify it—if the state decided the law violated its own liberty. Although similar protests had been made a few times in the past, it appeared that this one by South Carolina might become very serious. It might even make the state try to break away from the Federal Union.

Although Calhoun did not sign his name to the South Carolina statement, his connection with it was an open se-

John Calhoun had resigned as Vice-President about four years before James Longacre made this portrait in 1834. *Courtesy of the National Portrait Gallery, Smithsonian Institution*.

cret. President Jackson decided he had to show the country he would not stand for any attempt at dividing it. He took a dramatic way to do so in February of 1830.

At a banquet in Washington, attended by every leading political figure, Jackson arose and solemnly lifted a glass to offer a toast. "Our Union," he said. "It *must* be preserved." There was a moment of tense silence.

Then it was the turn of the Vice-President at the other end of the table. Calhoun, his eyes blazing, held out his own glass and said: "The Union. Next to our liberties, most dear."

From then on, Calhoun put his Southern loyalty above any other consideration. Immediately he resigned as Vice-President, preferring to lead his campaign on behalf of the South as Senator Calhoun from South Carolina.

For the next twenty years, Calhoun tirelessly carried out the mission he had undertaken. By doing so, he gave up his ambition to be President. Instead of engaging in political dealing, he did his best to play the part of a high-minded statesman whose only goal was fair treatment for his part of the country.

His fierce defense of the South made him the hero of his own region. At the same time, it made him hated in the North during this period when sectional enmity grew increasingly bitter. But even his enemies were touched by his final appearance in the Senate early in 1850.

By then, his health had failed. So weak and ill that his speech had to be read for him by one of his Southern allies, he sat wrapped in a long black cloak. The words of his speech were not very important. What he said to one of his aides as he tottered home was much more moving.

"The South—the poor South!" he murmured. "God knows what will become of her!"

His final political act was, at least unofficially, to pick his own successor as the leader of the Southern cause. He chose Senator Jefferson Davis of Mississippi. On March 31, 1850, Senator Calhoun died at the age of sixty-eight.

Henry Clay

1777–1852   U.S. Congressman; Speaker of the House; Secretary of State; U.S. Senator.

"I would rather be right than be President."

That's what Henry Clay said in 1850, toward the end of his long political career. For almost forty years he had been a leading figure on the national scene. But why did he fail, time after time, to win the country's top office?

It is a story filled with drama, and it started in a part of Virginia locally known as The Slashes. Not too far from the sea, the area was torn by fighting against the British during the American Revolution. At the height of the trouble, on April 12, 1777, the wife of a Baptist preacher gave birth to her seventh child.

The boy named Henry had three sisters and the same number of brothers. Another baby boy came after him. Then tragedy struck the family. When Henry was only four, his father died. The Reverend John Clay left no money at all, just the small farm on which they lived.

Henry's mother had to manage as well as she could. Her name had been Elizabeth Hudson, and her relatives, like her husband's, were plain folk, originally from England. None of them could do much to assist the widow, but she turned out to be very capable herself.

For ten years Mrs. Clay kept her children from suffering any real hardship—by making sure they all helped on the farm. Barefoot, young Henry walked behind a plow. Riding a pony with a bag of corn as his saddle, he delivered grain to a local miller.

Yet he did go to school. In a log cabin with a hard-packed dirt floor, he spent three winters learning to read and write and do a little arithmetic. The lessons were easy for Henry, who seemed extra fast at grasping any new idea.

Then, in 1791, when Henry was fourteen, his mother married again. His stepfather moved the family to the city of Richmond, the capital of Virginia. There Henry was set to work as a store clerk, selling molasses and measuring tape.

A tall, lanky boy with a gift for getting along with people, Henry soon impressed his stepfather as being more than usually bright. As a result, a new job was found for him—copying official papers at the courthouse. No matter that his country clothing made some of the other clerks tease him, his work impressed one of Virginia's most famous men.

George Wythe had signed the Declaration of Independence. Now he was a judge of his state's highest court, and he chose young Henry Clay to be one of his own clerks. In the next four years, the quick-witted youth absorbed enough about legal procedure to think of becoming a lawyer himself. Then Wythe asked one of his friends to give Clay some training.

At twenty, Clay earned a license to practice law. But how would he find any clients? It struck him that Richmond already had more than enough lawyers. Boldly, he decided to move West to Kentucky and "grow up with the country" there.

The town of Lexington, where Clay settled, was just emerging from its rough frontier days. While it had some fine buildings and bragged of being the cultural center of the West, a visitor from Massachusetts thought it was still rather wild. "Drink whiskey and talk loud," he said, "and you will hardly fail of being called a superior fellow."

This atmosphere delighted Henry Clay. Cheerful and high-spirited, he swiftly won renown as the best lawyer to consult if you had a serious problem. A good many Kentucky men carried guns, and murder cases came up often. In a few years, people were saying that nobody young Clay defended ever did hang.

But Clay also defended poor widows and orphans. What's more, he took an active interest in local politics and was elected to the state legislature. There, his ability and his likeable personality quickly made him a leader. He stood out to such an extent that, in 1806, when he was twenty-nine, something remarkable happened.

In those days, members of the United States Senate were chosen by the legislatures of the various states. A Kentucky

Senator had died before his term ended and, to fill the seat for the time being, Clay was selected. Neither he nor anybody else remembered that the United States Constitution specified that a Senator must be at least thirty years old.

Early in 1807—three months short of his thirtieth birthday—Clay took the oath of office, just as if no problem existed. Throughout the year, until his term expired, Young Harry from the West was by no means shy. He spoke up on many subjects, he introduced a bill to build a bridge across the Potomac River, he played cards almost nightly with some of his fellow lawmakers. Altogether, he thoroughly enjoyed this first experience in the nation's capital.

Again, in 1809, he filled out another unexpired term. During a debate about the British reaction if the United States acquired part of Florida from Spain, Clay gave a fine example of his lively style of speaking and of his patriotic spirit.

"Sir," he demanded of a cool New Englander, "is the time never to arrive when we may manage our own affairs without the fear of insulting his Britannic majesty?"

Back in Kentucky, Clay resumed his post as leader of the state legislature's lower house, telling his friends how much he relished being home again. Around the time he had first entered politics, he had married Lucretia Hart, the daughter of a prominent family, and they lived on a 600-acre estate called Ashland, where he hospitably played the role of a gentleman farmer.

In 1810 he jumped at a chance to run for a seat of his own in the national House of Representatives. He was elected by a very large majority—and then he burst into national fame.

As soon as he turned up in Washington again, Young Harry was chosen to fill the important office of Speaker of the House. It was certainly unusual for a brand-new member to be selected to preside over this branch of Congress. But Clay, at the age of thirty-four, had already convinced quite a number of people that he was an exceptional man.

And the time had come when America needed new leaders. Most of the men in charge of the government had helped to establish the United States and were now getting old. In 1811, their ideas struck a new generation as much too cautious. Especially in the field of foreign affairs, Clay's high-spirited outlook seemed like a breath of fresh air.

In Europe, England and France were fighting each other on land and at sea. To these mighty powers, the United States was merely a minor irritation, so they had been chasing and even seizing American trading ships.

In effect, Clay and some other young

"war hawks" forced President Madison into the War of 1812. They wanted to show the world that the United States would not stand for being treated as less than a major nation. No matter that this war against England was really quite a brash undertaking—and some historians believe it could have been avoided—it did serve the purpose Clay had intended.

Thanks to General Andrew Jackson, America won one outstanding victory at the Battle of New Orleans just as the war was ending. As a result, America's position among other nations was surely strengthened.

Henry Clay's own position as a national leader was immensely enhanced. President Madison made him a member of the commission that negotiated the peace treaty in 1814. After Clay came back from Europe and was again presiding over the House of Representatives, it was widely assumed that in the not too distant future he would run for President himself.

His chance came in 1824, during the so-called "era of good feeling," when political parties had practically faded away. Four major figures representing different areas of the country vied for the presidency that year, creating a very bitter contest.

In the actual election, General Andrew Jackson got the most votes, fol-lowed by Secretary of State John Quincy Adams. Clay and another lesser candidate had enough support, however, to prevent Jackson from receiving a majority. That put the issue up to the House of Representatives.

By the terms of the Constitution, members of the House were charged with choosing between the top vote-getters. Clay not only had to swallow a harsh dose of personal disappointment but also had to cast a public ballot favoring one or the other of the rivals he really felt were unfit for the presidency.

Clay's opinions were colored, of course, by his own ambition. At the age of forty-seven, he still had plenty of time ahead of him to run in future campaigns, so the way he voted struck many Americans as unforgiveably self-seeking. Clay voted for Adams, even though the legislature of Kentucky had instructed him to support Jackson. From that day onward, he never stopped explaining that he sincerely believed the stiff, uncompromising Adams was a better choice than the hot-tempered Jackson.

Nevertheless some held that Clay had "made a deal" with Adams—that, in exchange for his support, Clay had insisted on being appointed Secretary of State. Traditionally, this post was the stepping-stone into the White House. Clay angrily denied that any such arrangement had even been thought of. Even so, the idea that he was too ambitious to be trusted would not die, for Adams did appoint Clay to be Secretary of State.

However, in 1828, and again four years later, General Jackson proved unbeatable. When he retired after two terms as President, his handpicked successor, Martin Van Buren, further postponed the realization of Clay's dream.

At last, in 1844, it seemed that Clay might finally win the presidency. By then, there existed something like the modern two-party system. While the

Henry Clay engaged in impassioned debate on the Compromise of 1850. *Courtesy of the Library of Congress*.

friends of Andy Jackson had become Democrats, the more conservative among the nation's voters belonged to the party known as the Whigs.

Nominated by this group, Clay received almost as large a popular vote as the Democrat, James Polk. Yet his loss was decisive enough for him—at the age of sixty-seven—to admit he probably would never reach his goal. But four years later he announced he was willing to run again. This time the Whigs nominated General Zachary Taylor, a hero of the recent Mexican War, because they thought he stood a better chance of being elected.

Despite Clay's repeated disappointments, he never ceased serving as one of Washington's leading lawmakers. Following his four years in the office of Secretary of State, it was as Senator Clay that he won increasing renown for his talent at smoothing over the increasingly heated differences between the North and the South.

His tireless efforts at bringing some measure of agreement in this pre-Civil War period earned him the title The Great Compromiser. A century later, it is possible to doubt whether all his maneuvering did more than merely delay the eruption of outright conflict. Yet there can be no denying that he was one of the most notable congressional figures in American history.

Would he have made a good President? Some experts think so, although others say he lacked the depth of mind that could have led to greatness. In any case, he himself never stopped regretting his missed opportunity.

After a last spurt of energy, when he secured the adoption of the Compromise of 1850, Clay began showing symptoms of serious illness. Still hoping that he had managed to save the Union, on June 29, 1852, at the age of seventy-five, Henry Clay died—in Washington, where he had spent such a large portion of his long life.

Sam Houston

1793–1863   U.S. Congressman; governor of Tennessee; president of the republic of Texas; U.S. Senator; governor of Texas.

They called him The Raven, after the bird that was much admired in Cherokee Indian myth. Fifteen-year-old Sam Houston received that name from the Chief of the Cherokees, Oo-loo-te-ka, who adopted him as a son.

For Sam, the ways of the Cherokees were much better than farm life with his mother, brothers, and sisters, or than working behind the counter of a general store. He didn't like either of those choices, so he had decided to run away.

Several weeks later, two of his brothers came to bring him home. They found him in front of the wigwam of Chief Oo-loo-te-ka, lying under a tree. When they asked him why he had run off, he said that he preferred finding deer tracks in the woods to measuring

tape in a store. Living with the Indians delighted Sam. He walked along river banks with Cherokee girls and played a ball game, something like modern lacrosse, with the boys. He hunted for deer and fished in the streams. In the evenings, he sat with his companions around an outdoor wood fire and smoked a pipe of tobacco.

His years among the Cherokees gave Sam a cause—to try to protect them against oppression from the whites. His support of the Indians was most unusual on the American frontier, where the commonly held view was that "the only good Indian is a dead Indian."

In the early 1800s, Sam's family was part of the westward migration that displaced the Indians from their ancestral lands. His father, Major Samuel Houston, was a military man who had fought in the American army during the Revolutionary War. His mother, Elizabeth Paxton Houston, was the daughter of one of Virginia's leading families.

Young Sam had been born on March 2, 1793, on a plantation near Lexington, Virginia. He did not attend school until he was eight years old, but he spent a lot of time in his father's library reading history and geography books, dreaming of adventure. One of his favorite books was the *Iliad*, the great adventure story of the ancient Greeks.

But the pleasant life on the Houston plantation did not last long. Away on military affairs for long periods, Major Houston let the plantation fall into debt. At the age of fifty, he decided to leave the army and go west to start a new life. He sold the plantation, paid his debts, and bought a tract of land in Tennessee. But he died before he could leave.

In the spring of 1807, widowed Mrs. Houston, with iron-gray hair and a steely determination, left her comfortable home. She rode in a wagon pulled by a five-horse team, followed by two other wagons carrying her nine children and everything they owned. Sam was then fourteen years old.

For weeks, the wagons slowly rolled along crude roads through the Allegheny Mountains into Tennessee. They passed through a wilderness with no roads at all, at last coming to the tract that Major Houston had bought.

Like other pioneering families, the Houstons set out to tame the wilderness, cutting down trees and clearing the land for farming. But they did it without the help of Sam, who came home only occasionally to buy powder and shot for his rifle.

His peaceful life with the Cherokees came to an end when the War of 1812 broke out. At the age of twenty, he enlisted in the American army to go off and fight the British. Before he left, his mother gave him a ring engraved on the inside with one word, *Honor*. He wore it proudly until the day he died.

She gave him a rifle, too, he recalled much later, and told him, "My son, take this musket and never disgrace it. For remember, I had rather all my sons should fill one honorable grave than one of them should turn his back to save his life."

Houston turned out to be a good soldier. He became a drill sergeant and soon was promoted to be an ensign commanding a platoon. They did not go off to fight the British, though, but rather the Creek Indians, who were allied with the British.

Under the command of General Andrew Jackson, the American force, led by Cherokee scouts, attacked the Creeks, who fought back fiercely, led by their famous chief, Tecumseh. As the battle began, Houston was hit by an arrow in the thigh. A fellow officer pulled it out and Houston limped off for medical treatment.

Despite his wound, he returned to the fighting and led another charge. This time he was stopped by two bullets. One rifle ball smashed his right shoulder and the other shattered his arm. The military surgeons gave him up for dead, but he was tough and somehow he survived.

When Houston left the army several years later, he turned to the law as a profession. Although he was admitted to the bar in 1818, he also kept active in the Tennessee militia. His fellow officers admired him so much that they elected him as their commander, with the rank of major general.

In 1823, with the backing of his close friend Andrew Jackson, Sam Houston was elected a Representative to Congress. A few years later, in 1827, as part of the Jacksonian campaign to capture the presidency the next year, Houston ran for governor of Tennessee.

In those days candidates met the electorate by speaking at barbecues, logrollings, and barn raisings, where people got together in the sparsely settled areas. Houston made a striking appearance. He wore a ruffled shirt,

shining black trousers, shoes with silver buckles, and an Indian hunting shirt encircled by a beaded red sash.

Houston won the election. He was thirty-five years old and had a reputation for gallantry with women, although he was unmarried. Then he met and fell in love with Eliza Allen, the eighteen-year-old daughter of a well-known family in Tennessee. They were married in 1829.

Within months, the marriage broke up and they were later divorced. Refusing to talk about his personal affairs, Houston resigned as governor. He left to go farther west into the wilderness in a sort of self-imposed exile. There he once again met his old friend, Chief Oo-loo-te-ka, who had been pushed west by the American army.

Although the Cherokees had signed treaties of peace with the United States government, the written words that guaranteed their lands did not stop the advancing tide of white settlers. Backed by American troops, the white men came and occupied the Indian lands.

For several years, Houston lived among the Cherokees once more, frequently going to Washington to plead for their rights. Over the years, he said, he never had been deceived by an Indian, only by his fellow white men who did not keep their word.

After a conversation in Washington with his friend Andrew Jackson, who was now President of the United States, Houston returned to the West, but this time he had a different destination—Texas, then a Mexican colony. Jackson wanted Texas to become part of the United States, and there were many Americans in Texas who shared that dream.

Houston opened a law office in Texas in 1833. He became a member of a convention that set up an independent republic on March 2, 1836—his forty-third birthday. He was named commander-in-chief of the armed forces of Texas.

The Mexicans, determined to hold Texas by force, sent an army into the disputed area. The war that followed started out badly for the Texans. While Houston was in the eastern part of the territory raising an army, the Mexicans attacked a fort called the Alamo in San Antonio.

Inside the Alamo were about 150 men under the command of Lieutenant Colonel William Barrett Travis. Outside was an army of six thousand, commanded by General Antonio Lopez de Santa Anna, the President of Mexico. The Texans could have retreated safely. Instead, confident of their own abilities, they moved into the two-story Alamo Mission, which was protected by thick stone walls.

After thirteen days of fighting, the Texans drooped with exhaustion. When

A photograph taken in about 1858 shows Sam Houston, once the president of Texas and then its senator. *Courtesy of the National Portrait Gallery, Smithsonian Institution.*

their ammunition ran out, they fought with clubs and knives. But their plight was hopeless. The Mexicans captured the Alamo, sparing only the women and children. Every Texas fighting man died, including Travis, Jim Bowie, and Davy Crockett.

The only hope for the survival of the new republic of Texas was Sam Houston and his army of nine hundred men. They had no uniforms. Some of them wore boots, some moccasins, and some

Mexican General Antonio Lopez de Santa Anna surrenders to Sam Houston, who is shown wounded and reclining beneath a tree. *Courtesy of the Texas State Department of Highways and Public Transportation, Austin.*

were barefoot. Many of Houston's men were not used to military discipline, but he drilled them as best he could. Faced by a much larger Mexican force, he led his small army in a series of retreats across eastern Texas. But he was confident. Sitting on his big white stallion, Saracen, Houston spoke to his weary troops on the eve of battle.

"Remember the Alamo!" he cried out.

Thus was born one of the most famous slogans in American history. It was the battle cry on the afternoon of April 21, 1836, when Houston led his men in an attack on a Mexican camp that obviously was unprepared. Only a handful of Mexicans fought back.

One shot hit Saracen, and the horse crumpled to the ground. Houston jumped off and mounted another horse, but that, too, was shot down. A bullet hit Houston in the right leg, breaking the bone. He mounted a third horse and continued to fight.

The Mexicans fled, but their commander, Santa Anna, was captured. Defeated, Santa Anna agreed to withdraw all Mexicans from Texas and return south of the Rio Grande River, back into Mexico.

The Mexican defeat at the Battle of

San Jacinto is regarded as one of the most decisive battles in American history. Not only did it secure the independence of Texas, it also cleared the way for the United States to expand to the Pacific Ocean.

Once again, Houston had paid a high personal price for victory; it was months before he had recovered from his wounds. During that time, however, he was elected the first president of the republic of Texas, taking office on October 22, 1836.

His personal life improved, too. On a visit to Alabama, he met and fell in love with a young woman, Margaret Lea. They were married in 1840 and over the years had seven children.

The question of statehood for Texas was not solved easily. Although most Texans wanted to become part of the United States, in Washington the question became bogged down in a controversy about slavery. Finally, in 1845, the debate ended and Texas was admitted to the Union as the twenty-eighth state.

The following year, Houston was elected the first Senator from Texas. He served in the United States Senate for fourteen years as a strong supporter of a united nation, speaking out firmly against the Southern threat to secede from the Union because of the slavery issue.

Houston's strong anti-secession views, which were not shared by many of his fellow Texans, cost him reelection to the Senate in 1859. In the following year, however, he ran for governor and won, largely because of his great personal popularity.

Despite that popularity, he could not reverse the tide for secession in Texas. In 1861, the state voted to join the other Southern states in the Confederacy. Houston refused to take an oath of allegiance to the new Texas government, which was ready to go to war with the United States. He was removed from office.

Even though his political views were unpopular, Houston was treated with great respect in Texas during the early days of the Civil War. He died there on July 26, 1863, at the age of seventy.

Andrew Jackson

1767–1845   U.S. Congressman; U.S. Senator; seventh President of the United States.

At the age of fourteen, too young to be a regular soldier, Andrew Jackson joined up anyway to fight the British in the Revolutionary War. He served as an aide, carrying messages on horseback from one group of American soldiers to another.

It was 1781, a dangerous time in the Carolinas where the Jacksons lived. Andrew's oldest brother, Hugh, had been killed in battle the year before. Then during another battle, Andy Jackson and his older brother Robert were captured by the British.

One of the British officers who took them prisoner ordered Andy to shine his boots. The boy refused, saying it was not fit work for a prisoner of war. The angry officer aimed a blow at him with a sword. Andy threw up his left arm to protect himself. The sword came down, cutting his arm to the bone and slashing his head.

Then the two boys were marched off to a prison camp, about forty miles away. There they caught smallpox, a deadly disease in those days. Their mother came and convinced the commander of the camp to release her sick sons. Although Robert died of smallpox, Andy, a tough, wiry boy, with blue eyes and a freckled face, recovered.

But things did not get better for the Jackson family. Andy's mother died of smallpox, too, leaving Andy on his own, an orphan. His father, an immigrant from Ireland, had died two weeks before Andy was born on March 15, 1767.

As he grew up in the days after the Revolutionary War and the death of his mother, Andy's main interest was horses. He loved to ride and to bet on horse races. When he received an unexpected inheritance from an uncle who had died in Ireland, he spent all his money on clothes and gambling. He was a wild young man. One neighbor called him "the head of the rowdies hereabout."

After his money ran out, Jackson changed his ways, though, and began to study law. After three years of study, he was admitted to the bar in Salisbury, North Carolina, at the age of twenty. When the road to the West opened up in 1788, Jackson joined the first party of settlers to the frontier town of Nashville, then far in the wilderness.

There he stayed at the boarding house of the Widow Donelson, who appreciated having a straight-shooting young man around when Indians made their occasional raids into town. Jackson fell in love with her daughter, Rachel Robards, who believed she had been legally divorced from her first husband. They were married in August of 1791.

Nashville proved to be a good place for an able, ambitious lawyer. Jackson attracted many clients, and he also got involved in politics. He took part in the convention that wrote a constitution for the new state of Tennessee. In 1796 he became the state's first Representative in Congress. Later he served a term as United States Senator from Tennessee.

Despite his high offices, Jackson was not able to control his quick temper. He was always ready to fight to defend his honor—and that of his wife. In those rough frontier days, some people did make nasty remarks about her divorce, which, as it turned out, had not taken effect back in 1791 as the Jacksons believed. After it did become official, they were remarried in 1794, but that was not enough to still some gossiping voices.

At one time the governor of Tennessee, John Sevier, a Jackson political opponent, made a public remark about Mrs. Jackson's divorce. Jackson challenged him to a duel, a way of settling disputes on the frontier. No one was hurt.

It was quite a different story in 1806, when a Nashville lawyer, Charles Dickinson, also commented on Mrs. Jackson's divorce. Jackson challenged him to a duel as well. Dickinson fired first, hitting Jackson in the chest. Despite his wound, Jackson stood erect, taking careful aim. He fired a shot that killed Dickinson and then collapsed. Jackson recovered, although the bullet was so close to his heart that it could not be removed.

At about that time, Jackson received the highest honor that men of the frontier could give to a fighting man. He was elected commander of the Tennessee militia, with the rank of major general. It was the beginning of a spectacular military career.

When the War of 1812 broke out, Jackson led his Tennessee militia into the Mississippi Valley. On one march, a soldier remarked that Jackson was "tough as hickory." Soon all the soldiers started to call him Old Hickory, a nickname that the whole nation adopted.

Later in the war Jackson was ordered to defend New Orleans against a British invasion. South of the city he assembled his men: sharpshooters from Kentucky and Tennessee, some free blacks, a few Indians from the Choctaw tribe, and followers of Jean Lafitte, the famous pirate of the Louisiana bayous.

On January 8, 1815, the British troops marched toward New Orleans. From behind earthen barricades, the sharpshooters poured volley after volley of gunfire into the advancing Redcoats. "That leaden torrent no man on earth could face," said a British lieutenant. It was a big victory for the Americans, and Jackson became a national hero.

He was an obvious candidate for President of the United States in 1824, but that election turned out to be a complicated one. There were four candidates, each representing a section of the country. Even though Jackson won the most

popular votes and the most votes in the electoral college, he did not have a majority.

As a result, the election was thrown into the House of Representatives, as required by the Constitution. There Jackson lost to John Quincy Adams, who became President. But Jackson and his followers believed that he had been cheated out of the presidency.

"Was there ever such barefaced corruption in any country before?" Jackson asked a friend. Still, he did not contest the election. Instead he and his friends started to organize for the next one. He resigned from the Senate, and the campaign of 1828 got under way three years before the election.

At first the Jacksonians called themselves Friends of Jackson, but later they changed their name to the Democratic party. They produced and circulated newspapers in support of their candidate. Because he was known as Old Hickory, they distributed hickory canes, sticks, and brooms everywhere. And they bitterly attacked President Adams, whom they accused of living in "kingly splendor" in the White House. When the President bought a billiard table and some ivory chessmen, they accused him of gambling at public expense. Nothing Adams did could stop the well-organized campaign against him.

As a result, Jackson was overwhelm-

Andrew Jackson defeated the British at the Battle of New Orleans in 1815. *Courtesy of the Louisiana State Museum.*

ingly elected in 1828 as the nation's seventh President. He was the first President from the West, the first who was not from Virginia or Massachusetts. His followers called him the People's President.

Thousands flocked to Washington to see him inaugurated. "People have come five hundred miles to see General Jackson and they really seem to think the country has been rescued from terrible danger," Senator Daniel Webster of Massachusetts remarked.

One journalist of the time noted that Jackson was plainly dressed, all in black, at the inauguration. He was in mourning for his wife, who had died a few months earlier. Thin and pale, he delivered his inauguration address so softly that many could not hear him.

That made no difference to his followers. As he rode on horseback to return to the White House after taking the oath of office, the crowd followed. They burst into the mansion, where tables had been set with refreshments. The crush was so great that women fainted, fistfights broke out, and glasses were shattered. Jackson himself escaped through a back door and went to a hotel.

Jackson looked much older than his sixty-one years. Although he was tall, six feet one inch in height, he weighed only one hundred and forty pounds. His hair was gray-white, he suffered from tuberculosis, and the bullet near his heart kept him in constant pain. But his poor health did not keep him from being a strong President.

In office, his first major crisis was a question of social manners. The proper ladies who were the wives of Cabinet officers refused to see or visit the wife of Jackson's friend, John Eaton, who was the Secretary of War. Eaton had married Peggy Timberlake, a tavern owner's daughter with a questionable past.

Jackson stood firmly behind his friends, the Eatons. For months the controversy overshadowed the business of government. It ended only with the resignation of the entire Cabinet, which took Mrs. Eaton out of the official social scene.

The major problem of the day, a much more important one, was whether or not a state could refuse to obey a federal law. It was the most serious question of states' rights versus the powers of the federal government.

The dispute was put into sharp focus at a dinner in 1830 attended by the capital's leading political figures. Jackson proposed a toast: "Our Union. It *must* be preserved."

John C. Calhoun, the Vice-President and a strong supporter of states' rights, stood up next. "The Union," he said. "Next to our liberties, most dear."

Andrew Jackson was already a national hero when James Longacre inscribed this stipple engraving in about 1820. *Courtesy of the National Portrait Gallery, Smithsonian Institution.*

The controversy came to a head in 1832, when South Carolina's legislature proclaimed that two tariff laws passed by Congress were unconstitutional and that the state did not propose to obey them. For Jackson, that was a direct attack on the federal government. Asked what he would do, he replied, "Suppress the rebellion, sir, root out the treason, sir, with a ruthless hand." He said he would hang every leader of the rebellion and prepared to send troops into South Carolina.

Jackson's strong position carried the day. The issue was settled, at least temporarily, a few months later when a compromise tariff bill was passed. Then the South Carolina legislature backed down.

During Jackson's second term, the main issue was the future of the Bank of the United States, a private bank that controlled the nation's money system. Jackson believed the bank favored the rich. His opponents thought that the bank was needed to manage financial transactions.

Determined to crush the bank, Jackson ordered federal funds removed from it. After his Secretary of the Treasury refused to do so, the President replaced him with another man. The funds were removed. The bank and its supporters fought back, but Jackson won. The bank went out of business.

Jackson's last act as President was to recognize the new republic of Texas, which had just achieved its independence from Mexico. On March 3, 1837, he appointed an American representative to Texas, thus making its diplomatic recognition official.

The next day, Jackson left Washington and returned to his home, the Hermitage, in Nashville. During his retirement, he continued to take an active interest in national politics. He died, at the age of seventy-eight, on June 8, 1845.

James Polk

1795–1849   U.S. Congressman; Speaker of the House; governor of Tennessee; eleventh President of the United States.

He was the first "dark horse" in American politics.

The Democratic National Convention in 1844 could not decide between two of its most prominent men, Martin Van Buren, the former President, and Lewis Cass of Michigan. Suddenly, on the eighth ballot, James Knox Polk of Tennessee received a few votes. On the very next ballot, the weary delegates unanimously voted to make Polk the Democratic candidate for President. And a new phrase was added to American politics. From then on, any candidate who came out of nowhere to win a nomination would be known as a "dark horse."

To the country, Polk's nomination was a complete surprise. Members of the opposition party, the Whigs, were delighted. With the famous Henry Clay as their candidate, they thought the election would be easy. Their campaign slogan was "Who is James K. Polk?" and they made fun of him in a song:

Ha, ha, ha, what a nominee
Is Jimmy Polk of Tennessee.

During the campaign, the nation learned who James K. Polk was. He had been born in Mecklenburg County, North Carolina, on November 2, 1795, the first in a family of ten children. His father was Samuel Polk, a prosperous farmer. His mother, Jane Knox Polk, was a strictly religious woman who believed in hard work and little amusement for her children.

When young Polk was ten, the family moved to Tennessee, where he grew

James Polk was Speaker of the House when Charles Fenderich made him the subject of this 1838 lithograph. *Courtesy of the National Portrait Gallery, Smithsonian Institution.*

up as a serious boy. In school, he never missed a class or failed to do his homework. Although he looked rather frail and sickly, he proved to be strong enough at seventeen to survive an operation for the removal of gallstones. In those days, surgery was a terrible ordeal because doctors had not yet discovered drugs that would render a patient unconscious during the operation.

Polk recovered well enough to go off

to the University of North Carolina. He graduated in 1818 with honors in mathematics and the classics. Then he studied law and was admitted to the bar in Tennessee in 1820. There he began a lifelong association with General Andrew Jackson, a friend of his father's.

Polk's political career began in 1823, when he was elected to the Tennessee legislature. A year later, on New Year's Day in 1824, he married Sarah Childress, the daughter of a farmer. Like his mother, she was a strictly religious woman who frowned on drinking and dancing.

In 1825, Polk became a Representative in Congress. As a strong supporter of Jackson, he opposed President John Quincy Adams on almost every occasion. He was such a close associate of Jackson that he was called Young Hickory, a reference to Jackson's nickname of Old Hickory.

But Polk differed notably from the quick-tempered Jackson. While Jackson was colorful, outspoken, and always ready for a fight, Polk was quiet, formal, and hardworking. He was slender, of medium build, with gray eyes and long hair swept back over his neck.

He worked hard on congressional business, rising to prominence among his fellow Representatives. He became chairman of the important Ways and Means Committee, the body that wrote tax laws. In 1835 he was chosen Speaker of the House of Representatives.

In the last years of Jackson's administration and the first years of Van Buren's, Polk was a strong supporter of their policies, running the House of Representatives with a firm but fair hand. Even his opponents, who attacked him bitterly, respected his skill in deciding complicated matters of procedure.

Although Polk would have preferred to stay in Washington, the Democratic party of Tennessee drafted him as its candidate for governor in 1839. He won the election but lost campaigns for reelection in 1841 and 1843. Although his political career seemed ended, it revived as the national election of 1844 approached.

In that year, the political climate of the nation changed dramatically because of a growing controversy about Texas and slavery. Texas, which had won its freedom from Mexico in 1836, was an independent republic, but most Texans and many Americans wanted it to become part of the United States. Yet that seemingly simple matter was caught up in the issue of slavery.

At that time, the United States was neatly balanced between slave and non-slave states; there were thirteen of each. Southerners wanted Texas admitted as a slave state. Northerners opposed that

because they did not want the South's influence increased.

Van Buren destroyed his own chance of getting the nomination by opposing the admission of Texas. He said that it might endanger our relations with Mexico, which had not accepted the independence of Texas. His stand cost him the support of Jackson, still a powerful influence in the Democratic party.

Jackson and Polk were firm believers in "manifest destiny," a phrase used by those who believed the United States should expand all the way to the Pacific Ocean. For two decades, American fur traders and explorers had blazed a way to the Pacific, followed by settlers looking for land and a new way of life.

By 1844, many Americans had crossed the western borders of the United States into lands occupied by Indians or claimed by foreign powers. Mexico still held title to California and disputed the annexation of Texas. In the north, the British claimed the land as far south as the Columbia River.

Expansion of the United States was now a political issue. Jackson summoned the leaders of the Democratic party, including Polk, to his home in Tennessee. He suggested making "All of Oregon, All of Texas" a campaign slogan that would draw the support of enough people to win the next election.

Polk was the man to lead the party

An early daguerreotype shows President and Mrs. Polk (*center*), Secretary of State James Buchanan (*far left*), and Dolley Madison (*second from right*). Dolley Madison's blurred image indicates that she moved while the picture was being taken—a not uncommon problem at that time, because a pose had to be held for at least forty seconds for the camera to fix an image. *Courtesy of the International Museum of Photography, George Eastman House.*

to victory, Jackson said, and his own supporters rallied to Young Hickory. Still, Polk's opponent, Henry Clay, was favored to win the election.

But then Clay adopted a compromise position on Texas. In doing so, he lost a large number of Northern antislave votes without gaining Southern votes. As a result, Polk won the election by a narrow margin.

At the age of forty-nine, the youngest President at that time, Polk was inaugurated on March 4, 1845. It was the first inauguration to be reported by telegraph. Sitting at the Capitol was Samuel F. B. Morse, the inventor, who tapped out the news of the event on a line to Baltimore.

In office, Polk proved to be a strong, able President. One reason was that he spent long hours at his desk, paying attention to all the details of government. He did not believe in vacations and took Sunday off only because it was the Sabbath, a day of rest.

Under his administration, the White House turned into a rather cheerless place. Because of her religious beliefs, his wife banned wine, dancing, and card playing. But she believed in hard work, too. She became an able assistant to her husband. At first, she clipped and read newspaper articles for him. Later, when it was clear that he was overworked, she became a competent personal secretary.

The White House also became a more comfortable place to live under Polk. The Polks were the first presidential family to have an icebox to cool foods. It was installed in 1845, at a cost of twenty-five dollars.

And Polk was the first President to be able to read by gaslight instead of candles or oil lamps. Gas chandeliers were installed in 1848 when gas mains were built down Pennsylvania Avenue in Washington. Mrs. Polk insisted that one chandelier be left with candles, and that proved to be a wise decision. At the very first reception after the change, the gas gave out, leaving the candle-lit chandelier the only illumination in the White House.

From his experience as Speaker of the House of Representatives, Polk knew how to get things done in Washington. And he knew what he wanted to achieve—his campaign promise to expand the United States westward to California and the Pacific Ocean.

First he turned his attention to the Oregon question. For years, the Oregon Territory had been jointly occupied by England and the United States. But many Americans believed that it was time Oregon became part of the United States. These expansionists had a slogan, "Fifty-four, forty, or fight." The numbers referred to the latitude of a suggested border for Oregon as far north as southern Alaska, and some Americans were willing to go to war for that.

In a private message to London, however, Polk made it known that he was prepared to accept a compromise. The British agreed. In June of 1846, the northern border of the United States was firmly established along the forty-ninth parallel of latitude on a straight line running west from Minnesota to the Pacific Ocean.

The northern agreement came just in time because the United States had become involved in a war with Mexico to the south. The Mexicans were angry about the annexation of Texas as part of the United States, which had been approved by Congress early in 1845.

In a dispute about the border between the two countries, Polk sent

American troops to the Rio Grande River, which Mexico said was part of her territory. When Mexican troops fired on the Americans there, Polk went to Congress and asked for a declaration of war against Mexico.

After war was declared, Polk ordered two armies into action. One was aimed at California, then part of Mexico, and the other directly at Mexico City.

A small army under the command of General Stephen Watts Kearny marched due west. Kearny's orders were to conquer New Mexico and California. On a map back in Washington, it looked easy. The map showed only distances, not the desert, rattlesnakes, thirst, mountains, or Indians.

The sun was scorching hot as Kearny's men marched west. They found and killed thousands of rattlesnakes and marched through lands so dry there was little water or grass for their horses. Finally, on August 18, Kearny's men reached Santa Fe. The Mexicans there surrendered without a fight.

Kearny and his men then proceeded on through an even worse desert in the southwest toward California. Unknown to them, a revolt had already started there. Americans in the Sacramento Valley had raised the flag of an independent republic, with the idea of following the example of Texas and becoming part of the United States.

They did not have long to wait. Shortly after, an American naval force occupied the coastal cities of California, taking possession in the name of the United States. When Kearny arrived, he began to organize a government for the new American territory.

The war in the West had ended before the main fighting even started against Mexico. The major enemy there was not soldiers, but heat, sickness, and lack of supplies. It was not until 1847 that an American army was ready to fight in Mexico.

In February, these Americans commanded by General Zachary Taylor were attacked by a Mexican force that outnumbered them three to one. But Taylor was an old Indian fighter, at his best when he was in danger. He defeated the Mexicans at the Battle of Buena Vista, a victory that would lead to his election as President in 1848.

Still, the war was far from over. Polk appointed General Winfield Scott to head a force that landed on the Mexican coast and fought its way inland through the mountains to Mexico City. In September of 1847, Scott captured Mexico City—and then the American triumph was secure.

Under the peace treaty that followed, Mexico yielded its claims to Texas, California, New Mexico, and parts of Arizona, Utah, Colorado, and Nevada. In return, the United States paid Mexico $15 million.

With these territories added to the United States, the nation now spread "from sea to shining sea." Polk felt that he had accomplished all that he had promised to do as President. Summing up his term of office, one historian said of him: "A moderate in the midst of radicals and reactionaries, he won the enmity of both sides and the admiration only of history."

Worn out by his long hours of work in the White House, Polk left office in 1849. Only three months later, on June 15, 1849, he died in Nashville at the age of fifty-three.

Daniel Webster

1782–1852   U.S. Congressman and Senator; Secretary of State.

In the hills of New Hampshire, Captain Ebenezer Webster was an important man. During the Revolution, one night he had personally guarded General Washington's tent. When he came home to take up farming again, he took up politics, too.

His farm sat on the main road between Boston and Concord, the New Hampshire capital, so Captain Webster used part of his big old house as a tavern, where he had plenty of opportunity for talking politics. Nobody listened to him more avidly than his own youngest son.

Daniel Webster, born on January 18, 1782, was only seven at the high point of his father's political career. As an official "elector," the captain helped to make George Washington the first

President of the new United States in 1789. To Dan, it seemed that just being connected this way with such a great event made him different from other boys.

He did strike many people as an unusual sort of boy. Although he loved to go skating or fishing, any ordinary farm chore could defeat him. Still, his brain appeared to be remarkably big and powerful, for his head was large compared with the rest of his body. In those days, many people believed this was a sign of superior intelligence. And didn't the boy's dazzling ability as a reader prove the case?

Somehow Dan had taught himself more than the teacher at the log-cabin school knew. He could pick up any newspaper a traveler brought to the tavern and read even the longest words easily. When he was thirteen, this gift changed the direction of his life.

A young lawyer from Boston had opened an office in the nearby village of Salisbury. Asking around for a lad who could mind the office while he was busy elsewhere, he was told to hire Dan Webster. He did. After just a few weeks the lawyer went to see the boy's parents.

Send him away to school, the newcomer urged. Dan's mother was a hardworking woman whose name had been Abigail Eastman before she married and began bringing up eight children. She'd always thought, she admitted, that Dan might amount to something.

Dan's father hesitated; money was tight. It would please him, though, if the brightest of his sons could have something he more and more felt the lack of himself: a real education. In May of 1796—by then Dan was fourteen—he and his father rode on horseback down to the high-toned Phillips Exeter Academy.

This was a school not far from Boston where the sons of gentlemen were prepared to enter college. Dan Webster, in his plain homespun clothes, felt more than somewhat of an outsider. Even so, he crammed in enough Latin and other learning to move on quickly. Hardly more than a year later, while

he was still only fifteen, he became a freshman at Dartmouth.

Founded only about thirty years previously, the college had been built in a former pine forest near the New Hampshire town of Hanover. Here Webster did outstandingly well. He amazed other students by skimming twenty pages of any book—then repeating the whole passage, almost word for word.

He also displayed a spectacular skill at making speeches. When he was eighteen, he gave the main address at Hanover's Fourth of July celebration. By then, he had grown enough so that, with his shaggy hair and high forehead, some people said he reminded them of a young lion. Although he never talked much about his goals in life, it was widely assumed that one day Dan Webster would enter politics.

After graduating at the age of nineteen, Webster went home to learn about becoming a lawyer from the man he had worked for in Salisbury. But handling routine cases in a small town did not appeal to him. It was only because he was so fond of his father that he stayed put—until the old man died in 1806.

When he was twenty-five, Webster moved to the New Hampshire seaport of Portsmouth. During nine happy years there, he laid the foundation for his future success. In this same period, he married Grace Fletcher, the daughter of a minister. Less happily, though, he also formed the habit of spending more money than he earned.

It was as if he felt driven to live in the highest possible style. By winning law cases for prosperous shipowners, Webster earned a handsome income in Portsmouth. But he could not be satisfied with buying just a good house— he had to have the best. In the same way, he was increasingly driven to seek a wider, grander stage for his talents.

Webster entered politics. By the age of thirty, he had become the leading spokesman for the Federalist party in New Hampshire. That year—it was 1812—he was first elected to Congress.

His loyalty to the Federalists could have been predicted. In New England, many solid citizens continued to support this conservative party that Alexander Hamilton had originally led. Around the rest of the country, however, the Democratic-Republicans, founded by Thomas Jefferson, had become far more popular.

So, when Webster reached Washington, his opinions had not much impact. He opposed the War of 1812, of course, because New England Federalists feared the war would ruin their foreign trade. But Webster's personality and his appearance made a deeper impres-

sion than what he said. There seemed to be a special charge of electricity around this new Congressman whenever he stood up to speak. No matter that he was really only of middle height, he managed to look like a giant. People who kept a close eye on Washington politics said it was a pity that Webster held such narrow, New England views. With a broader outlook, what a national leader he might be!

But midway in his second term, Webster's money problems caused him to give up politics, at any rate for the time being. Because he could think of no other way to pay his debts, he decided to move his family to Boston. He felt sure that in this large city he could earn much more as a lawyer handling really major cases than he could in Portsmouth. The move meant, however, that he could no longer represent New Hampshire in Congress.

Still, Washington had by no means seen the last of Daniel Webster. During the next several years, he kept turning up there as an attorney, bringing many notable cases before the United States Supreme Court. By 1820, some experts were calling him the foremost lawyer of the era.

He proved to be brilliant at arguing fine points of law in the highest court of the land. On behalf of dozens of different clients, he won cases that went down in legal history. Among these, the so-called Dartmouth College Case did much to strengthen the Supreme Court itself, because Webster convinced a majority of the Justices that the Constitution did give them the power to settle disputes that some had thought were beyond their scope.

As a resident of Boston, Webster also made his mark. Invited to give the main speech at ceremonies observing the two hundredth anniversary of the Pilgrims' landing, he surprised some listeners. "I was never so excited by public speaking before in my life," a Harvard professor said.

Webster went back to Congress, representing Massachusetts, in 1822. Within five years, at the age of forty-five, he became Senator Webster, just in time to win national fame. When South Carolina threatened to break up the country by leaving the Union rather than abiding by a tax measure it could not approve, Webster delivered one of the outstanding speeches in American history.

It was 1830, and South Carolina aimed to "nullify" the tax law on the grounds that this interfered with the liberty of the state's residents. Clearly, the next step could be an outright clash between loyal states and those that put their own interests first.

In this crisis, Webster was inspired to rise above the interests of his own part of the country and speak on behalf of the nation. For more than three hours he poured forth the kind of emotional oratory that was much admired at the time. He finished:

When my eyes shall be turned to behold for the last time the sun in heaven, may I not see him shining on the broken and dishonored fragments of a once glorious Union. . . . Let their last feeble and lingering glance rather behold the gorgeous ensign of the republic . . . not a stripe erased . . . nor a single star obscured, bearing for its motto . . . dear to every true American heart—Liberty *and* Union, now and for ever, one and inseparable!

More than 150 years later, it may be hard to see why this speech of Webster's had such an extremely strong appeal during his own time, but he became a great hero to the young United States. Copies of his talk were printed, and in schools around the country countless students recited portions of it at speaking contests.

Some historians say that Webster became so famous because he provided a symbol—the symbol of the Union. As tensions between the North and South grew from 1830 onward, his passionate words in favor of preserving the Union gave patriotic citizens in the

This 1860 lithograph by Eliphalet Brown shows Daniel Webster debating the Compromise of 1850. *Courtesy of the National Portrait Gallery, Smithsonian Institution.*

North and the West a clear sense of purpose.

Not surprisingly, Webster himself tried to win the presidency several times. Since he was, without any doubt, a leading figure, why couldn't he be elected? It proved impossible, however, because of his personal problems.

In matters involving money Webster's judgment never did improve. In 1829, after the death of his first wife, he had married a wealthy New York woman named Caroline LeRoy, and it

seemed he would no longer be burdened with debts, but he still made risky investments and continued getting into financial trouble.

In addition, Webster showed less and less self-control when the time came that he could afford to indulge his taste for high living. He not only ate too much, becoming more like an elephant than a lion, he also drank too much, sometimes even in public.

While he still struck many people as godlike when he rose in the Senate and made one of his eloquent speeches, it was widely believed that Webster had a devilish streak, too. One writer said of him, "I have no question that he is the ablest man in public life at this time." But many felt that from a moral standpoint he could not be trusted.

So Webster had to give up his White House ambition. In 1840, President Harrison appointed him Secretary of State and in this important Cabinet post he worked hard to solve a long-standing controversy over the boundary between Maine and Canada. The resulting Webster-Ashburton Treaty was considered a diplomatic victory for the United States.

In 1844 Webster returned to the Senate. There he continued defending the Union fervently. His last great speech came in March of 1850, when he urged adoption of a compromise plan to settle the burning issue of whether slavery should be allowed in new territory acquired after the Mexican War.

"I wish to speak today," Webster said, "not as a Massachusetts man, nor as a Northern man, but as an American. I speak today for the preservation of the Union." Then he went on:

I hear with pain, and anguish, and distress, the word "secession" . . . Secession! Peaceable secession! Sir, your eyes and mine are never destined to see that miracle! I see that it must produce war, and such a war as I will not describe. . . . No, sir! There will be no secession!

Just ten years later, Webster's worst fears were realized with the outbreak of the Civil War. But he did not live to see it. On October 24, 1852, at the age of seventy, he died at his country home in Marshfield, Massachusetts.

PART III

The Civil War through the First World War

William Jennings Bryan

1860–1925   U.S. Congressman; Secretary of State.

It turned out to be the most famous speech in the history of American political conventions. The speaker was William Jennings Bryan of Nebraska at the Democratic National Convention on a hot day in Chicago in June of 1896.

By that speech, Bryan, until then a relatively unknown man, turned himself into a national figure. He became "the Silver Knight of the West" and ran for President of the United States three times.

But at that convention in 1896, Bryan was only one of several speakers on the most important issue facing the nation. It was a complicated subject—whether silver as well as gold should be used as the basis for the nation's money.

The silver issue represented a wave of protest from the farming communi-ties in the Middle West against the growing power of the industrial North-east. Farmers and others who worked with their hands were angry at what they considered to be the evils of the bankers on Wall Street, who controlled the nation's money.

Already the Republicans had adopted a party platform backing gold, and they had nominated Governor William McKinley of Ohio as their candidate for President. Now it was the turn of the Democrats.

Before their convention opened, the Democrats did not consider Bryan as a serious candidate to lead the party. But he was ambitious, and he saw an opportunity to win the nomination by strongly supporting silver.

An experienced orator, Bryan knew

he had the power to move audiences by his words. Ever since he had been in high school, he had practiced public speaking. Now he faced the biggest test of his life—but he was confident. Before he rose to speak, a reporter handed him a note: "This is a great opportunity." Bryan sent the note back with the words, "You will not be disappointed."

Standing before twenty thousand noisy delegates and guests at the convention, Bryan seized their attention immediately by attacking the financial leaders of the nation. In a mellow voice that reached out to the ends of the vast convention hall, he said:

We have petitioned and our petitions have been scorned; we have entreated and our entreaties have been disregarded; we have begged and they have mocked us when our calamity came. We beg no longer, we entreat no longer, we petition no longer, we defy them.

Bryan had found the words to move his audience. They cheered every sentence. Then he roused them into a tumult with these words: "We will answer their demand for the gold standard by saying to them, 'You shall not press upon the brow of labor a crown of thorns, you shall not crucify mankind upon a cross of gold.'"

A wave of excitement passed through the hall. In a frenzy of excitement, the delegates waved handmade banners saying, "No crown of thorns" and "No cross of gold." They paraded through the hall for almost an hour, cheering Bryan.

The next day, on the fifth ballot, Bryan was nominated as the Democratic candidate for President, at the age of thirty-six, the youngest man ever nominated by either party for the nation's highest office.

A son of the Middle West, Bryan had been born in Salem, Illinois, on March 19, 1860. His father, Silas Bryan, was a lawyer and later a judge in Illinois. His mother, Mariah Jennings Bryan, was a strong-minded religious woman. Young Willy was brought up in a strict, religious household.

From his boyhood, he had two major interests, politics and public speaking. When he was sixteen, he took a train all by himself to St. Louis because he wanted to see what the 1876 Democratic National Convention looked like. Unable to get in because he had no ticket, he looked and listened through a window.

Later, he confided to a friend that his ambition was to become a United States Senator. But that was a long way off for Willy, then a student at the Whipple Academy in Jacksonville, Illinois. As his first step, he joined the debating society.

The early verdict of his professors was discouraging. Willy was a poor speaker, they said. He was too timid and did not pronounce his words clearly. But his cousin Lizzie, who lived in Jacksonville, had faith in him. Together, they went to a nearby farm, where Willy stood on the stump of a tree and practiced speechmaking until he could hardly stand. He talked and talked, while she listened, until he could get the words out clearly and without hesitation.

At last, Cousin Lizzie thought he was ready for his first public-speaking competition. He entered a school contest, made his speech, and was awarded third prize. The audience thought he had a fine baritone voice that carried to the listeners at the back of the room.

Bryan continued to speak wherever anyone would listen through his years at Illinois College in Jacksonville and later at law school in Chicago. After graduating as a lawyer, in 1884 he married Mamie Baird, a classmate he had known for years. She, too, had studied law, but instead of becoming a lawyer she decided to have a family and help her husband.

After three years as a beginning lawyer in Illinois, Bryan decided that he was not getting ahead. On a trip to Nebraska to visit a friend, he made up his mind to leave Illinois. He would move to Lincoln, Nebraska, and start all over again.

It was a good choice for an ambitious young man. Even though Nebraska usually voted Republican, there were opportunities for a young lawyer, even a Democratic one. Bryan was twenty-seven years old, personable, tall, and handsome, with a wealth of black hair combed straight back from his forehead.

He plunged into politics in Nebraska. In the election of 1888, Bryan spoke in every corner of the state for the Democratic ticket. Two years later, he was nominated for a seat as a Representative in Congress, and he won. The Lincoln *Herald* described him then as "able, brilliant, young, magnetic, hopeful, candid, honest and poor."

In Washington, Bryan continued to work hard to improve his speaking ability. Mrs. Bryan often met her husband in Arlington Cemetery after Congress adjourned for the day. There, amid the tombs of the war dead, he practiced word for word, gesture for gesture, until he had his first speech to the House of Representatives just right.

For three hours, in that first speech, he spoke against a new tariff bill. Without notes, he quoted statistics, marshalled arguments, and answered hecklers, without losing his poise. BRYAN DOWNED THEM ALL, said a headline in the New York *World*. It was not only his eloquence but his facts and logic that convinced his colleagues that he was a comer.

His moment came with the "cross of gold" speech in 1896. After he got the nomination, he traveled all over the country, making as many as ten speeches a day in his campaign for the presidency. By contrast, his opponent, Governor McKinley, stayed at home in Canton, Ohio, greeting trainloads of visitors who came to see him.

Bryan won the hearts of the people of the Middle West with his attacks on high interest rates and his demand for regulation of railroad rates. His admirers called him The Great Commoner, because they felt he spoke for the common man. But the Republicans attacked him vigorously, calling him irresponsible, a rabble-rouser, and even a revolutionary. McKinley won the election.

Despite that defeat, Bryan retained the backing of the Democratic party. Once more, in 1900, he was its candidate for President, running against McKinley again. For Bryan, the campaign was more than just a political contest. To him, it was a battle between good and evil. The evil was the monied class of bankers and industrialists who supported McKinley, while the good was the working people who backed his own cause. McKinley won once again.

Bryan ran for President a third time in 1908 against William Howard Taft. "Shall the people rule?" Bryan asked repeatedly in speeches across the nation. To him and to his supporters, the choice before the voters was either a government devoted to the people, which he would provide, or a government favoring the privileged, represented by Taft and the Republican party.

Bryan was stunned by the election results. He lost by a bigger margin than before, despite the fact that there were more voters in the growing nation. It was the worst defeat for Bryan in all his three presidential campaigns. For political analysts, the explanation was simple. The nation was prosperous, and Taft's association with the popular Theodore Roosevelt gained him widespread support.

Although Bryan was out of the running for the Democratic nomination in 1912, he played a prominent role in the convention that year. When the delegates were deadlocked between Champ Clark of Missouri, the Speaker of the House of Representatives, and Woodrow Wilson, the progressive governor of New Jersey, Bryan threw his support behind Wilson. After Wilson won the election, he named Bryan as Secretary of State.

Despite unfamiliarity with foreign af-

William Jennings Bryan, shown here as Secretary of State, held that office from 1913 to 1915, when he resigned in protest of President Wilson's foreign policy. *Courtesy of the Library of Congress.*

fairs, Bryan learned quickly and gained the respect of foreign diplomats in Washington. When war broke out in Europe in 1914, Bryan insisted on not taking sides. But the question of American neutrality became a major issue in 1915 after a German submarine sank the British ocean liner *Lusitania,* with a loss of over a hundred American lives. Wilson sent a strong note of protest to Germany that Bryan considered a step on the road to war. In protest, Bryan resigned.

Over the years Bryan gradually withdrew from politics, moving to Florida in semiretirement but keeping busy in church affairs. He made headlines again in 1925 when he helped the prosecution in the famous Scopes trial.

John Scopes was a school teacher in Tennessee who talked about the theory of evolution in his classroom. That disturbed people who believed in a literal reading of the Bible. It was also a violation of the law in Tennessee.

Bryan, who had read and studied the Bible all his life, was called to testify. Under defense lawyer Clarence Darrow's questioning, Bryan finally exploded in anger. "The purpose here is to cast ridicule on everybody who believes in the Bible," he shouted.

"We have the purpose," Darrow replied, "of preventing bigots and ignoramuses from controlling the education of the United States."

Scopes was convicted, but Bryan took no joy in the verdict. He felt that the Bible and his religious faith had been made objects of mockery.

After that, he stayed out of the limelight. He died on July 26, 1925, at the age of sixty-five, and was buried in Arlington National Cemetery.

Jefferson Davis

1808–1889   U.S. Congressman; U.S. Senator; Secretary of War; President of the Confederate States of America.

Was he a hero? Or a traitor?

Over a hundred years have passed since the Civil War, when Jefferson Davis was the president of the Confederate States of America, but even now opinions about this leader of the South differ remarkably.

Those who admire him call him "the most misunderstood man in history." Other experts say his leadership lacked any real spark of greatness. On just one point they all agree: Jefferson Davis himself had a very sad and interesting life.

Born on June 3, 1808, he was the youngest and favorite son in a family of ten children, five boys and five girls. Clearly, his father had grand hopes for him because he named him after the man then occupying the White House,

President Jefferson. Young Jeff's surroundings also gave evidence of the same ambitious outlook. No other log home in their part of Kentucky had four separate rooms, besides windows of glass.

Still, Samuel Emory Davis was not satisfied. He had heard that fortunes were being made by planting cotton much farther south, along the Mississippi River. When Jeff was two, the family packed up several wagons and traveled 800 miles, mostly through wilderness, a journey of more than two months.

They settled in the southwestern corner of what would soon become the new state of Mississippi. There, Jeff's father and older brothers helped the twelve slaves they had brought with

121

them build a brick house with a wide front verandah. Not big enough to be called a mansion, neither was it the home of a poor family.

Ever since his own boyhood on a Georgia farm, Samuel Davis had been trying to better himself. After fighting in the Revolution, he had married Jane Cook and, as their family grew, he had kept moving south and west, seeking to join the upper rank of prosperous planters.

By the time he reached Mississippi, he was getting old. It would be his first son, Joseph—twenty-three years old the year Jeff was born—who did become rich. But Jeff's father seemed to ease his personal disappointment indirectly, becoming more and more occupied with grand plans for his golden-haired, blue-eyed youngest son.

At the age of only seven, Jeff was taken by horseback through the wilderness again to attend a highly regarded boarding school in Kentucky. He stayed there two years, until his mother missed him so much that he was allowed to come home. This time, he traveled on one of the new paddle-wheel river steamboats, a tremendous adventure for a nine-year-old boy.

At thirteen, Jeff once more left Mississippi, bound for Lexington, Kentucky. Here he enrolled at Transylvania University, where he learned Latin and

Greek. Growing up to be an extremely handsome young man, he also enjoyed the occasional dances in the homes of local families, to which some of the college students were invited.

A year before Jeff was to have graduated, his father succeeded in arranging something even more impressive. Just as Jeff was turning sixteen, in the spring of 1824, he received a letter telling him that he had been accepted as a cadet by the United States Military Academy at West Point, New York.

Despite all the rugged travel experiences of his boyhood, young Davis much preferred reading to playing any sort of game, so he did not long for the active life of a soldier. His father pointed out, however, that West Point offered a fine education at no cost. "Knowledge is power," old Mr. Davis assured him.

Jeff would always feel relieved that he had made his father happy by accepting the West Point offer. Otherwise, he might have blamed himself for the old man's sudden sickness and death a few weeks later. From then on, it was Jeff's oldest brother Joseph who assumed the role of guiding him.

At West Point, Cadet Davis did not relish the strict routine of studying and marching from dawn till ten at night. He was two years younger than most of his classmates, and he ranked twenty-third in his class of thirty-three when he graduated in 1828.

More important, though, he had become well acquainted with several future generals, notably Cadet Robert E. Lee. Because Davis had been brought up to believe he was capable of accomplishing anything he set his mind to, he no doubt dreamed of becoming a general himself someday. Meanwhile, as a brand-new lieutenant, he was assigned to duty out West.

He spent the next seven years in the territory that would later be carved into the states of Wisconsin and Iowa. There his days were filled with rough, mostly boring work like supervising the building of a new sawmill or the repairing of an old fort. Only rarely was the monotony interrupted by trouble with hostile Indians.

In 1835, Davis decided to give up his Army career. The break was not easy because he had made some good friends and he liked the prestige of being a military officer. Still, he felt he must try his luck elsewhere—in order to marry the young woman he loved.

Sarah Taylor was the daughter of his own commanding officer, Colonel Zachary Taylor. The colonel knew how hard life was for the wives of army men, so he had forbidden Sarah to marry a soldier. That started a chain of events, both joyous and tragic.

First, Davis wrote a letter formally resigning from the Army. Shortly afterward, on June 17, 1835, he married Sarah at the home of one of her aunts in Louisville. Then the young couple boarded a boat going south toward Mississippi, where they stayed at the plantation of the bridegroom's brother Joseph. Meanwhile, their own home was being built on an adjoining tract he had given them as a wedding present.

Three months after their wedding day, Jefferson Davis and his wife both fell seriously ill with malarial fever. It seemed for a time that neither of them would live, but he recovered, only to hear that Sarah had died.

During the eight years following his wife's death, Davis grieved and saw hardly anybody except his brother Joseph. He read countless books about history, which they discussed together. Because he hated owing Joseph money, he put some effort into directing the planting of cotton on the land he had been given. His interest in the world around him did not revive, however, until a seventeen-year-old girl with sparkling eyes accompanied her parents on a visit to Joseph's plantation.

Varina Howell belonged to one of the most prominent families in the area. Davis was twice her age when they met, but they both fell in love. About two years later—he was thirty-seven by that time, and she nineteen—her parents agreed to their marriage.

During these years of waiting, Davis quickly emerged as a bright new star on the Southern political scene. After just a brief term in the Mississippi state legislature, he was elected to the national House of Representatives.

He arrived in Washington with his young bride early in December of 1845. There, too, he immediately attracted attention, partly because of his handsome appearance and his manner of being a person of some importance. Yet what he said had even more impact.

By 1845, slavery had become a burning issue, causing bitter antagonism between the North and the South. The South urgently needed a convincing new spokesman for its own point of view because its longtime leader—the stern, old Senator Calhoun of South Carolina—was getting weaker every year. Congressman Jefferson Davis from Mississippi filled this need, for he passionately believed that slavery provided many benefits to "a childlike race." He also insisted that slaves in the South were treated better than many factory workers in the North. Above all, he defended the principle that every state had the right to do as it wished on this matter, without interference from outsiders.

Only six months after Davis began making his mark in Washington, the Mexican War erupted, propelling him to further prominence all over the country. As a retired Army officer, he volunteered to lead a regiment of Mississippi riflemen into combat.

At the Battle of Buena Vista, Davis boldly won the day for the Americans. It was actually his first experience under fire, but even though he received a painful leg wound, he behaved like a hero. President Polk immediately promoted him to brigadier general.

By now politics interested Davis more than warfare. To guard the South's interests, he decided he would rather accept another offer, and he became a member of the United States Senate. As a Senator, then as Secretary of War under President Pierce, then as a Senator again, Davis increasingly seemed the voice of the South in Washington. He repeatedly said he hoped the Union could be saved—but saved under terms protecting the South from any Northern dictation about its own way of life.

Still, Davis could not stop less temperate supporters of the Southern cause from deciding to quit the Union after the election of President Abraham Lincoln in 1860. A congress of Southern delegates met in Montgomery, Alabama, to set up their own Confederate States of America, and on February 8, 1861, this congress elected Jefferson Davis as president of the new country.

Jefferson Davis is pictured entering the Battle of Bull Run. *Courtesy of the National Portrait Gallery, Smithsonian Institution.*

An unidentified artist based this lithograph on photographs of the Confederate generals. From left to right are Leonidas Polk, John Bankhead Magruder, Thomas Jefferson Simmons, George Nichols Hollins, Benjamin McCulloch, Jefferson Davis, Robert E. Lee, Pierre Gustave Toutant Beauregard, Sterling Price, Joseph Eggleston Johnston, and William Joseph Hardee. *Courtesy of the National Portrait Gallery, Smithsonian Institution.*

Even if Davis had been able to organize his government peacefully, he would have faced tremendous problems. As it was, outright war between the North and the South started in April of 1861, when Confederate troops seized the federally owned Fort Sumter in the harbor of Charleston, South Carolina.

Throughout the next four years of fighting, President Davis never had a day off, and he suffered from increasingly severe headaches. That was why he often acted coldly or high-handedly, his friends explained; those who knew him well said he was really warm-hearted.

Davis had a wonderful gift for swiftly making up his mind about complicated issues. Yet even in the South, his leadership sometimes upset people more than it inspired them. They blamed him for interfering in military matters, as if he considered himself a better general than any commander in the field, including the much-loved head of the Southern army, General Robert E. Lee. Moreover, the individual states constituting the Confederacy often complained that President Davis did not understand their own viewpoint.

Much of this criticism struck admirers of Davis as unfair. A century later, experts on the history of the Civil War agree with them—to a certain extent. Whatever they think of Davis personally, they agree that nobody could have led the South to victory.

In size and economic power, the North was vastly superior, so it was bound to triumph. Most historians agree that only the amazingly strong spirit of the South kept it from going down to defeat much sooner.

When General Lee surrendered early in April of 1865, President Davis still could not accept the fact that his cause was lost. He left his capital of Richmond in Virginia, vowing to carry on the fight somehow. Several weeks later, he was finally captured in Georgia.

He was thrust into prison—even chained, for a few days. The terrible assassination of President Lincoln had aroused fierce anger over what appeared at first to be some sort of conspiracy by the leaders of the South. "Hang Jeff Davis!" people chanted all over the North.

Davis was released after two years in a Virginia prison. No trial was ever held; nobody could say what crime he should be accused of, and it surely seemed that he had suffered enough.

In the next twenty-two years Davis went to Canada and to England and became involved in numerous business ventures that failed. He died in New Orleans on December 6, 1889, at the age of eighty-one.

Robert LaFollette

1855–1925   U.S. Congressman; Governor of Wisconsin;
U.S. Senator.

During his first year at the University of Wisconsin, in 1875, Bob LaFollette had an exciting time. Two things happened that set him on the path toward political fame. He heard a speech about the need for reducing the power of rich business leaders—and he fell in love.

The speech by a judge of the state's highest court stirred him deeply. Following the Civil War, executives of railroads and other large corporations had acquired increasing influence over the government. "Which shall rule?" the judge demanded. "Wealth, or educated and patriotic free men?"

But it was sixteen-year-old Belle Case, one of his fellow students, who gave LaFollette more specific prodding to work for changing the system. Why, she asked, shouldn't educated and pa-

triotic women also share in running the country?

When Bob and Belle were both juniors in college, they became engaged. In effect, they formed a team that started one of America's major reform movements. At that time many people disapproved of female involvement with public service, so Belle remained mostly in the background while the spotlight focused on Bob.

Robert Marion LaFollette had the sort of magnetism that made him stand out even in his youth. Born on June 14, 1855, near a Wisconsin town called Primrose, he went through some unhappiness as a child. His father, Josiah LaFollette, died when Bob was only eight months old.

Josiah had been an ambitious man,

descended from a farming family that had left France to settle in New Jersey back in the 1700s. He was more interested in politics than plowing, though, and before his health failed he had held several local offices. No matter that his son never knew him, Bob grew up determined to achieve the political success his father would have been proud of.

Probably Bob thought so much about the parent he could only imagine because his mother—a tiny, strong-minded woman named Mary Ferguson—married again. Her new husband was a prosperous storekeeper with extremely strict religious beliefs, and Bob did not like him at all.

Although there was just a one-room school in Primrose, Bob set his mind very early on going to college. Instead of seeking help from his stepfather, he went around selling books and doing any other work he could find to earn the money he would need. Then he spent a few years at a private academy, preparing to enter the university in the state capital of Madison.

LaFollette was twenty when he finally qualified as a freshman. Besides being older than most of his classmates, he had the kind of bouncy personality that attracted attention. Short and stocky—he measured just five feet five inches—he also used a rather startling

method for appearing taller. He had his thick, sandy-colored hair cut so that it stood straight up above his high forehead, adding several inches to his height.

He and Belle Case got along marvelously together. A small, bubbly farm girl, she was the best student in their class. She was aiming to become the first female admitted to the university's law school. Meanwhile, she thoroughly enjoyed helping Bob get better marks, and she worked hard with him on polishing the speeches he delivered in various contests. Orators were nearly as highly regarded on this campus as athletes, and Bob LaFollette was determined to shine at public speaking. By his senior year, he was ready to try for the Midwest championship.

Newspapers all over the region carried long stories about the competition in Iowa City, Iowa. LaFollette had chosen the character of Iago, in Shakespeare's play *Othello*, as the subject for his oration. He not only analyzed the reasons why Iago told such evil lies, but also he gave his own interpretation of some of Iago's words. "Put money in thy purse," he hissed impressively.

And so he won the Interstate Oratorical Contest in May of 1879. The victory made him a hero on his own campus, where he graduated a month later. It even made him famous among residents of Madison, very much simplifying his entry into politics.

Hardly more than a year after getting his diploma, LaFollette had crammed enough legal knowledge into his head to pass the bar exam. Then he opened his own law office right in Madison. But sitting and waiting for clients struck him as not really necessary, so in the autumn of 1880 he boldly set out to become the county district attorney.

Thanks to the splash he had made by winning the speaking contest, LaFollette got the job. Even though he had to ask experienced lawyers what in the world he was supposed to do, he did well enough to win reelection two years later.

By then, he and Belle were married. She had also managed to break through the prejudice against women at law school, where she was getting a far better legal education than her husband had. All during his career, he cheerfully admitted that he depended on her legal advice.

In 1884, when he was twenty-nine, LaFollette took a great step forward politically. Because of some complicated feuding in the state's Republican party, he was able to get the nomination to run for Congress. Although there were several issues on which he felt the party needed to change its position, he still

considered himself basically a Republican.

If the Wisconsin branch of the party had not been torn by disputes among some of its leaders, LaFollette could not have decided on his own that he wanted to go to Washington. As in many other states, powerful bosses controlled the selection of officeholders very tightly. After LaFollette won the post he wanted, however, he was more or less accepted by the Milwaukee Ring— the top command of Wisconsin's Republicans—because he seemed to be such a good vote-getter.

LaFollette went along pretty dependably with the Ring's policies, but after serving six years in the House of Representatives he felt it was time to speak up on his own ideas about taxes. He had just begun showing some independence when, in 1890, he suffered a rude awakening. He, along with several other Republican candidates from Wisconsin, went down to defeat in the November election because the state's farmers and working men were angry about the way the party appeared to be favoring the rich. While the defeat upset LaFollette, it really started his political career.

Soon after he resumed practicing law in Madison, he was summoned to a private meeting with the head of the Milwaukee Ring. This man had become

After two defeats in previous elections, Robert LaFollette won the race for governor of Wisconsin in 1900. *Courtesy of the State Historical Society of Wisconsin.*

wealthy from his dealings in every sort of business where a lot of money was to be made, from lumbering to railroad building. When LaFollette returned to Madison, he told reporters that the ringleader had dared to offer him a bribe.

The story made a sensation in Wisconsin newspapers. According to LaFollette, he had been offered some high-paying law business to make sure of his future loyalty to the Ring. The man he named denied the charge, of course.

From then on, though, LaFollette openly fought to "clean up" Wisconsin politics. He became a familiar figure at county fairs all over the state—speaking to voters by the thousands, waving his arms and striding around the platform, arousing great enthusiasm. "Go on, Bob!" his audiences would holler delightedly.

Still, the Ring had so much power that it took LaFollette ten years to get elected governor. In 1901, Bob and Belle LaFollette, along with their two sons and two daughters, moved into Wisconsin's imposing executive mansion on the shores of Lake Mendota in Madison.

By then, LaFollette had developed a program of reforms that newspapers all over the country publicized as the Wisconsin Idea. It had three main points:

1. Candidates for public office should be chosen by direct primaries open to every voter, instead of being hand-picked by political bosses.

2. Tax laws should be changed so that large corporations and rich businessmen paid their fair share.

3. To ensure fair play, the rates charged by railroads and other corporations serving the public should be regulated by governmental commissions.

During two terms as governor, LaFollette secured adoption of these basic reforms in his own state. Owing to the influence of Belle LaFollette, Wisconsin also pioneered in giving women a more important role politically. By 1905, the governor and his wife were ready to move on to Washington.

As Senator LaFollette, he strove then to extend the Wisconsin Idea throughout the nation. Although the Republican party was still basically conservative, an increasing number of its members called themselves Progressives. It was no secret that LaFollette hoped eventually to lead the growing Progressive movement—from the White House.

To advance his cause, LaFollette founded his own weekly magazine. It provided a fine example of his hard-hitting approach to politics. On its front page, the slogan of his publication proclaimed: It Will Be Conservative When Good Things Are to Be Conserved. It

Robert LaFollette campaigned with great oratorical skill and earned wide popular support. *Courtesy of the State Historical Society of Wisconsin.*

Will Be Radical When Bad Things Are to Be Uprooted.

"Fighting Bob" LaFollette's influence was felt all over the country as many other states adopted the direct primary method for picking candidates for public office. His ideas about reducing the power of big business and using natural resources for the benefit of all the people resulted in the passage of new laws.

All through American history, there have been waves of reform from time to time, and the early 1900s saw the cresting of one of the most notable of these waves, so in 1912 LaFollette thought he had a real chance of being nominated for the presidency.

But former President Theodore Roosevelt came out of retirement that year to tear apart the Republican party. When its national convention renominated the conservative President Taft, Roosevelt himself led a third party he called the Progressives. As a result, La-Follette was left out in the cold.

Yet even the dynamic T.R. could not be elected without the support of a major party. All he accomplished was to split the Republican vote, thereby assuring the election of the Democrat Woodrow Wilson.

Worse was in store for Senator LaFollette. When a great war broke out in Europe in 1914, he kept insisting the United States must not take sides. Neutrality was the only wise policy, he contended. Even after German submarines were ordered to attack American ships, he voted in 1917 against helping England and France to defeat Germany.

LaFollette's antiwar stand made him extremely unpopular for several years. He had to stop making speeches because a chorus of booing drowned out his every word. But public opinion changed after the war ended. Americans had fought, in President Wilson's words, "to make the world safe for democracy," so the squabbling that broke out among former allies as soon as peace returned caused deep feelings of dis-

illusion around the country.

Then Senator LaFollette easily won another term in 1922. His White House dream revived, even though Americans had become less interested in reform than in making money. In 1924, he did run for President—as the candidate of his own newly formed Progressive party.

About 5 million people around the country voted for him, but over 8 million voted for the Democrat John W. Davis, and more than 15 million cast their ballots to elect the conservative Republican Calvin Coolidge.

Less than a year after this defeat, Senator LaFollette died on June 18, 1925, at the age of seventy.

His son, Robert M. LaFollette, Jr., who had served many years as his secretary, took over his seat in the Senate. "Young Bob" LaFollette continued to work for tax reform and many other causes his father had supported until his own retirement in 1947. Another son, Philip, also carried on the family's political tradition, holding office as the governor of Wisconsin for six years during the 1930s.

Abraham Lincoln

1809–1865   Sixteenth President of the United States.

When historians rank Presidents of the United States, Abraham Lincoln is always named as one of the greatest, along with George Washington. The reason is that Lincoln, with personal courage and strength of character, held the country together in the time of its greatest peril, during the Civil War.

More than a hundred years have passed since the end of that terrible war, when brother fought against brother, but Lincoln's reputation as the man who saved the Union has not dimmed.

In his time, he was loved and hated. He was called Honest Abe and Father Abraham by those who loved him. He was also called The Tyrant and the Illinois Baboon by those who opposed him.

What kind of human being could inspire such affection and hatred?

Lincoln emerged from a background of rural poverty. He was born in a one-room log cabin with a dirt floor in Hodgenville, Kentucky, on February 12, 1809. Little is known about his mother, Nancy Hanks Lincoln. His father, Thomas Lincoln, was a carpenter. Unable to make a living in Kentucky, he moved his family to Indiana when Abe was seven years old.

After his mother died in 1818, his father remarried. Abe's stepmother, a kindly woman, made sure he received some schooling. But because his work was needed on the farm where they lived, he attended various schools for less than a year.

Abe grew up tall, lanky, and strong. From using an axe to cut down trees and to split logs, he developed tremendous strength in his arms and shoulders. He became a top-notch wrestler. Fleet of foot, he won recognition as the best athlete in the area.

Above all, he loved to read. Since his family had no books, he walked miles to borrow and return them. He read by the dim light of wood burning in a fireplace. He took books to the fields while plowing, stopping to read when he let the horses rest.

The Lincoln family did not prosper in Indiana either, so his father moved them once more, this time to Illinois in 1830. Abe was twenty-one years old then, six feet four in height, with gray eyes and coarse black hair.

In Illinois he worked as a farmhand, as a ferryboat operator, and as a clerk in a New Salem general store. His employer there boasted that his new man had no equal in running, jumping, or wrestling. That, of course, brought

Legend has it that Abraham Lincoln was born in this one-room log cabin in rural Kentucky. *Courtesy of the Library of Congress.*

challenges from many other young men in town. Lincoln won them all.

But it was not all rough-and-tumble. Lincoln joined the local debating society and learned to argue with force and vigor. He enlisted during a war with Indians in 1832 and was elected captain of the local company. In that same year, he ran for the state legislature. Even though he lost, the campaign gave him experience and confidence.

Then, with a partner, he opened a general store. That failed, however, because his partner liked to drink and Lincoln spent much of his time reading books. It took him fifteen years to pay off their debts, but he did.

Lincoln's luck changed in 1833, when he was named postmaster of New Salem. He kept his postal receipts in an old blue sock and the mail in his hat. A faithful mailman, he would walk miles to deliver a letter—and he made friends.

The following year he ran for the state legislature once more. This time he won and found a profession that he could excel in—the law. It was not easy to study law because there were no lawyers or even law books in New Salem. Lincoln borrowed books in Springfield, walking forty miles to get and return the books he needed. He was admitted to the bar in 1836.

During that period, he met and fell in love with Ann Rutledge, the blue-eyed, blonde daughter of a local tavern owner. Unhappily, she died in 1835 of what is thought to have been typhoid fever. She is remembered even today as the lost love of Lincoln's life.

Several years later, Lincoln met Mary Todd from Lexington, Kentucky. They were married on November 4, 1842, and made their home in Springfield. They had four sons.

In 1846, Lincoln ran for a seat in the House of Representatives and was elected. In Washington he opposed what he thought was an unjust war with Mexico. That lost him support at home and he was not nominated to run again.

In those days, the most important political issue was slavery, and whether new states in the West should be admitted to the Union as "slave" or "free" states. Lincoln himself was opposed to slavery, but he did not believe that the federal government had any right to interfere with slavery in the states where it already existed.

When the new antislavery Republican party was formed in 1856, Lincoln joined it. In 1858, the new party chose him as its candidate for United States Senator from Illinois. In accepting the nomination, Lincoln made a memorable speech. "A nation divided against itself cannot stand," he said.

Lincoln and his Democratic oppo-

Thomas Le Mere was one of many artists and photographers who captured Abraham Lincoln's likeness. *Courtesy of the National Portrait Gallery, Smithsonian Institution.*

nent, Stephen A. Douglas, debated the slavery issue all over the state of Illinois. Although many people thought that Lincoln won the debates, Douglas won the election. However, Lincoln's moderate stand and his ability to express his views convincingly attracted attention all over the country.

Early in 1860, Lincoln was invited to speak at Cooper Union in New York City. He supported a policy of not interfering with slavery in the states where it existed but opposed the extension of slavery into new territories and states. The speech convinced many people that he was the right man to be President during such troubled times.

At the Republican state convention in Illinois, his backers entered the hall carrying split logs that they said Honest Abe had cut himself as a young man. From those logs, Lincoln gained the nickname The Rail-Splitter, which may have helped make him better known.

At the Republican National Convention in 1860, Lincoln was the choice of the party's moderates, but public opinion was so divided by then that there were four candidates for President. Lincoln faced Douglas of the Northern Democrats, John C. Breckinridge of the Southern Democrats, and John Bell of the Constitutional Union Party. Lincoln won the election.

Two things happened before he took office. He grew a beard at the suggestion of an eleven-year-old girl, Grace Bedell of Westfield, New York. She had written him a letter saying that he would look a great deal better with a beard because his face was so thin.

More important, drastic action was taken in the South. Even though Lincoln was considered a moderate on the slavery issue, the South saw his election as a threat. On December 20, 1860, South Carolina seceded from the Union. Two months later, on February 4, 1861, the Southern states met in Montgomery, Alabama and proclaimed themselves the Confederate States of America.

In his inaugural address on March 4, 1861, Lincoln said he had no intention of interfering with slavery—but, he added, the Union was indivisible. Under the Constitution, he said, his duty was clear: to enforce the laws of the United States everywhere.

Despite that mild speech, the South prepared for war. It seized all federal forts and navy yards in the states it controlled, except Fort Sumter in the harbor of Charleston, South Carolina. At 4:30 A.M. on April 2, the South fired on Fort Sumter to force it to surrender. The Civil War had begun. It was to last four years and cost the lives of 600,000 Americans.

In military terms, the war began with a series of defeats for the North. Al-

After the Battle of Antietam in 1862, Alexander Gardner photographed Abraham Lincoln with officers at the headquarters of the Union Army near Harper's Ferry. *Courtesy of the Library of Congress.*

though the South was smaller and had fewer factories, it had better generals than the North. For Lincoln, those early days of the war were very trying. He was faced by a divided Cabinet, incompetent generals, abolitionists calling for an immediate end to slavery, and abuse in the press.

In addition, his personal life was bitter. His eleven-year-old son, Willie, died in the White House in 1862, and his wife became nearly insane with grief.

Through all the troubles he faced, Lincoln remained a tower of strength to the nation. As the war progressed, the Union slowly began to show its power. After a victory at the Battle of Antietam, Lincoln issued his famous Emancipation Proclamation on January 1, 1863, which freed the slaves in the states where the Confederacy was still in rebellion.

The turning point of the war came at the Battle of Gettysburg in July of 1863. Southern forces under the command of General Robert E. Lee had invaded the North but were turned back in one of the fiercest battles of the conflict.

Several months later, on November 19, 1863, a cemetery for the war dead was dedicated at Gettysburg, Pennsylvania. There Lincoln made what is probably the most famous speech in American history. It was only ten sentences long, but it captured in simple terms what the war was all about. It ended with these words:

. . . that we here highly resolve that these dead shall not have died in vain; that this nation, under God, shall have a new birth of freedom; and that government of the people, by the people, for the people, shall not perish from the earth.

Throughout the war, Lincoln had been looking for a fighting general. He finally found his man in Ulysses S. Grant, who had won a string of victories along the Mississippi River. Promoted to command the Union forces in 1864, Grant

Herman Faber drew Abraham Lincoln on his deathbed in a house across the street from Ford's Theatre. *Courtesy of the Library of Congress.*

immediately began to pound away at the Confederate Army.

But the nation grew weary of death and casualties as the presidential election of 1864 approached. In a move toward unity, the Republicans changed their name. Together with some Democrats who supported the war, they formed a National Union party, with Lincoln as its leader. As his vice-presidential running mate they chose Andrew Johnson of Tennessee, the only Southern Senator who had stayed loyal to the Union when the South seceded.

The Democratic party, at its convention, called the war a failure and favored negotiations with the South. It nominated General George B. McClellan, who had been fired by Lincoln, as its candidate for President. The campaign was bitter, and even Lincoln thought he had little chance of victory.

But before Election Day, the tide of war turned. Admiral Farragut captured Mobile Bay. General Sherman captured Atlanta and began his famous march through Georgia to the sea. With

victories at last being won, Lincoln was reelected by a wide margin.

In his second inaugural address, on March 4, 1865, he again spoke words that stirred the nation:

With malice toward none; with charity for all; with firmness in the right, as God gives us to see the right, let us strive on to finish the work we are in; to bind up the nation's wounds; . . . to do all which may achieve and cherish a just and lasting peace among ourselves, and with all nations.

The final victory came at the Appomattox Court House in Virginia on April 9, 1865, when Lee surrendered to Grant. The nation rejoiced, and Lincoln made plans to welcome the South back into the United States.

But then a terrible thing happened. On April 14, Lincoln and his wife went to Ford's Theater in Washington to see a play, *Our American Cousin*. As they sat in their box, a proslavery extremist, John Wilkes Booth, fired a shot into Lincoln's head. He died on April 15, at the age of fifty-six, the first President in American history to be assassinated.

Justin Morrill

1810–1898 U.S. Congressman; U.S. Senator.

All his life, Justin Morrill regretted that he had not had the opportunity to go to college. In the small Vermont village where he grew up, children had to go to work at an early age to help keep their families going.

He never forgot that. Even when he was eighty years old, near the end of long years of public service in Washington as a member of the House of Representatives and as a Senator, he still remembered it. In a speech to college students, he recalled that during his own youth he had had to read in the evenings or by the light of candles after church on Sunday. From sunrise to sunset, he had no time for anything but chores on the farm.

After he was grown, though, he did a lot to make up for what he had missed.

Morrill not only educated himself so well that he became a major leader in the political life of his country, he also devoted his life to making it easier for others to go to college.

Because of his efforts, agricultural colleges were established across the nation in the mid-1800s. They gave millions of young Americans in rural areas the opportunity that he himself had lacked, and they sparked the scientific research in agriculture that has made the bounty of American farms the envy of the world.

Morrill's determination to help others had its roots in the rocky soil of his native Vermont. His ancestors were among the earliest settlers of the wilderness of eastern Vermont shortly after the Revolutionary War. They arrived

143

in 1795, ready to farm near Strafford in the valley of the Ompompanoosuc River.

Making a living in the short growing season of Vermont was not easy, so Grandfather Morrill became a blacksmith, too. Using a forge to heat metal and a hammer to shape it, he made shoes for horses as well as axes, scythes, and hoes for other farmers.

One of his sons, Nathaniel, when he was only fifteen years old, saw a way of making the hard work easier. Why not use waterpower instead of muscles to hammer metal and sharpen tools? With a neighbor, he built a dam across the valley so that paddle wheels could turn the grindstones and other tools of the blacksmith's trade.

When he was twenty-six years old, in 1816, Nathaniel was a successful blacksmith. He had married Mary Hunt, the daughter of a neighboring farmer, and they made their home on a farm near the blacksmith's shop. The oldest of their ten children, Justin was born there on April 14, 1810.

As a boy, Justin helped with the farm chores, feeding the animals, spreading hay, planting corn, and digging potatoes. One of his favorite jobs was turning the handle of the churn filled with cream—turning it tirelessly, until the cream became butter. In between these chores, his mother taught him to read.

Like the other children in the area, he attended a small, red-brick schoolhouse. But the school year was short. In that farming community, school started the first Monday after Thanksgiving, in late November, instead of the usual September, because the boys and girls were needed on the farms to help with the fall harvest.

Justin continued in school until he was fifteen years old. It was then that he suffered his great disappointment. "I desired to obtain a college education," he recalled much later, "but my father said he was unable to send all his boys to college and felt he ought to give them all an equal chance." As a result, none of the boys or girls in his family went to college.

It was time for Justin to go to work. He was offered a job with Judge Jedediah Harris, the leading storekeeper of the village. His pay was $45 for the first year of work and $75 for the second year. Despite those low wages, it was the best job in town for a boy his age.

In those days, the village store was more than just a place to buy things. It was the center of local life, where everybody came sooner or later to meet their neighbors as well as to buy what they needed. They talked about the crops, the weather, births, marriages, deaths and, above all, politics.

The village store turned out to be

an excellent school of politics for young Morrill. He also had an experienced teacher in Judge Harris. In addition to being a merchant, Harris was the local representative to the state legislature. Listening to Judge Harris talk about his cases was an education in itself.

But that did not satisfy the ambitious young man. He wanted to read more, to learn more himself, but he had no books. So he founded a library. By talking to everybody in the village and around it, he managed to get fifty subscribers. Each paid two dollars a year as a membership fee. But the library failed because, as Morrill put it, "the books went out like doves from the Ark of Noah, never to return."

After two years in the store, Morrill moved for a short time to Portland, Maine, where he worked as a bookkeeper, but soon he returned to Strafford and became a partner in a new store with his old employer, Judge Harris.

As Vermont grew, the store flourished. The business expanded until the partnership operated four stores in the area. Morrill prospered, so much so that he was able to retire in 1848, at the age of thirty-eight, with sufficient money to live on.

He settled down to life on his small farm, growing flowers, raising sheep, and improving his orchard. Now he had

Justin Morrill represented Vermont in Congress for forty-four years.

enough time to browse in his small library among the books that he had missed when he was growing up.

Two things changed his life in the next few years. He met a young woman from Massachusetts, Ruth Swan, and they were married in September of 1851. Then, in 1854, his neighbors decided that Morrill knew enough about politics to represent them in Washington.

At the age of forty-four, Morrill began a distinguished career in Congress that was to last forty-four years. He served in Congress longer than any other man of his time, earning the respect of his colleagues for his hard work on "bread and butter" issues like taxes and finance.

He was an exceptionally skillful legislator, noted for his sound reasoning and courteous behavior. He and his wife were frequent hosts at their home, and his birthday parties were among the most important social events in the capital. Year after year, the voters of Vermont sent Morrill back to Washington to continue his work for them—in the House of Representatives through 1866, and thereafter as a Senator.

Looking down from the press gallery one day, a writer described him as tall and thin, with abundant dark hair, blue eyes, and a kindly smile. "Here is a face to believe in without any reservation," he wrote.

From the beginning of his service in Washington, Morrill felt his most important work was in the field of education. Only a few years after he entered Congress, he introduced legislation to establish colleges in each state that would specialize in the scientific study of agriculture and mechanics.

It was a revolutionary idea because at that time a college education was reserved for the leisured class or for training leaders in government or professions such as medicine and the ministry. It seemed to most educators that agriculture was a field beneath the dignity of an institution of higher education.

By the middle of the nineteenth century, there was the beginning of a revolt against that idea. Agricultural societies in many states insisted that colleges must be available where new methods of farming could be studied. From his experience on the rocky soil of Vermont, Morrill was convinced that agricultural colleges would benefit not only farmers but the entire nation.

His major contribution was an ingenious way of paying for them. He saw that the federal government owned vast tracts of empty land that it was giving away to railroads, for example, as a means of helping them construct tracks to the West. Why not use some of the land to pay for the new colleges?

In 1857, Morrill presented his proposal to Congress. It would establish at least one college in each state "where the leading object shall be to teach such branches of learning as are related to agriculture and the mechanic arts to promote the liberal and practical education of the industrial classes."

Congress adopted his proposal, but it was vetoed by President Buchanan. He thought it was a violation of the traditional policy of the federal government to leave education to the states.

But Morrill persisted. He worked quietly behind the scenes to convince his colleagues and others that the new kind of college was needed in a growing country. Once again, Congress passed the Morrill Bill in 1862. Despite the fact that the nation was engaged in a great Civil War, President Lincoln signed it into law.

The colleges became known as land-grant colleges, because the federal government gave each state 30,000 acres for each Senator and Representative. The land could be held or sold to pay for the new colleges.

Altogether, the government gave more than eleven million acres to the states to establish the land-grant colleges. Today there is at least one such college in each of the fifty states, as well as in the District of Columbia, Puerto Rico, Guam, and the Virgin Islands. At the last count, there were seventy-two land-grant colleges in the United States.

From the beginning, the colleges were engaged in agricultural research as well as in education. The results of the new research were so impressive that Congress in 1887 established agricultural experiment stations connected with each state's land-grant college. Out of them came new seeds and new methods of growing that produce the food that feeds America and a large part of the world.

Today, more than a century later, the nation's land-grant colleges stand as a permanent memorial to Justin Morrill. A president of Cornell University in New York, itself one of the land-grant colleges, said Morrill's work should rank in historical importance with Jefferson's purchase of the Louisiana Territory.

Visitors to Washington today can see other signs of Morrill's contributions to his country. As chairman of a congressional committee, he was largely responsible for the construction of terraces and fountains for the stately Capitol building. And more than any other legislator, he fought for years until he finally won funds to build a suitable home for the Library of Congress. As a leader of the Senate until the end of his long life, he became known as "the grand old man of the Republican party."

Despite his lack of a college degree, Morrill was honored by his native state with an appointment as trustee of the University of Vermont.

He died in Washington on December 28, 1898, at the age of eighty-eight, and is buried overlooking his native village of Strafford.

Jeannette Rankin

1880–1973   First U.S. Congresswoman.

How would she act? And what would she wear? Washington was buzzing with questions about Jeannette Rankin on the morning of April 2, 1917.

At noon that day she would make history, taking her seat as the first woman ever to serve as a member of Congress. The voters of Montana had amazed the rest of the country by electing her. In most states, women were still not allowed to cast ballots, let alone run for office.

But women's suffrage, the matter of whether females should have the right to vote, had become a major issue. Committees all over the nation were staging parades and protests. In Washington, on that spring morning, a festive breakfast was held instead.

Before the guest of honor drove off to the Capitol, she was presented with a large bouquet of yellow flowers. She liked them too much to leave them behind. When she entered the House of Representatives, escorted by the senior man among Montana's members, one reporter joked that she reminded him of a bride.

Yet the ceremony welcoming Jeannette Rankin to Congress was not really like a wedding. Four hundred and thirty-four men stood up, clapping their hands as she walked down the aisle toward her seat dressed in a simple dark-blue suit. Twice, after she had sat at her place, she had to rise and bow as the applause and cheering continued.

From the visitors' gallery, the wife of a leading Congressman watched Miss Rankin with great interest. It pleased her that the new member smiled cheerfully at all the excitement and, when men came over to greet her, the object of so much attention shook hands in the most natural sort of way.

The Congressman's wife kept a diary about the Washington scene. That night, a whole page was devoted to the debut of the first Congresswoman. "She was just a sensible young woman going about her business," this writer concluded.

On that historic day, Jeannette Rankin was thirty-six years old. Already, she had stepped out of the usual path that the females of her era were supposed to follow. And her streak of independence would make her keep on defying public opinion throughout her very long life.

No doubt her childhood in the wide open spaces of the West had a lot to do with her free-thinking outlook. She had been born on June 11, 1880, on a ranch six miles from the nearest settlement in the Montana Territory. Not until she was nine years old would the area become part of the nation's forty-first state.

Jeannette's mother, as Olive Pickering, had taught school in New Hampshire until her spirit of adventure made her decide to try teaching out West. Shortly after arriving in Montana, she met John Rankin, a rancher and lumber

dealer, who soon asked her to marry him. Jeannette was the first in their family of six daughters and a son.

No matter that she and her sisters were expected to help cook meals for the ranch hands, the Rankin girls all grew up without any feeling of having a more limited future than their brother. He became a lawyer, and so did two of the girls. Two others became professors at the University of Montana.

As the eldest, Jeannette had the special responsibility during her early years of helping her mother care for the younger children and manage a complicated household. These duties brought her home again after she had gone off to the state university and earned a teaching certificate, for her father died in 1904, when she was twenty-four, and her mother needed her. She spent the next few years wondering how she could ever get to be more involved with important events in the great world back East. At twenty-eight, she finally left Montana.

Using some money she had inherited from her father, she went to New York City and studied social work. A small, trim young woman with crisp brown hair, she had no interest in marrying. She thought that a career of helping women and children would be more satisfying.

Yet New York seemed too confusing.

After not much more than a year there, she took a train all the way across the country to the state of Washington. It was 1910, and a tremendous campaign to gain the right to vote was being conducted by the woman's suffrage organization in that state.

Helping on this campaign—which succeeded—Jeannette Rankin, at the age of thirty, found her life's work. Besides women's suffrage, she discovered another cause to which she would devote herself wholeheartedly. It was the cause of peace.

Among the friends she made in Washington, a journalist from New Jersey influenced her deeply. Minnie Reynolds convinced her that one of the most important reasons why women should strive for their full rights as citizens was so that, as voters, they would be able to make sure the United States never again went to war.

In the long run, Rankin's commitment to the cause of peace absorbed much more of her energy than any other activity, but suffrage, and then politics, occupied her during the next several years.

Tirelessly, she traveled around making speeches at suffrage rallies. In New York, Ohio, and California, she helped state committees pushing for the right to vote in their own state. In a dozen other states, she prodded lawmakers to support the campaign's national goal: the adoption of an amendment to the Constitution, forbidding any state to deny females the basic right to vote.

But Jeannette Rankin's main effort was in her own state of Montana. STOP! LOOK! LISTEN! That headline on posters captured attention wherever she went. Using humor to disarm the men who would have to be won over, because only men could vote in the special election on the suffrage issue, the posters announced meetings where

Miss JEANNETTE RANKIN
Will Discourse Eloquently on the
Latest Agricultural Stunt of
Making 2 Votes Grow Where Only 1
Grew Before

The men of Montana did vote in favor of women's suffrage, so they were not too alarmed when Miss Jeannette Rankin decided it was time for a female to take the next step politically. At her first opportunity—in the 1916 election—she ran for, and won, a seat in Congress. Her victory created a great flurry of publicity elsewhere, some of it very foolish.

Some newspapers told their readers that the Lady from Montana liked to carry a six-shooter. A woman columnist rejoiced at the falsity of such rumors and wrote: "I am glad, glad, glad that Jeannette is not freakish or mannish."

Jeannette Rankin addressed a crowd from the headquarters of the National American Woman Suffrage Association in April 1917 before being installed as the first female member of Congress. *Courtesy of the Library of Congress.*

Yet the Louisville *Courier-Journal* thought she must be incredibly daring, for: "Breathes there a man with a heart so brave that he would want to become one of a deliberative body made up of 434 women and himself?"

Despite all this frivolous comment, the nation was on the brink of one of the most serious decisions in its history. Since 1914 the major countries of Europe had been fighting the fierce con-

flict that would later be known as the First World War. By the spring of 1917, when the recently elected Congress had not yet been sworn in, a crisis had developed.

President Wilson had promised that he would keep the United States out of the war. But when Germany ordered its submarines to sink any American ships crossing the Atlantic because they might be bringing supplies for England or France, most Americans felt the time had come to join the Allies in fighting the Germans.

The day after the new Congress convened, Wilson himself came to address it. He asked the Senate and the House of Representatives to approve America's entry into the war on the Allied side.

Congresswoman Rankin faced a terrible problem. Many leaders of the suffrage movement warned her that she would hurt the cause enormously if she refused to go along with the majority opinion about entering the war. But her own conscience would not let her take this advice.

Her first vote in the House of Representatives—just two days after her friendly welcome there—was on the Wilson request to support going to war. When her name was called, she spoke up simply. "I want to stand by my country," she said, "but I cannot vote for war."

Fifty-six other members of Congress also refused to vote "Aye" on the war resolution. Some of them weathered the storm of disapproval that followed their unpopular decision. For Congresswoman Rankin, however, this first vote just about ended her political career.

She ran for a second term in 1918—and was soundly defeated. Still, she had

no regrets. The following year, after the war was over, she attended a meeting of women from many countries in Switzerland. There she helped to organize a new group called the Women's International League for Peace and Freedom.

During the next twenty years of increasing tensions, Jeannette Rankin kept very busy working for the league and for several other groups aiming to improve health care or working conditions among American women. In a way, she was still in politics because much of her effort went into talking with lawmakers, attempting to sway their votes on issues important to her.

Then, by a remarkable turn of fate, she ran again for Congress in 1940. So she was once more a member of the House of Representatives when the Japanese attacked Pearl Harbor in Hawaii on December 7, 1941. The following day, President Franklin Roosevelt went to the Capitol and asked the nation's lawmakers to approve America's entry into World War II.

This time, only one person voted "Nay." By then, a handful of other women sat in the Senate or the House of Representatives. All of them endorsed the declaration of war, except Congresswoman Rankin. Once more her unpopular stand led to defeat in the next election.

For another twenty years, most people forgot about her. By the 1960s, Jeannette Rankin was in her eighties—still small and trim and outspoken. Then, finally, a new generation of feminists recognized her as a heroine.

During the rising tide of protests against America's undeclared war in Vietnam, some youthful leaders of the antiwar movement were astonished to find that a very old lady living in California could help them.

At the age of eighty-eight, Jeannette Rankin spoke up with surprising energy against any further American involvement with fighting in Asia. It turned out that during the years when nobody had heard of her, she had repeatedly visited India, absorbing the peaceful teachings of the great Indian leader, Mahatma Gandhi.

In 1968, the amazing Miss Rankin once more arrived in Washington. Like a general who had finally found an army, she led 5,000 young women in a demonstration on the steps of the Capitol demanding that America quit fighting in Vietnam. The Jeannette Rankin Brigade, her antiwar followers were called by the newspapers.

Although she announced that she was planning to run again for Congress, so she could vote—if necessary—against American involvement in a third World War, nothing came of this campaign. Still Jeannette Rankin kept issuing strong antiwar statements. Without any physical or mental failing, she continued supporting the cause of peace.

Two weeks before she would have reached her ninety-third birthday, on May 18, 1973, Jeannette Rankin died peacefully in California.

Theodore Roosevelt

1858–1919   Governor of New York; twenty-sixth President of the United States.

"Teedie" Roosevelt was a sickly boy who had trouble breathing. When he was twelve years old, a doctor recommended exercise to improve his health. Day after day, a determined Teedie went to a gymnasium, swinging weights to strengthen his muscles.

A year later, for the first time in his life, he had no health problems. He read constantly and had private tutors to teach him German, French, and Latin. But what he liked to do best of all was to collect birds and preserve them by stuffing them. To help him gather more birds, his father presented him with a rifle.

But then another problem arose. Shooting his rifle, Teedie found that he could not hit his targets. One day, the reason suddenly came to him. Looking at a nearby billboard, he found that

he could not read the letters on it.

Outfitted with a pair of glasses, he began to see the world around him. "I had no idea how beautiful the world was until I got those spectacles," he said.

Teedie—called Teddy as he grew older—lived in comfortable surroundings in New York City. He had been born there on October 27, 1858, just before the Civil War. His father, Theodore Roosevelt, Sr., was an importer and a strong Union supporter. His mother, Martha Bulloch Roosevelt, a native of Georgia, never wavered in her Southern views. But it was a happy marriage. Teddy had two sisters and a younger brother. Together the whole family traveled all over Europe and the United States.

Even as a boy, though, Teddy sometimes went off on trips by himself. One summer, on a stagecoach going to Moosehead Lake in Maine, two strange boys made fun of his city manners. With fists flailing wildly, he tried to fight back, but the tough bullies handled him easily. Angry at his own weakness, he made up his mind that he would take boxing lessons.

He learned so well that a few years later, at Harvard College, he fought his way to the lightweight boxing finals. After defeating several opponents, he lost the championship—but won much admiration for his courage.

At Harvard, Teddy showed the characteristics that were to mark the rest of his life—boundless energy, an ability to speak out forcefully for what he believed in, and a very good mind. Besides being elected to Phi Beta Kappa, the scholastic honor fraternity, he started writing a book while he was still a student. It was *The Naval War of 1812*, which became required reading at the United States Naval Academy.

Shortly after graduating in 1880, at the age of twenty-one, he married Alice Hathaway Lee, the daughter of a well-to-do family in Boston. They went to live in New York City. There Roosevelt kept busy by going to law school in the mornings, finishing research for his book in the afternoons, and going to parties with his wife in the evenings. Still, that was not enough for the ambi-

tious young man. He began attending meetings of the local Republican Club as well.

That was an unusual choice for someone with his social standing. Gentlemen of the upper class did not stoop to politics, according to the code of his family and friends. But it was a challenge to Roosevelt—something he could never resist. "I intend to be one of the governing class," he told his family when they complained.

At the age of twenty-three, he was elected a member of the New York State legislature. His boyish, high-pitched voice was frequently heard in the Assembly chamber, attacking what he called "that most dangerous of all classes, the wealthy criminal class." By that, he meant businessmen who bribed judges or lawmakers.

Roosevelt quickly made a name for himself by calling for reform of the civil service, supporting proposals for awarding government jobs on merit and not on the basis of friendship. As just a junior member of the legislature, however, he did not accomplish much. The old-time lawmakers called him a "Harvard goo-goo," a term they used to laugh at anyone committed to good government.

But in his first public office Roosevelt demonstrated courage in speaking out against injustice. He showed persistence and self-confidence. By being himself, he gained the respect of even his opponents.

Almost everything he was involved in was dramatic, even when tragedy struck. On the same day in February of 1884, his mother and his wife, who was only twenty-two years old, died. He was left with an infant daughter, Alice.

Leaving her in the care of one of his sisters, the grief-stricken Roosevelt went off to the wild Dakota Territory where he owned a ranch. Cowboys there dismissed him at first as a "four-eyed tenderfoot," but he earned their respect by riding horses and branding cattle with the best of them.

He liked the quiet of the empty land, its rivers and mountains, and he loved to hunt. "I now look like a regular cowboy dandy," he wrote to his sister. "You would be amused to see me in my broad sombrero hat, fringed and beaded buckskin shirt, and cowboy boots with braided bridle and silver spurs."

Roosevelt also admired the code of the West, which meant taking care of yourself. On one occasion, he rode up to a hotel late in the evening. In the bar was a man shooting at the clock on the wall. As soon as he saw Roosevelt, he said, "Four-eyes is going to treat." Roosevelt replied mildly, "Well, if I've got to, I've got to."

With that, Roosevelt advanced and hit the man on the jaw with his right fist. He hit him again with his left and then once more with his right. The bully fell. Then Roosevelt calmly reached over and took his guns away.

While many men would consider merely keeping alive in that hostile country sufficient work, Roosevelt did not. He even managed to finish the manuscript of another book, a biography of Missouri's Senator Thomas Hart Benton, before returning to New York.

It was 1886 and Roosevelt was twenty-eight years old. Back in New York, a group of Republican party leaders asked him to run for mayor of the city. The youngest man ever to seek the post, he lost the election.

But in that same year, his personal life changed for the better. He married Edith Carow, an old childhood friend, in December during a trip to England. They later had five children.

On their return to New York, Roosevelt started to write several other books, including one of his best known, *The Winning of the West*. And together with about a dozen wealthy animal lovers, he organized a society to protect the American wilderness. Yet that was not enough to keep the active Roosevelt busy.

He welcomed an appointment as head of the United States Civil Service Commission in 1889 and served in that post until 1895. Then he became police commissioner of New York City, making quite a splash with his efforts to root out corruption.

A newspaper article described his method of gathering information: "When he asks a question, Mr. Roosevelt shoots it at the trembling policeman as he would shoot a bullet at a coyote . . . . But Mr. Roosevelt's voice is the policeman's hardest trial. It is an exasperating voice, a sharp voice, a rasping voice."

Two years later Roosevelt was named to the job he really wanted, Assistant Secretary of the Navy in Washington. It combined his love of the sea and ships with a chance to do something important. For Roosevelt, nothing was more urgent than building a modern fleet to help the United States maintain its growing stature as a world power.

When war with Spain broke out in 1898, he resigned to become colonel of a regiment of mounted soldiers that was soon being called The Rough Riders. He led them in a charge up San Juan Hill in Cuba later that year, gaining a victory for the United States and fame for himself.

As a war hero, Roosevelt became an obvious choice of the Republican party to run for governor of New York. He won that election in 1899. In office, however, he made enemies of his own party leaders by coming out for a tax on corporations. At that time, in dealing with local politicians, he coined a phrase that would be one of his best known: "Speak softly and carry a big stick."

Within a year, the leaders of the party had had enough of the independent Roosevelt. They found a rather strange way of getting rid of him. They engineered his nomination for Vice-President of the United States.

Elected with McKinley in 1900, he was inaugurated on March 4, 1901. Within months, McKinley was assassinated—and Roosevelt assumed the nation's highest office. On September 14, 1901, not yet forty-three years old, he became the youngest President the country ever had.

He was also the most active President the country had ever seen. He started antitrust actions against combinations of businesses and, when a nationwide coal strike began, he stepped in to force a settlement. All he wanted, he said, was "to see to it that every man has a square deal."

In foreign affairs, Roosevelt also believed in direct action. When a proposed Panama canal between the Atlantic and Pacific Oceans was delayed, a revolution backed by the United States took place in Panama in 1903. The new government immediately agreed to the construction of a canal by the United States.

"I enjoy being the President," Roosevelt said. And the nation enjoyed watch-

Colonel Theodore Roosevelt (*center*) and his Rough Riders pose for a photograph by William Dinwiddie after their dramatic capture of San Juan Hill. *Courtesy of the Library of Congress.*

ing him and his family in the White House. He boxed every day, played football on the lawn, and went hunting panthers in Colorado. His children slid down the bannisters, played with animals in the White House, and even brought a horse into the mansion to comfort a sick brother.

Roosevelt gave his name to one of the most loved toys in the world. After a hunting trip during which he refused to shoot a lame bear, a cartoonist drew a picture of the event. A toy manufacturer made some cuddly bears and asked Roosevelt for permission to name them after him. It was the birth of the Teddy bear.

A man of volcanic energy, Roosevelt was stocky in appearance. With bushy eyebrows above steel-rimmed glasses, a droopy moustache, and prominent teeth, he made it easy for cartoonists

Theodore Roosevelt inspects the construction of the Panama Canal. *Courtesy of Underwood & Underwood.*

An unidentified photographer took this shot of Theodore Roosevelt during his tenure in the White House. *Courtesy of the National Portrait Gallery, Smithsonian Institution.*

to draw pictures of him. Still, he was extremely popular.

Easily reelected in 1904, Roosevelt continued his reforms by pushing through the nation's first pure food and drug law. But his most notable achievement was settling a war between Russia and Japan in 1905. For that he received the Nobel Peace Prize the following year.

After arranging for the nomination of his friend and colleague, William Howard Taft, to succeed him as President, Roosevelt left office in 1909. Only fifty years old, he was still full of vigor and went off to Africa to hunt big game.

On his return to the United States, he was unable to keep out of politics. He felt annoyed because his successor, Taft, showed signs of independence. Anxious to return to power, Roosevelt said, "My hat is in the ring," creating a phrase that is still used to indicate that someone is running for a nomination to political office.

Despite losing the Republican nomination to Taft, Roosevelt ran in 1912 as the presidential candidate of the new Bull Moose, or Progressive, party. In doing so, he gained more votes than Taft but split the normal Republican vote, so the Democratic candidate, Woodrow Wilson, won the election.

Once more Roosevelt left on a hunting expedition. When World War I broke out, he offered to serve, but Wilson did not accept his offer. He died unexpectedly on January 6, 1919, at the age of sixty.

Woodrow Wilson

1856–1924 Governor of New Jersey; twenty-eighth President of the United States.

Tommy Wilson had a lively imagination. When he was growing up in Virginia, he created a play world in which he commanded a great army, leading his men in heroic deeds. He called himself The Duke of Eagleton, commander-in-chief of the Royal Lancer Guards.

Many years later, during the First World War, Tommy had grown up to be President Woodrow Wilson. Then he really did serve as commander-in-chief—of all the armed forces of the United States.

Nobody knows, of course, whether his early dreams influenced his decisions as President. But there is no question about another matter. In much of his boyhood imagining, he pictured himself as an English admiral or general. That undoubtedly came from the emphasis his parents put on their own British ancestry.

Both his parents had strong religious backgrounds. His father, the Reverend Joseph Ruggles Wilson, was an imposing figure, tall and strong. He was a leader in the Southern Presbyterian Church, a scholar and a preacher of remarkable ability. But his mother, Jessie Woodrow Wilson, probably had a stronger influence on Tommy's life. She had come to the United States from England with her parents at the age of five. Her father, Thomas Woodrow, had been a minister, too.

Jessie Woodrow met the man who was to become her husband in Ohio, where she was a student in a female seminary and he was a teacher. After they were married in June of 1849, he got a job teaching in Virginia. Thereafter, they lived in the South and considered themselves Southerners.

Their first son, born on December 28, 1856, was named Thomas Woodrow Wilson after his mother's father. At the time, the boy's own father was a minister in Staunton, Virginia. Tommy had two older sisters and a younger brother.

His first recollection as a child was of a man standing at the gate of his house, shouting, "Mr. Lincoln's elected. There'll be war." But Tommy was sheltered from the Civil War in the peaceful backwater of Augusta, Georgia, where the family had moved.

He was raised in a loving home. His father read the children stories, almost all of them by English authors. Mrs. Wilson kept a close watch over Tommy, who was a sickly boy, so much so that he became a "mama's boy." He didn't go to school until he was nine years old and was eleven before he learned to read well.

By the time he was sixteen, however, he was ready to go off to Davidson College, a small Presbyterian school in North Carolina. Away from home for the first time, he was frail and timid, but while there he showed two of the interests that were to stay with him until the end of his life—debating and base-ball. He joined the debating society and played second base for the freshman team. But Wilson became ill while at college and was forced to return home at the end of his freshman year.

His life changed in September of 1875, when he entered Princeton College in New Jersey. Not only did his health improve, he became a hardworking student both in class and outside the classroom. He excelled in oratory and debate and remained fascinated by sports, football as well as baseball.

He played on his boarding house baseball team, called The Bowery Boys, and was the nonplaying captain of the college baseball association. In addition, he was the president of the football association, not playing but taking part in the coaching. As a coach, he worked out plays for the team so well that the 1879 football team won all six of its games, beating Harvard and Yale. That made it a year of sports triumph for Princeton, largely because of Wilson's insistence that the team play "a scientific game."

At Princeton, Wilson was also active on the staff of the college newspaper, the *Princetonian*. He was elected editor of the paper in his senior year and devoted much of his editorial attention to the better financing of student activities.

In those undergraduate days, Wilson

started to break the cords that tied him to his parents. He decided that he would not enter the ministry, as they had hoped, but instead planned for a career in government.

And he changed his name. Tommy was not a suitable name for a rising young man, he decided. He began to sign letters home T. Woodrow Wilson, and then even dropped the initial. From then on, he said, he would be known as Woodrow Wilson.

He also decided to study law. He enrolled at the University of Virginia, but bad health caused him to withdraw from classes. He completed his law education at home and was admitted to the bar in 1882.

Then Wilson changed his mind. What he really wanted to do, he decided, was to learn more about American government, so he entered Johns Hopkins University in Baltimore. It was there that Wilson, at the age of twenty-nine, emerged as a brilliant scholar. He earned his doctorate, and his thesis, *Congressional Government,* was published to enthusiastic reviews.

During that period, he met and fell in love with Ellen Louise Axson, the daughter of a minister in Rome, Georgia. They were married in June of 1885 and went off to Wilson's first teaching job, at Bryn Mawr College near Philadelphia.

After teaching there for a short time, Wilson accepted another teaching job, at Wesleyan College in Connecticut. Besides teaching, he renewed his interest in football. When the 1889 season opened with a series of defeats, Wilson stepped in and became one of the coaches.

The team held meetings in Wilson's classroom, where he used his teaching skills to help plan for future games. He did something unusual at that time— he diagrammed plays on the blackboard. And he emphasized speed in running off plays, to catch opponents by surprise. As a result, the Wesleyan team improved notably.

In the classroom, Wilson made a hit with students. They thought he was an enthusiastic teacher who had a mastery of his subjects. He also worked on writing a book, *The State,* in which he came to the conclusion that it was not only proper but necessary for government to intervene in a nation's economy in order to equalize opportunity for all.

Wilson left Wesleyan in 1890 to take up the teaching job he really wanted, as a professor of government at his beloved Princeton. His elective courses for juniors and seniors were so popular that sometimes there was standing room only for other students who wanted to come and hear his lectures.

He became a familiar sight on the campus, riding his bicycle from home to class every day. He built a towering reputation as a teacher, author, and lecturer. His standing was so great that in 1902 the college turned to Wilson, then forty-five years old, as its new president.

As head of Princeton, Wilson showed a zeal for reform. He established a system of tutoring, along the lines of English universities, and he fought against the snobbish system of private eating clubs. He lost that fight, but he earned a reputation as a fighter for democracy against the privileges of the rich.

A group of influential Democrats saw in Wilson a potential President of the United States. Wilson was willing, even eager. It was clear, though, that first he had to establish a record in government, so he resigned from Princeton and ran for governor of New Jersey. He was elected in 1910.

Governor Wilson showed that he was a progressive leader. To start with, he forced through a law by which direct primaries would select candidates for office. Then he sponsored programs to regulate public utilities and to provide insurance payments for workers injured on the job.

In 1912, Wilson the reformer became a major candidate for the Democratic nomination for President. But there were others as well. Forty-six ballots were cast at the Democratic Convention that year before Wilson won the nomination.

He won the election mainly because the Republicans were split. On Inauguration Day, March 4, 1913, Wilson was fifty-six years old. He was almost six feet tall, lean, with a stern-looking face, his blue-gray eyes hidden by steel-rimmed glasses. He moved into the White House with his wife and three daughters.

In office, Wilson lived up to his reputation as a reformer. He pushed through Congress a law to lower tariffs to aid consumers. Then he sponsored legislation to set up a Federal Reserve System to regulate banks and a Federal Trade Commission to monitor business.

For the Wilson family, life in the White House was rather pleasant. One of his daughters, Jessie, was married there in 1913 and another daughter, Eleanor, the following year. Wilson himself never gave up his interest in baseball. He became the first President ever to attend a World Series game on October 9, 1915, when he watched the Philadelphia Athletics play the Boston Red Sox.

But in 1914 personal tragedy struck the Wilsons. Mrs. Wilson died suddenly, leaving her husband a sad and lonely man until he met and married Mrs. Edith Bolling Galt, a Washington widow, the following year.

Also in 1914 war in Europe had broken out between Germany and Britain and France. Hoping to keep the United

President Woodrow Wilson poses with the American delegation to the Paris Peace Conference in 1919. *Courtesy of the National Portrait Gallery, Smithsonian Institution.*

States out of the conflict, Wilson issued a neutrality proclamation.

"He kept us out of the war," was Wilson's campaign slogan when he ran for a second term in 1916. But it was a very close election, so close that even Wilson thought he had lost to the Republican candidate, Charles Evans Hughes. When the late returns came in, it was clear that Wilson had won a narrow victory.

Despite the close margin, Wilson be-

lieved he had won a mandate from the people to act as a peacemaker. In a speech before the Senate, Wilson called for "a peace without victory" in Europe. But the European powers did not listen.

In 1917, the third year of the war in Europe, Wilson's efforts to keep the United States out of the conflict failed. In January the Germans announced that their submarines would sink ships in the Atlantic Ocean without warning in

Woodrow Wilson had already left the White House when Edmund Tarbell painted this portrait in 1921. *Courtesy of the National Portrait Gallery, Smithsonian Institution.*

order to prevent supplies from reaching England.

Then Wilson asked Congress for permission to arm United States merchant ships to protect themselves against German attack. That was held up by what he called "a little group of willful men" in the Senate, but Wilson armed the ships anyway.

After German submarines began sinking American ships, Wilson asked Congress to declare war. "The world must be made safe for democracy," he said. Congress approved a declaration of war against Germany in April of 1917.

Soon millions of American soldiers were in Europe. The fresh American troops defeated a last-ditch German attack in France in 1918 and then started to push the enemy back. On November 11, 1918, Germany surrendered and the war was' over.

Wilson then embarked on a great personal crusade, an attempt to eliminate future war through a League of Nations that would enforce the peace. He went to Europe, the first American President ever to go abroad, to draft a peace treaty. When he brought back the Treaty of Versailles, however, he found opposition from many Senators who thought it meant giving up some of America's rights as a nation.

Stubbornly, Wilson refused to compromise. He went on a speaking tour of the nation to gain public support, but he collapsed in the autumn of 1919, suffering a stroke that paralyzed his left side. Suddenly he was an invalid, hardly able to leave his bed. The seriousness of his condition was kept from the public, however, and he continued in office, with Mrs. Wilson acting as a screen to keep visitors to a minimum. Years later some writers would claim that she became, in effect, the acting President during the final year and a half of her husband's second term.

Despite Wilson's efforts, American membership in the League of Nations was rejected by the Senate. The world recognized his leadership for peace, however, when he was awarded the Nobel Peace Prize in 1920.

Wilson left office in 1921 and continued to live in Washington. He died in his sleep there on February 3, 1924, at the age of sixty-seven.

PART IV

Modern Times

Dwight Eisenhower

1890–1969   Allied military commander during World War II; thirty-fourth President of the United States.

"I come from the very heart of America."

These words were spoken by a victorious war leader at a moment of great emotion. Many people who heard them thought they were being used the way a poet uses words—to express a feeling, not an actual fact. But the moving phrase voiced both feeling and fact.

Dwight David Eisenhower had really grown up near the center of the United States, in the small town of Abilene, Kansas, and this friendly man with such a beaming smile surely gave the impression of being a typical American. Still, his remarkable career as a commanding general, and later as one of the most popular Presidents the country has ever had, proved that he possessed far more than average talents.

He was born on October 14, 1890, in the dusty Texas community of Denison, where his family had moved temporarily while his father was working for a railroad. Before Dwight reached his first birthday, the Eisenhowers returned to Kansas.

Dwight had two older brothers, and three more boys would come after him. When he became famous, it struck reporters that his early years were like a simple, wholesome story of life during the horse-and-buggy days. His family lived in a white cottage with a large vegetable garden out back. They also kept their own cow, a flock of chickens, and a pig or two to provide milk and meat.

But the reason for all this old-fashioned raising of their own food was that

171

they had very little money. David Eisenhower, Dwight's father, would have
liked to become an engineer. At the
small college where he met and fell in
love with a wonderfully cheerful young
woman named Ida Stover, he had been
studying toward this goal. Then he decided he would rather get married.

David was as quiet as Ida was lively.
Yet they shared a deep religious faith,
and they had similar backgrounds.
Their ancestors had been hardworking
German or Swiss farmers who settled
in Pennsylvania or the western part of
Virginia. After the Civil War, the young
people had come out to Kansas with
some of their relatives.

David Eisenhower spent most of his
working life tending the machinery at
a plant where cream was separated from
milk and put into bottles. He never
earned more than $100 a month, which
made them not quite as poor as it might
seem because, in those days, eggs cost
only five cents a dozen. Even so, his
wife had no easy time bringing up a
houseful of husky boys on such a low
income.

As a result, Dwight had to work if
he wanted to buy a football. He and
his brother Ed—a year older, and the
closest friend he had—would load up
a wagon with surplus vegetables from
their garden, then peddle them at the
back doors of richer families on the
other side of the railroad tracks.

Something Dwight never could explain was how he acquired his nickname. Maybe because such a likeable
boy needed a nickname, practically
everybody called him "Ike." Since he
was good at every sort of game, Ike
was elected president of the Abilene
High School Athletic Association.

Studying did not interest him nearly
as much, but a speaker at his high school
graduation captured his attention. "I
would sooner begin life over again with
one arm cut off than attempt to struggle
along without a college education," this
man said.

Ike had no idea what he would like
to be—except that George Washington
was his private hero. Ike's brother, Ed,
though, had set his mind on becoming
a lawyer, so the two of them came up
with a plan for helping each other.

They decided to take turns working
and attending college. One would go
away and study a year, while the other
stayed home earning money for the student's expenses. Because Ed was older
and already knew what he wanted to
study, he went away first.

But during the year Ike worked at
the creamery, a man in town told him
about a way he might be able to get a
fine education absolutely free. Yet he
would have to pass a pretty stiff entrance
exam. Ike boned up on math and some

President Eisenhower met his future wife, Mamie Doud, while he was a second lieutenant at Fort Sam Houston, Texas. *Courtesy of the Dwight D. Eisenhower Library.*

other subjects until he finally took, and passed, the test. Late in the summer of 1911, when he was almost twenty-one, he left home to enter the United States Military Academy.

At West Point, Cadet Eisenhower had one severe disappointment. He had been elated to make the football team. Even if he was not quite six feet tall and weighed only 174, his fierce urge to gain ground had impressed the coach. But as Ike plunged through the opposing line in the next-to-the-last game of his sophomore year, he injured his knee badly. The doctor told him a few weeks later that there would be no more rugged sports for him. Ever.

Eisenhower thought of quitting West Point, but his friends kept trying to cheer him up and he remained to graduate with the Class of 1915. Popular as he was, he ranked only 61st among the 164 men who were commissioned with him as second lieutenants in the United States Army.

On his first assignment—at Fort Sam Houston in San Antonio, Texas—something important happened to Lieutenant Eisenhower. He met an attractive young woman from Denver who was spending a few months visiting in Texas. On Valentine's Day of 1916, he and nineteen-year-old Mamie Doud became engaged.

While her family liked him, as almost everybody did, they thought their daughter ought not to marry for another few years. However, two war threats made the young couple impatient. When it seemed that Lieutenant Eisenhower might soon be fighting in Mexico, the Douds relented and there was a wedding at their Denver home on July 1, 1916.

As it turned out, war with Mexico was averted. The following year, however, the United States entered the great conflict in Europe that would go down in history as the First World War. Instead of being assigned to fight in France, Captain Eisenhower found himself training troops and coaching football at various posts around the country.

He was extremely distressed by his failure to get into the fray. Under his easygoing manner was a deep ambition, pushing him toward excelling in whatever he did. Having chosen soldiering as his career, he could not help dreaming of becoming a general someday—and wouldn't the Army's future generals be men who had made outstanding records during this war?

Yet Eisenhower did attract the attention of some important military figures by his notable gift for organizing new training camps. As a result, during the 1920s he was sent to the Army's special school at Fort Leavenworth in Kansas, where promising young officers received advanced courses in military planning.

Here, Major Eisenhower finally emerged at the head of his class. It was the turning point of his career. When he left Fort Leavenworth in 1926, his name went down on a secret list in Washington. If the United States ever fought a war again, he would surely receive an important assignment.

Yet hardly anybody outside the Army had ever heard of Eisenhower. Then, on December 7, 1941, the Japanese attacked Pearl Harbor in Hawaii. A few days later the telephone rang at the camp in Texas where Brigadier General Eisenhower was directing training maneuvers. An aide to the Army's Chief of Staff in Washington spoke crisply: "The Chief says for you to hop a plane and get here right away."

That began Eisenhower's wonderfully successful four years as one of the major leaders in World War II. After a brief stint of working on war plans in Washington, he was sent to England and took command of a series of campaigns, culminating with the greatest invasion of all history, when Allied forces stormed the beaches of France on June 6, 1944.

Besides his military mastery, General Eisenhower proved to have marvelous skill at smoothing over tensions between the nations fighting together against Nazi Germany. After the Germans surrendered in 1945, the people of England gave him a hero's welcome on his return to London. That was when he made his touching speech starting: "I am not a native of this land. I come from the heart of America. . . ."

What he was trying to say was that the Allies must remain united to defeat Japan, and then to preserve peace once the fighting stopped. Yet reporters watching his warm smile when huge crowds turned out to greet him on his return home jumped to another conclusion. "This man is absolutely a natural for the White House," they said.

General Eisenhower laughed heartily the first time somebody told him he ought to run for President. Why, he didn't have the least interest in politics, he kept remarking. In fact, most people had no idea whether his political sympathies were Republican or Democratic.

Privately, though, Eisenhower considered himself a Republican. That party's conservative outlook appealed to him, but he believed that military officers should keep their political opinions to themselves. After the war was over, however, he retired from the Army and put away his uniform with five stars on the shoulder. Only a handful of men in American history had ever

Thomas Edgar Stephens painted this 1947 portrait of Dwight D. Eisenhower, then a five-star general. *Courtesy of the National Portrait Gallery, Smithsonian Institution; transfer from the National Gallery of Art, Washington.*

Eisenhower was inaugurated on January 20, 1953. Richard Nixon, waiting to be sworn into the office of Vice-President, is shown at the far right. Nixon himself would be inaugurated in 1969. *Courtesy of the Dwight D. Eisenhower Library, National Park Services.*

been promoted to more than a four-star rank.

Since Eisenhower liked the prospect of spending time among young people, he accepted the post he was offered as the president of Columbia University in New York. But campus life proved not as exciting as being in the thick of world-shaking events, and important Republicans kept urging him to let them nominate him as President of the United States.

Eisenhower escaped all this political discussion briefly by putting on his uniform again. He accepted an appointment by President Truman to direct a new association of Allied nations called the North Atlantic Treaty Organization. But even at NATO headquarters in Europe, he kept receiving political requests.

In 1952, General Eisenhower finally let his friends know that if he were nominated to be President he would consider it his duty to run for the office. When the Republican Convention chose him, the Democrats countered by nominating a former governor of Illinois, Adlai E. Stevenson.

The slogan Eisenhower supporters adopted was, "I Like Ike." Millions of people all over the country, including quite a number who considered themselves Democrats, signified that they did like Ike, for he won the election easily.

Sixty-three years old when he entered the White House, President Eisenhower gave a lot of responsibility to the aides he appointed. Some said he played golf too often and took too frequent vacations, but most people clearly approved of him. Although he had a heart attack toward the end of his first term, he recovered to beat Stevenson by an even bigger margin when he ran for a second term in 1956.

During the years Eisenhower served as President, Democrats criticized him for not taking a more active role in running the country. Even his supporters thought his main accomplishments were securing statehood for Alaska and Hawaii and convincing Congress to pass a law calling for the construction of a vast new interstate highway system.

After Eisenhower left office, however, some of his critics changed their minds and decided he had influenced the government more than anybody suspected at the time. Despite several international crises—especially in the Middle East and Indochina—this former general had upheld American interests without permitting a single American soldier to be killed by enemy fire.

No matter that he did not provide strong leadership in dealing with some domestic problems, notably the civil rights struggle of black Americans, President Eisenhower won lasting renown because of a warning he issued on the eve of his retirement. In a farewell address to the nation, he said the country must guard against the increasing power of what he called "the military-industrial complex."

Leaving the White House in January of 1961, at the age of seventy, President Eisenhower was still immensely popular. He and his wife retired to a farm they had bought in Gettysburg, Pennsylvania. He died on March 28, 1969, at the age of seventy-eight. After solemn ceremonies in Washington, attended by high officials from dozens of nations, a special train carried his body across the country to its final resting place in Abilene, Kansas.

Oliver Wendell Holmes

1841–1935   U.S. Supreme Court Justice.

It was no fun, having a famous father. The boy even had the same name as Boston's most noted doctor and nonstop talker—who also wrote verses children all over America learned to recite, for instance, "Old Ironsides," starting:

Ay, tear her tattered ensign down!
Long has it waved on high,
And many an eye has danced to see
That banner in the sky.

Into the bargain, Dr. Oliver Wendell Holmes wrote a regular column in the popular magazine, the *Atlantic Monthly*, about what went on in his own household. His son could never speak up at the breakfast table without wondering whether his words would soon appear in print. One day when he was thirteen, he told his favorite uncle John he could hardly bear this lack of privacy.

"Don't take it so hard, Wendell," his uncle said with a smile. "You'll get used to your father. I did, long ago."

And Uncle John was right. What's more, Oliver Wendell Holmes, Jr. became such a major figure himself—one of the greatest judges ever appointed to the United States Supreme Court—that his own fame outdistanced his father's.

The future judge, born on March 8, 1841, actually had dozens of relatives who were well-known, at least in Boston. Both sides of his family could boast of sturdy Yankee forebears going back many generations. His mother, Amelia Jackson Holmes, had been the daughter of an eminent chief justice of the highest

Oliver Wendell Holmes was twenty years old and a Union solidier when he posed for this photograph in 1861. *Courtesy of the National Portrait Gallery, Smithsonian Institution.*

court in Massachusetts. His father's father, a leading minister, also gained renown by compiling one of the first histories of the United States.

But if young Wendell sometimes felt buried under a ton of ancestors, he realized very early that belonging to Boston's inner circle had its advantages, too. Being a boy with a bent for thinking, he was much impressed when that deep-thinking author, Mr. Emerson, called him by his first name. So did Mr. Longfellow and Mr. Lowell, the poets. Another family friend who fascinated him was Mr. Hawthorne, the novelist.

In fact, Wendell really had no serious worries during his growing-up years. He did well at school, he went ice-skating in the winter, and he read a lot of books. Like his father and uncles and cousins, when he was sixteen he entered Harvard. Then in the spring of his senior year—in April of 1861, soon after his twentieth birthday—trouble that had seemed far away from his own safe surroundings suddenly affected him.

War broke out between the North and the South, and President Lincoln called for 75,000 men of the North to take up arms. Young Holmes, to his own quiet satisfaction, had shot up to be over six feet tall. Now, feeling very manly, he joined a regiment of Massachusetts volunteers.

Fighting in the Civil War ended Wendell's sense of always being in his father's shadow—but at quite some cost. Only a few weeks after climbing aboard a train with his fellow soldiers, amid band music and cheering, Lieutenant Holmes was camped on the banks of the Potomac River. Without warning, a band of rebels came yelling out of the woods to start the Battle of Ball's Bluff.

Less than ten minutes later, Holmes fell to the ground. In the field hospital to which he was carried, a doctor said he was an extremely lucky young man. The bullet that had hit his chest had only narrowly missed his heart and lungs.

In Boston, reports that young Holmes might have been killed made his family frantic. Dr. Holmes himself took a southbound train and at last found the hospital where his son was, pale but on the mend. The lieutenant was allowed to go home with his father to complete his recovery.

During the next few months, Lieutenant Holmes was treated like a hero by his Boston relatives, but they all knew this happy interlude could not last. The war was going badly for the North, and as soon as the lieutenant's wound had healed, off he went again to rejoin his comrades.

Then Holmes really began learning how boring and horrible war could be. Throughout the summer of 1862, under the broiling Virginia sun, he marched across fields and into swamps where the mud was knee-deep. Repeatedly, the opposing armies met in fierce, bloody combat with pistols and sabers. On September 17, at the famous Battle of Antietam, Holmes was wounded again.

This time he was shot through the neck. In the confusion, he somehow found his way to a farmhouse where a kind woman took care of him. It was several days before his family received a telegram reporting that Captain Holmes—for he had been promoted because of his bravery—was alive, after all.

Again, Dr. Holmes rushed southward and brought his son home to recover. The captain just shook his head when relatives asked about his experiences. He would hardly ever speak of the terrible sights he had seen, and this time it was much harder for him to return to duty.

A third wound hurt him most severely—during fighting near Fredericksburg, Virginia, on May 3, 1863. As he lay helpless after an enemy shell hit him, he thought at the very least he would lose his leg. But the leg was saved, even though it took nine months for the shattering injury to heal. By then, the tide had turned and a Union victory seemed certain within another few months. Finally, at the age of twenty-four, Captain Holmes felt free to face the question of how he wished to spend the rest of his life.

He chose to study law. Returning to Harvard, Holmes soon had an impulse to concentrate instead on philosophy. The word itself pleased him. It came from the ancient Greek words meaning "love of wisdom." Over the years it had become the general term for the science that inquires into basic ideas about human existence—seeking solutions to such puzzles as the reason for wars.

Much as Holmes enjoyed mulling over ideas, he decided he could not retreat to the ivory tower of a philosopher. "I think it is required of a man that he should share the action and the passion of his time," he later explained. Besides, he had a strong streak of common sense, and since he preferred not to be supported forever by his father, it struck him that he had better become a lawyer and start earning some money.

Yet Holmes soon found, when he opened a law office, that day-by-day dealings with clients did not interest him much. What did fascinate him were the reasons why the practice of law had developed along certain lines. He kept asking himself whether the body of legal doctrine by which cases were settled could be adjusted to suit the changing world around him.

Holmes discovered that he was spending a lot of time talking over these questions with a young woman he had known since his boyhood. Indeed, Fanny Dixwell was the daughter of the headmaster at the school he had attended. Finally, Wendell realized it was not just her keen intelligence that attracted him and, in 1872, at the age of thirty-one, he married Fanny.

She encouraged him then to start writing down some of his ideas about legal philosophy. After hours, during the next ten years, he studied deeply and wrote a series of essays. These were published in a book called *Common Law*, which made Holmes' reputation as a brilliant legal thinker.

The following year, in 1882, he became a professor at the Harvard Law School. Just six months later there was a vacancy on the bench of the Massachusetts Supreme Court, and nobody was surprised when the governor of the state appointed Professor Holmes to be an associate justice.

So, at the age of forty-one, Holmes started a new career that he enjoyed thoroughly. Serving as a judge in a court that decided whether or not lower courts had reached a fair verdict proved to be a perfect spot for him. Lawyers who presented cases that were being appealed often felt awed by the quickness of his mind.

It seemed, one of them said, that after just a few words of an argument were spoken, "he had already seen the end of it." Furthermore, a Holmes opinion was likely to be a new sort of mixture of learning and common sense.

In this period, the United States had begun turning into a great industrial nation, and the process brought increasing tensions between employers and workers. Instead of applying old legal standards when disputes arose, Holmes insisted there was a "secret root from which the law draws all the juices of life."

By that he meant that judges had to base their decisions not merely on legal principles established in the past but also on what was now best for the whole community. Because the owners of large factories were getting to be so powerful, Holmes thought that workers, too, should have new ways of protecting their own interests.

His outlook, favoring the growth of labor unions, made some solid citizens regard him as a dangerous radical. Holmes himself felt that by speaking up as he did he had ended any possibility of being appointed to a more important judicial position. But this judgment of his proved to be mistaken.

In 1899, when the chief justice of the high court of Massachusetts retired, Holmes was promoted to fill his place. Then three years later, when he was sixty-one—a time of life often marked by thoughts of retiring—exactly the opposite happened to him. In 1902, President Theodore Roosevelt appointed him to fill a vacancy on the United States Supreme Court. That opened a thirty-year era, during which Justice Oliver Wendell Holmes made legal history.

Roosevelt had chosen him because he wanted a progress-minded judge who would favor his own efforts to break up powerful combinations of big business that were taking over the nation's railroads and other major industries. But anyone who expected Justice Holmes to follow any particular political course was in for a surprise.

What Holmes did was much more attention-getting. He applied his own combination of legal learning and common sense to every case he considered. Time after time, he came to a conclusion that differed from that of the majority of his fellow justices. The Great Dissenter, the newspapers took to calling Holmes.

Old as he was, his opinions struck a good many people as much more in tune with the changing times than the majority verdicts. One of his first dissents came in the case of a man named Lochner, who operated a bakery in New York. That state had recently passed a law limiting the working time in bakeries to ten hours a day. Lochner sued to have the law declared unconstitutional because it interfered with his own freedom as the operator of his business.

The majority on the Supreme Court upheld his point of view. But Justice Holmes differed. To him, it was obvious that the New York law regulating working hours was an attempt to protect working people. And why shouldn't a state be allowed to experiment with

Olive Wendell Holmes

February 23 . 1926

Holmes was eighty-five and a legendary jurist when Samuel Johnson Woolf sketched this portrait in charcoal in 1926. *Courtesy of the National Portrait Gallery, Smithsonian Institution.*

new ways of serving the best interests of the whole community?

Ordinarily, the opinions of a Justice who is outvoted by his colleagues do not attract much attention, except among lawyers. But Holmes over the years became more and more of a celebrity. The young and the liberal-minded predicted—rightly—that the passage of time would bring general acceptance of his point of view. Also, even those who disagreed with him were impressed by his amazing vigor, both mental and physical, as he reached old age.

In his eighties, he still took daily walks along the streets of Washington. At eighty-seven, he broke a record by becoming the oldest Justice ever to serve on the Supreme Court. The following year, his wife died and his friends feared he would begin failing.

But he continued working until January of 1932, when he himself decided the time had come for him to resign. He spent the next three years at his Washington home, catching up on books he had been too busy to read previously. On March 6, 1935, Justice Holmes died, just two days before his ninety-fourth birthday.

George Marshall

1880–1959   U.S. Army Chief of Staff; Secretary of State; Secretary of Defense.

"That Marshall, he'll never make a soldier."

The words were the verdict of an upperclassman in September of 1897 when a tall, blue-eyed, seventeen-year-old freshman with a pug nose showed up at the Virginia Military Institute in Lexington, Virginia. He was awkward in drill and unable to follow the simple commands of "Right, face," or "To the rear, march."

But he learned quickly and well. In the years to come, George Catlett Marshall, Jr. became the foremost soldier of his time. In World War II, he commanded the largest army the United States ever had. And his service to his country did not end with the military. As a civilian, his work to eliminate the causes of war was so outstanding that

he received the Nobel Prize for Peace.

Ever since he could remember, George had wanted to be a soldier. From his boyhood days in Uniontown, Pennsylvania, where he was born on December 31, 1880, his chief interests had been horses and the military, perhaps because there was a military tradition in the Marshall family.

His father, George C. Marshall, Sr., had been called into service in the Civil War at the age of seventeen. His brother Stuart had graduated from V.M.I. a few years before his own arrival there. And a distant cousin had been one of the famous V.M.I. cadets who had marched directly into battle in 1864 to fight for the Confederacy in the Civil War.

Now George was determined not to

let them down, even though he was put in the "awkward squad" for those whose feet could not seem to follow the orders. From six in the morning to ten at night, the awkward squad marched and drilled. Gritting his teeth, George tried to follow instructions.

As the days went by, he began to grasp and even enjoy the precision of military drill. His earlier clumsiness disappeared and he gained confidence in his own abilities, both military and academic. Without protest, he endured the hazing of the upperclassmen—like standing at attention, or shining their shoes, or singing "Dixie" frequently.

What he did in his spare time showed him to be different from the other cadets. He walked around nearby battlefields of the Civil War, studying how professional soldiers had used the terrain to help their movements, making his own maps to show the military maneuvers.

In his senior year, Marshall was ranked first of all the cadets in military efficiency. He was appointed captain of cadets, the highest officer among the students. He played football with such skill that he was selected as tackle on the 1900 all-Southern football team.

One evening as he left football practice, Marshall passed by a private home near the campus and heard the sound of piano music. He and some friends stopped to listen. Then a young woman with red hair leaned out of the window and said, "Would you gentlemen like to come in and listen to the music?"

It was Lily Coles, the leading belle of Lexington. George, approaching his twentieth birthday, fell madly in love with Lily. Risking dismissal from the Institute, he slipped out of the dormitory at night to visit her. They decided to get married, but first he had to get an appointment as an officer in the United States Army. It was not easy, even for the top-ranking cadet at V.M.I., because the Army at that time was so small. Determined to become an officer, Marshall went off to Washington.

Unable to get a hearing at the War Department, he decided he would go to the top. He went to the White House and sat there patiently but was not admitted to the President's office. Finally, an usher escorted in a man and his daughter, the last ones besides George who were waiting to see President McKinley. George marched in right behind them.

President McKinley stared at the intruder. "What can I do for you, young man?" he asked.

"I would like an appointment as an Army officer," George replied, quickly listing his qualifications.

There is no record that his invasion

of the President's office brought results, but shortly after, in January of 1902, he received a commission as a second lieutenant.

He and Lily were married the following month, but they were soon separated, for his first assignment as an officer was in the Philippine Islands, where the climate was too hot for the delicate Lily, who had a heart problem.

In the years that followed, Marshall learned the soldier's trade in the Philippines and at a succession of army posts in the United States. His slow upward climb in the Army began when he finished first in a class of officers at a special school in Fort Leavenworth, Kansas, where future generals were trained to organize combat forces.

At the beginning of the First World War, Marshall was a captain training troops. After the United States entered the conflict against Germany in 1917, Marshall was among the first to go off to France. His job was to prepare untrained American troops for fighting.

Among Army men, he gained the nickname, The Wizard of the Meuse-Argonne, because his careful planning and precise orders got a million American soldiers to the right place at the right time so they could fight and win. Others got credit for winning battles, but in the inner Army circles generals knew that Marshall, then a colonel, was responsible.

They recommended that he be promoted to the rank of general, but the war ended before any action could be taken. After the war, he served in various posts in the United States and in China before returning to Washington in 1927.

In that year, his wife died. The grieving Marshall was sent to Fort Benning, in Georgia, to take command of the infantry school there. His job was to train young officers for war. While serving at Fort Benning, he met Katherine Tupper Brown, a widow. In 1930, they were married and Marshall, who had no children, acquired a ready-made family—his wife's three children by her previous marriage. Together, they went all over the country on a variety of assignments in the peacetime Army.

It was not till 1936 that Marshall became a general, eighteen years after he had been recommended for that rank at the end of World War I. Two years later, when another war in Europe seemed to be at hand, Marshall was called to Washington to head the war plans division of the Army.

On September 1, 1939, German troops invaded Poland, starting World War II. On that same day, Marshall took the oath of office as Chief of Staff, commanding officer of the entire Army. Although he had been thirty-fourth in seniority on the list of generals, President Franklin Roosevelt selected him

George Marshall posed for a Signal Corps photographer in 1938, two years after he had been made a general. *Courtesy of the George C. Marshall Research Foundation.*

above all the others because he believed Marshall was the best officer in the Army.

At the time, Marshall was fifty-nine years old, a dignified man who permitted no familiarity. Once President Roosevelt called him George, but after he saw the frosty look on Marshall's face, he never did it again. His family called him colonel, dating back to his long years of holding that rank.

In Washington, Marshall plunged into his major task: preparing the Army for possible action in war. While the United States policy was to remain neutral, experienced military officers foresaw dangerous times ahead.

Marshall found out that his job had two parts. Not only did he have to supervise an expanding army, he had to educate the public and the Congress about the need for a strong defense. Once, when he appeared before a Congressional committee to request funds for training, he said, "You wouldn't send a team against Notre Dame before it had a scrimmage, would you?" He got the money.

When Japanese planes attacked Pearl Harbor in Hawaii on December 7, 1941, the United States was at war. Still unprepared, the nation suffered a series of defeats in the Pacific. During those dark days, Marshall had all the money he needed but little time to train his troops for battle.

One of Marshall's chief functions was to coordinate the American war effort with that of its allies, Great Britain and the Soviet Union. He sent a promising younger general, Dwight Eisenhower, to London to prepare for the invasion of Europe.

It was two years before this huge operation could be undertaken. As the planning advanced, the question of who would be its commander arose. To almost everybody in Washington, there was one clear choice—Marshall, the top soldier in the United States Army.

President Roosevelt called him to a conference and tried to get Marshall himself to make a choice. Did he want to be commander or did he prefer to remain as Chief of Staff in Washington? Marshall replied that the war was too big for any personal feelings.

Finally, Roosevelt said, "I feel that I will not be able to sleep nights with you out of the country." Marshall hid his own regret with a simple, "Yes, sir." But it was the greatest disappointment of his life.

Shortly afterward, Eisenhower was appointed to command the Allied invasion—and began his rapid rise to fame and, later, the presidency. Marshall, as his superior officer in Washington, gave him the tools and the men that brought Allied victory in Europe in 1945.

After Japan surrendered later in

1945, President Truman awarded Marshall the Distinguished Service Medal and said of him: "Statesman and soldier . . . he takes his place at the head of the great commanders of history." On November 30, 1945, Marshall at the age of sixty-five retired from the Army.

But his retirement lasted only a few weeks. Truman called him back as a special ambassador to try to end the civil war in China. By January of 1946, Marshall was in China, meeting with both Communist leaders and those of the National government. But each side thought it could win by war, and his mission failed.

Once more, in 1947, Truman needed Marshall, this time as Secretary of State, a most unusual post for a soldier, but Marshall's job as Chief of Staff in World War II had trained him for dealing with foreign powers.

In June of that year, Marshall made a speech at Harvard that had a world-wide impact. He called upon the war-torn nations of Europe to come together with a plan for economic recovery. If they did that, he said, the United States would aid them financially. Thus was born the Marshall Plan, which resulted in a rebirth of prosperity in Europe.

Marshall retired from government service for the second time, but that retirement did not last long either. Truman named him as Secretary of Defense in 1950, when the Korean War broke out. He served until September of 1951. Then, at last, he went home to Leesburg, Virginia.

In those later years, Marshall received two honors. In 1953, the Nobel Peace Prize was awarded to him as "a soldier, statesman and benefactor of peace." But the honor that pleased him most was given by his alma mater, the Virginia Military Institute.

Back on the campus where he had been an awkward cadet fifty years earlier, he stood at attention while the Institute named the entrance hall to a cadet barracks for him. To an outsider, that might not seem like much, but for an old soldier, it was the highest praise. It put him in the company of only two other great soldiers, George Washington and Stonewall Jackson.

For the next several years, Marshall lived quietly in Leesburg. He died on October 16, 1959, at the age of seventy-eight.

Thurgood Marshall

1908–   U.S. Supreme Court Justice.

In 1967, he became the first black Justice of the United States Supreme Court. Before then, some newspapers had called him Mr. Civil Rights. To Thurgood Marshall's friends, though, he was affectionately known as Turkey.

He liked the nickname, not being the least bit stiff or solemn. While he took the law itself with a deep seriousness, outside court he looked at life more humorously than most other lawyers, whatever the color of their skin. Still, the dark color of his skin, without any question, was the most important influence on his whole career.

He never forgot that he was the great-grandson of a slave brought over from Africa in the 1800s, a slave who behaved so independently that his owner decided he was more trouble than he was worth—and set him free. It happened, therefore, that some years later a free black on the eastern shore of Maryland volunteered to fight on the Union side in the Civil War. He was the son of this former slave and the grandfather of the future Supreme Court Justice. When he enlisted, he had a little problem regarding his name.

He said everybody called him Marshall. Soldiers, however, were supposed to have a first name as well as a last name. Pressed to provide another name, the volunteer came up with an invention of his own. "Thorough-good," he said. So he went down on the army records as Thoroughgood Marshall. About fifty years later, the same name was given to his grandson.

Born in Baltimore on July 2, 1908,

the boy had parents who had both achieved a respected standing among the city's black community. His father, William Canfield Marshall, had risen from being a waiter on railroad dining cars to running the restaurant of a country club. His mother, Norma Williams Marshall, taught young children at a public school.

In those days, many states operated two separate school systems—one for white children and the other for blacks. This racial segregation applied to teachers, too, so Mrs. Marshall taught at the school her own two sons attended. Right under her watchful eye, the younger of them did something all by himself about his complicated first name.

It was too much to keep spelling and explaining, he decided, so he simply shortened it to Thurgood. This was a good example of the way he found reasonable solutions that someone else might have missed.

Still, the rest of his family had plenty to say about what Thurgood ought to be when he grew up. His grandmother, who lived with them, kept luring him into the kitchen to watch her make biscuits or crab soup. "No one ever yet saw a jobless Negro cook," she would tell him. His mother insisted that being a dentist was a better idea. Thurgood loved to eat, so he didn't at all mind learning how to cook. As for his moth-

er's plan, which seemed not very enjoyable, he just joked about it.

His father, however, had a real influence on him. "He never told me to become a lawyer, but he turned me into one," Marshall recalled years later. "He did it by teaching me to argue, by challenging my logic on every point, by making me prove every statement I made."

Even so, Marshall did not study much during his first two years at the all-black Lincoln University, in Pennsylvania. "I got the horsing around out of my system," he cheerfully explained. Then he began dating a young woman who had the same idea about the career he ought to aim for that his father had.

At the beginning of his junior year, on September 4, 1929, the twenty-one-year-old Marshall married Vivien Burey—and from then on, he settled down to making an outstanding record. Despite working part-time at a variety of jobs to pay his tuition expenses, he graduated with high honors and won a lot of attention by shining on the debating team.

It was not easy in 1930 for a black student to gain admission to a nonsegregated law school, no matter how bright he appeared to be, so Marshall was not too surprised when the law school at the University of Maryland rejected him. Instead, he entered the leading center for the higher education of black students—Howard University, in Washington, D.C.

At Howard, Marshall learned more than just law because several of its professors were closely involved with the organization they always called the N.A.A.C.P., the National Association for the Advancement of Colored People. Early in the 1930s, the N.A.A.C.P. was about to embark on a new sort of drive toward reducing unfair treatment of black Americans.

Since Marshall was the top student in his class, he got to attend the professors' strategy meetings. There he heard them talk about using laws already on the books to end some forms of discrimination—by starting test cases and carrying them all the way to the Supreme Court, if necessary.

While this may not sound very complicated more than fifty years afterward, at the time Marshall was in law school the Supreme Court itself was extremely conservative. It took a strict and narrow view of the meaning of some basic parts of the Constitution. A great deal of legal spadework was necessary before the N.A.A.C.P. could prepare solid statements defending its own stand—and actually begin filing test cases.

Meanwhile, Marshall finished his law training and opened a law office in Baltimore. It was 1933, the low point of the Great Depression. Not many clients showed up to consult him, and even the few cases he worked on gave him no feeling of satisfaction, for he found that he was much more interested in helping blacks with a problem involving race discrimination than with ordinary legal work. "He had a genius for ignoring cases that might earn him any money," his secretary recalled.

In 1935, Marshall was asked by the N.A.A.C.P. to handle a lawsuit against the University of Maryland. It was just five years since he himself had been turned down by its law school—and now another qualified black had had the same experience. On his behalf, the N.A.A.C.P. was suing to make the university admit him.

In the Maryland Court of Appeals, Marshall won this case. No doubt the victory particularly pleased him because of his personal rebuff by the same institution not too long before. The victory also greatly affected his own future, for it led to his joining the N.A.A.C.P.'s legal staff the following year.

Marshall spent the next twenty-five years associated with this group, heading its legal arm from 1938 onward. Nobody knew better than he did that his first success—forcing the admittance of the first black law student at just one university—was only a beginning.

On the issue of segregated schools,

Betsy Graves Reyneau painted this portrait of Thurgood Marshall in 1956. Eleven years later, he would become the first black man to serve on the Supreme Court. *Courtesy of the National Portrait Gallery, Smithsonian Institution; gift of the Harmon Foundation.*

three words had long been used to justify keeping blacks and whites apart. In 1896, the Supreme Court had ruled that segregation did not violate the rights of black citizens if "separate but equal" facilities were provided for them. As a result, twenty-one states had set up all-black school systems that were certainly separate from the schools for whites.

But were they equal, too? Although a mere look at most of the schools for blacks showed inferior buildings and equipment, proving this in a court of law was no easy matter. It was especially difficult because many whites did not want to see segregation ended.

But few states had separate law schools for blacks. That was why the N.A.A.C.P.'s early efforts toward equal educational opportunity concentrated on law and similar special schools. Yet there was a deeper reason, too.

In the long run, Marshall and the people he worked with wanted full equality for black students at every level. Yet they realized that, before such a major change could take effect, public opinion among white Americans would have to come around to believing that the change ought to be made. By going slowly, securing small victories involving just a single university, they hoped to gain increasing support—until the Supreme Court itself changed its old "separate but equal" ruling.

That happened, finally, in 1954. When Thurgood Marshall won the historic case outlawing all segregated schools—the case known to lawyers as *Brown v. Board of Education*—he was hailed as the mastermind of one of the most significant reforms the country had ever seen.

By then a substantial number of white Americans were ready to admit that integrating the schools was the right thing to do. So Marshall himself received much praise, even though bitter opposition to letting black children enter formerly white schools continued in many areas.

But Marshall, before and after this landmark case, had little time for worrying over the reaction of bigots. Altogether, he brought thirty-two major cases before the Supreme Court—cases involving discrimination in housing, on public transportation, and in the registering of voters, as well as the famous education case.

Of these thirty-two cases, Marshall won the amazing total of twenty-nine. Not many other lawyers had ever achieved any such batting average in the nation's highest court. Besides having a great effect in broadening the civil rights of black Americans, this record made Marshall himself something of a celebrity.

In his youth, he had been tall and very thin. By now, though, his love of eating had broadened him physically. "A great, rumpled bear of a man," *Newsweek* magazine called him. He had endured a personal tragedy when his wife died of cancer not long after his triumph on the school segregation case, but on December 17, 1955, he married Cecilia Suyat from Hawaii. They were living happily together in their New York City apartment with their two young sons in 1961 when President Kennedy telephoned Mr. Civil Rights. Would he be willing to become a judge on the United States Court of Appeals?

Marshall served nearly four years on the bench of this federal court in New York. He realized, of course, that there were political reasons why Kennedy had offered him the job. The President hoped that by appointing a black to the second highest federal court, he would convince the black community that it had a friend in the White House.

There were people, however, who thought the civil rights movement was causing too much strife. They criticized Marshall's appointment, saying he lacked the well-rounded legal experience to qualify him as a judge making important decisions on all sorts of cases involving big corporations. Marshall went back to his books and boned up on subjects like tax law. During the next several years, he wrote more than 150 opinions—and he must have done his homework admirably. Not a single one of them was reversed by the Supreme Court.

That highest court of all was where he surely wished to end his own career. When Lyndon Johnson took over the presidency, political experts wondered if he might break with tradition and appoint the first black Justice.

Instead, in 1965, Johnson asked Marshall to be Solicitor General, an important post in the Justice Department. After a two-year period there, in which he got acquainted with the Washington scene, Marshall was summoned to the White House in June of 1967.

In the Rose Garden, President Johnson was holding a surprise press conference. A vacancy had just occurred on the Supreme Court—and the President announced he wanted Thurgood Marshall to fill it. "He deserves the appointment," Johnson said.

Marshall was fifty-nine when he took his seat as one of the nine members of the Supreme Court. In a way, his long service as a Justice was less exciting than his days as Mr. Civil Rights. He quietly took the liberal side in hundreds of decisions over the years until he retired in 1991. Yet his place in history is secure because he proved that the great-grandson of a slave could reach the very top rank in the legal branch of the American government.

Richard Nixon

1913–   U.S. Congressman; U.S. Senator; thirty-seventh President of the United States.

In the long history of the United States, only one President ever resigned in disgrace—Richard Milhous Nixon. He left the White House in 1974 to avoid removal from office by Congress for crimes committed during his administration.

Only once before had a President been formally charged and tried by Congress, in 1868 just after the Civil War. President Andrew Johnson stood charged with misconduct by the House of Representatives in an obvious political dispute. In a trial, the Senate found Johnson not guilty, and he stayed in office.

The Nixon case was different. The charges were that he not only abused the powers of the President but also obstructed justice, a serious crime that could lead to a jail sentence. Clearly

there was evidence to prove the charges.

It was an astonishing turnaround in Nixon's long political career. Only a year earlier, in 1973, he had been sworn into office for a second term as President after one of the most lopsided victories ever in an election. How could a man who had been the overwhelming choice of the people leave the White House tarnished?

For the answer, one has to go back to the life and character of Nixon. He was born on January 19, 1913, in Yorba Linda, California, not far from Los Angeles. His father tried to raise lemons there but failed, so the family moved to Whittier, where his parents operated a combination gas station and general store.

Richard's father, Francis A. Nixon,

disappointed in almost everything he tried, had a foul temper, frequently yelling at his family. His mother, Hannah Milhous Nixon, was a gentle Quaker, liked by everybody. Living in back of the store, the Nixons had five sons. One died as a young boy and another while in his twenties. It was far from a rich household and Richard, like the other boys, had to work as soon as he could.

When he was big enough, he worked as a farm laborer, picking beans. In the store, he picked out rotten apples and potatoes and delivered groceries. He worked as a floor sweeper in a packing-house and as a janitor at a public swimming pool.

Despite those many jobs, Richard was a good student. He maintained a four-year average of A in his Latin classes in high school and graduated with honors. His biggest disappointment was being defeated for the student presidency of Whittier High School.

In those growing up years, the Nixons lived near the tracks of the Santa Fe Railroad. Young Richard at first wanted to become a railroad engineer. "The train whistle was the sweetest music I ever heard," he once said. But he also was an eager newspaper reader—and that changed his mind about what he wanted to be when he grew up.

As his mother recalled it, he was reading a newspaper article about the Teapot Dome oil scandals in the 1920s, when he called out to her, "Mother, I would like to become a lawyer, an honest lawyer, who can't be bought by crooks."

Nixon did grow up to be a lawyer. In school at Whittier, he won prizes for public speaking and debating. At college, too, he was a top-notch debater. He represented Whittier College in more than fifty debates, winning most of them. In his senior year, he was elected president of the student body.

He graduated from college in 1934, in the middle of the Great Depression, when there were few jobs. But Nixon knew that he wanted to go to law school, and he found one that gave him a scholarship, Duke University, in Durham, North Carolina.

When he graduated in 1937, he returned to Whittier to practice law. Shortly after his return, he heard about a glamorous new schoolteacher in town who was acting in an amateur theater production. He went to the rehearsals and met Thelma Catherine Ryan, usually called Pat. He proposed to her the night they met, but she did not consent until two years later. They were married in June of 1940.

In those early Whittier years, Nixon was a rising young lawyer. He was elected a trustee of Whittier College at the age of twenty-six and there was even talk that he might become its president. But World War II broke out, and Nixon felt he had to do something.

At first, he went off to Washington to work as a lawyer in a government agency. Then, despite his Quaker upbringing, he joined the Navy and was sent as an officer to serve with an air transport group in the South Pacific.

When Nixon returned home from service in the Navy, a friend suggested that he run for Congress. The Republicans in Whittier needed a candidate, and Nixon, an ambitious lawyer, seemed a good choice.

Politically unknown, he made a name for himself by engaging in a series of debates with his opponent. In his first campaign, he also found a powerful political weapon—attacking his opponent as a left-winger. Nixon won.

In the House of Representatives, Nixon made a national reputation as an anti-Communist. As a member of the Committee on Un-American Activities, he investigated communism in various phases of American life. He made his biggest impact in a case involving charges that Alger Hiss, a former State Department official, had furnished materials to the Communists.

Using his reputation as a hunter of Communists in government, Nixon ran

for the Senate in 1950. His opponent was Helen Gahagan Douglas, a well-known Democratic liberal. As he had before, Nixon based his campaign on charges that his opponent had supported Communist policies. Once more, he succeeded.

He won the election and became Senator Nixon. His supporters admired him as a hard-hitting anti-Communist, but his opponents criticized him as Tricky Dick, charging that he used devious tactics.

When Dwight D. Eisenhower became the Republican nominee for President in 1952, he turned to Nixon as his vice-presidential running mate. During the campaign, Nixon's rapidly rising political career almost ended. Newspapers published accounts of wealthy Republicans in California who had set up a secret fund for Nixon's use when he was in the Senate.

In a television speech to the nation, Nixon defended himself by talking about the plain and simple style in which he and his wife and two daughters lived. He mentioned that one of the gifts his family had received was a black-and-white cocker spaniel named Checkers. And then he said, "Regardless of what they say about it, we are going to keep him."

An avalanche of telegrams poured into Republican National Headquar-

Richard Nixon, painted here by Norman Rockwell, was the first President to resign from office. *Courtesy of the National Portrait Gallery, Smithsonian Institution.*

ters, and Eisenhower decided not to drop Nixon from the ticket. Because of the personal popularity of Ike, the Republicans won in 1952 and 1956. Nixon served as Vice-President for those eight years.

In 1960, Nixon became the Republican nominee for President. He lost the election to John F. Kennedy, mainly because of his poor showing in the first television debates ever held between presidential candidates.

Two years later, after Nixon ran for governor of California and lost, his political career seemed ended. He moved

to New York City and entered private law practice. But he continued to make political speeches around the nation. As a result, in 1968 he emerged once again as the Republican candidate for President.

Avoiding television debates this time, Nixon was elected, defeating a Democratic ticket headed by Senator Hubert Humphrey. He took the oath of office as the thirty-seventh President on January 20, 1969. He was fifty-six years old.

The major issue confronting him was the unpopular war in Vietnam. Nixon began to withdraw American troops from that far-off Asian land, but nationwide protests against any fighting in Southeast Asia increased as Nixon sent troops into a neutral country, Cambodia, and started to bomb bases in that country.

Nixon had two foreign policy triumphs in the early years of his presidency, however. He reversed twenty years of American policy by flying to Communist China to open relations with that country. He also flew to Moscow, the capital of the Soviet Union, for a summit meeting with the head of that Communist nation in a spirit of friendship.

After he was reelected in 1972, Nixon signed an agreement ending the war in Vietnam. It seemed that peace at last had come to the United States. But then the Nixon presidency began to fall apart.

Within a year after Nixon took office for his second term, his Vice-President, Spiro T. Agnew, resigned on October 10, 1973. In court that same day, Agnew pleaded guilty to a charge of evading income tax payments after the government had made public evidence that he had accepted bribes while he was the governor of Maryland. Nixon appointed Gerald R. Ford, a leader of the House of Representatives, as the new Vice-President.

From the very first day of his second term, Nixon was confronted by what became known as the Watergate scandal. It started when five burglars were arrested trying to break into the office of the Democratic National Committee in the Watergate Hotel in Washington.

That minor incident turned into a major scandal because the Watergate burglars were tied to the Nixon reelection committee and the White House. A series of investigations disclosed wrongdoing at the highest level of Nixon's administration, including Cabinet officers, senior White House staff members and, finally, Nixon himself.

The crimes included misuse of campaign funds, destruction of official documents, illegal wiretapping, lying to a grand jury, and the payment of "hush money" to the Watergate burglars. Even worse, the evidence showed that the White House tried to use the Federal Bureau of Investigation and the Central Intelligence Agency to cover up the misdeeds.

Nixon made many speeches to the nation, trying to explain away the Watergate affair. At one time, he even said, "I am not a crook." But day after day new disclosures of wrongdoing by members of his staff were made public in official court hearings, investigations by congressional committees, and in the press.

One of the most startling revelations was that Nixon had ordered all conversations in the Oval Office of the White House to be secretly taped; he hoped to provide a record for future historians. Instead, his own voice on tape provided the evidence that convinced a committee of the House of Representatives to vote to impeach him.

He faced certain impeachment by the full House, which would have brought him to a trial before the Senate and removal from office. And so, on August 9, 1974, Nixon resigned. In a nationwide television speech, he said, "It has become evident to me that I no longer have a strong enough political base in Congress" to remain in office.

Many of Nixon's chief aides, including two Cabinet officers, were convicted of crimes for their actions, but Nixon himself received a full pardon "for any offense" committed by him during his administration. The pardon was granted in September of 1974 by the man Nixon had appointed as Vice-President and who succeeded him as President, Gerald Ford.

In granting the pardon, Ford said his purpose was "to heal the wounds" inflicted on the nation by Watergate. Accepting the pardon, Nixon said, "That the way I tried to deal with Watergate was the wrong way is a burden that I shall bear for every day of the life that is left to me."

George Norris

1861–1944   U.S. Congressman; U.S. Senator.

Growing up in Ohio, George Norris became the champion corn shucker of Sandusky County. After the harvest, he and the other boys in the area would gather to see who could strip the green leaves off ears of corn the fastest. George won every time.

The corn-shucking contests were a welcome chance for George to play a little. Every morning as the sun rose, he got up to begin a long day of farm chores. He pumped water from the well outside the house, milked the cows, sawed wood for the kitchen stove, and gathered eggs from the chickens.

Born on July 11, 1861, George was the eleventh of twelve children in the Norris family. His only brother, John, who had been much older, died as a soldier in the Civil War. His father, Chauncey Norris, had died around the

same time, so George, from a very early age, took on a lot of responsibility.

His mother, Mary Mook Norris, managed the farm with the help of her girls, but she often told George he was the man of the household. As soon as he could lift an axe, he went out to cut away stumps of trees, clearing land for planting. In the summer, he weeded between long rows of growing corn, and in the fall he picked corn. Winters, he worked along with neighbors at keeping the county roads clear.

From such humble beginnings, George William Norris rose to become one of the most famous statesmen in the United States. History has ranked him, along with Henry Clay and Daniel Webster, among the nation's outstanding lawmakers.

His rise began because his mother

insisted that he and his sisters had to go to school as well as work on the farm. He walked a mile and a half to get to school and the same distance home. Yet studying seemed like a vacation to him, compared with the hard work on the farm.

George applied himself so well to his studies that soon he was tutoring other children who had learning problems. He earned some money that way and by doing chores on other farms as well as his own.

When he finished school, he still did not have enough money for college. The Norris family solved that problem in a cooperative way. George and two sisters went off to Baldwin University in Berea, Ohio. They lived in an old house, where George sawed and chopped wood for heat and Clara and Emma did the cooking and cleaning. By chopping wood and clipping lawns for other families, George earned enough to pay their tuition.

Somehow, he also found time to join the debating and literary societies as well. During these busy college years, George made up his mind that he would become a lawyer. Still, he faced the same old problem of a lack of money.

He arrived at a way of paying for his legal education by alternately working and attending law school in Valparaiso, Indiana. At night, instead of collapsing from overwork, again Norris took part in debating contests. He turned out to be one of the best debaters at law school.

In 1883, Norris received his law degree, but he still did not have enough money to rent an office so he could begin practicing his profession. Instead, he packed his few possessions and traveled west to the state of Washington. There, he worked in orchards and taught school. With some of his savings, he returned eastward, to Nebraska.

At the age of twenty-four, he set up a law practice in Beaver City, the center of a large corn- and wheat-farming district. Clients were few, however, and so he accepted an appointment as a district attorney. He became known as a stern but fair prosecutor. His financial problem eased to the extent that, in 1890, he married Pluma Lashley, the daughter of a banker in Beaver City.

After serving as district attorney for several years, Norris in 1895 was elected a district judge. In that job, he became well-known for his sympathy for farmers faced with eviction from their farms because they could not pay their debts.

Norris' life changed dramatically in the opening years of the twentieth century. It started with a tragedy. His wife died, in 1901, giving birth to their third daughter. Two years later he met and married Ella Leonard, a former school-teacher in McCook, Nebraska, which became his home.

In 1902, the year before his second marriage, Norris had decided to run for Congress. At that time a conservative Republican, he won a narrow victory over his Democratic opponent and went off to Washington as a strong supporter of his party and its policies.

But soon he began to show his independence. He was disturbed to see how the Republican political machine tried to control his every vote on the basis of party loyalty instead of on the merits of each piece of legislation.

Norris joined a small group of Representatives opposing the Speaker of the House, Joseph Cannon, who maintained an iron grip on all of the lawmaking process. Cannon did it by controlling the appointment of members of the House's powerful Rules Committee. That committee determined which proposed laws could be voted on—and which would not even be considered.

It was years before the rebels were strong enough to attack the man who was called Czar Cannon because of his power. The opportunity came in 1910, when Norris arose on a point of procedure. He moved that members of the Rules Committee should be ap-

pointed by the full House, not by the Speaker.

That simple motion became the focus of a major fight between the leaders of the House, who wanted to maintain their control, and the rebels, who wanted a more democratic way of proceeding. After a thirty-six-hour battle, Norris and his supporters won. They took away Speaker Cannon's power. Some historians have called that the most important reform in the history of the House of Representatives.

With that victory, Norris became an important national figure and a leader in the growing Progressive movement. Still, he retained his ties to the Republican party, even though its leaders disapproved of him.

In 1912, Norris entered a new phase of his career. He was elected to the United States Senate, taking office at the age of fifty-one. He served in the Senate for thirty years, gaining in stature because of his independence and integrity.

He showed his independence when war broke out in Europe shortly after he took his seat in the Senate. As the United States seemed to be gradually edging toward participating in the war, Norris spoke out strongly for peace. He was one of twelve Senators who opposed President Wilson's plan to arm American merchant ships in 1917 because he thought this was a step toward war.

Wilson attacked Norris and the others as "a little group of willful men representing no opinion but their own." But Norris believed Wilson was leading the nation down the path toward war. When Wilson asked for a declaration of war against Germany in April of 1917, Norris spoke out.

He opposed the war, he said, because "we are going to risk sacrificing millions of our countrymen's lives in order that other countrymen may coin their life-blood into money." Norris was one of only six Senators who voted against the declaration of war.

For that he was bitterly attacked all over the nation as unpatriotic. But when he returned to Nebraska, he told the voters back home, "I have come to tell you the truth." After listening to him, they showed their confidence in him by returning him to the Senate in the 1918 election.

A mild-mannered man ordinarily, Norris was a tiger when he thought that partisan politics or private privilege were affecting issues important to the public. He had many admirers, and even his opponents never questioned his devotion to the good of the public. Indeed, a book about him bore the title *Integrity: The Life of George W. Norris.*

In the Senate chamber, Norris sat quietly most of the time. When he arose to speak, he used conversational tones, without raising his voice. He had a knack of making complicated matters seem simple. In his personal life, he liked to keep things simple, too.

He always wore a plain black suit with a black bow tie. In his office, he kept two pictures, one of Theodore Roosevelt and the other of Abraham Lincoln. His door was always open to visitors from back home and he loved to chat with them, smoking his corncob pipe.

In the summers, he and Mrs. Norris went to their cabin in the woods in Wisconsin. There, he chopped the wood they used in their fireplace and stove. "I still haven't forgotten the Sandusky County days," he once said.

And he never forgot the struggling farmers of Nebraska and the rest of the Middle West. As a skilled user of the rules of the Senate, he pushed through measures for farm relief, rural electrification, and the rights of labor. He was also chiefly responsible for the adoption of the Twentieth Amendment to the Constitution, which shifted the inauguration day of Presidents from March 4 to January 20.

His major contribution, however, came in the field of public power. All by himself, he waged a battle to preserve waterpower facilities built by the government during World War I at Muscle Shoals, Alabama.

First, he prevented the sale of the valuable dam there to private industry. Then he slowly persuaded his colleagues to support government operation of Muscle Shoals by convincing them that public power would be cheaper for consumers than power bought from private companies. But when Congress passed bills to create public power facilities, they were vetoed by Republican Presidents.

To the nation's power interests, the defeat of Norris became a major objective. They found another George W. Norris, this one a grocer in Broken Bow, Nebraska, and entered him in the Republican primary election of 1932. They hoped that would confuse the voters and the real George Norris would go down to defeat. When the tricky scheme was uncovered, however, Norris was easily returned to his Senate seat.

Around that time, Norris began to

George Norris (*second from right*) is shown with employees of the Tennessee Valley Authority, the agency he created in 1933. *Courtesy of the Tennessee Valley Authority Archives.*

In 1938, George Norris visited the first dam built by the Tennessee Valley Authority, which was named Norris Dam in his honor. *Courtesy of the Tennessee Valley Authority Archives.*

break his ties with the Republican party. In 1928, he opposed the election of Herbert Hoover, the Republican candidate for President. In 1932, he endorsed Franklin D. Roosevelt, the Democratic candidate. When Roosevelt was elected, Norris strongly supported his New Deal measures.

Roosevelt supported Norris when he wrote the law that created the Tennessee Valley Authority in 1933. In recog-

nition of his contributions to the vast T.V.A. system, the first dam built in that region, near Knoxville, Tennessee, was called the Norris Dam.

But Norris did not neglect his home state of Nebraska. He also pushed through legislation that made Nebraska the only state in the nation with a one-house legislature. Its members were to be elected on a nonpartisan basis, with no indication of political party. "There is no difference between a Democratic and a Republican machine," Norris said.

When World War II broke out, Norris reversed his antiwar position because he thought that the security of the United States was threatened. After the attack on Pearl Harbor, he voted for declarations of war against Germany and Japan.

In 1942, at the age of eighty-one, Norris decided to retire, but then he changed his mind and ran for reelection to a seat in the Senate as an independent. This time, however, the voters of Nebraska decided it was time for the old man to step down, and he was defeated.

He returned to his home in McCook and wrote an autobiography. Its title was a fitting summary of his life, *Fighting Liberal*. He died in McCook on September 2, 1944, at the age of eighty-three.

Eleanor Roosevelt

1884–1962   First activist First Lady; U.S. delegate to the United Nations.

It was past midnight when the new First Lady started writing a letter to one of her friends. On very impressive paper—with gold printing across the top that said THE WHITE HOUSE—she scrawled several pages about all the excitement since her husband had become the President.

Then Eleanor Roosevelt added a few simple words. "I begin to think there are ways in which I can be useful," she confided.

And so, early in March of 1933, something entirely different arrived on the American scene. Every previous First Lady had stayed out of the public eye as much as possible. From Martha Washington onward, the wives of Presidents had concentrated on family duties and welcoming guests.

But the wife of Franklin D. Roosevelt took such an active role in public affairs that many people consider her the most influential woman of the twentieth century. In part, she owed her prominence to her husband's position. After his death, however, she reached an even higher status on her own.

Then her work on behalf of the United Nations—along with her unofficial efforts to help improve life for the less fortunate everywhere—won her a title nobody else had ever earned. The First Lady of the World, she was called.

Her full name was Anna Eleanor Roosevelt, and she had been born, on October 11, 1884, into one of New York City's leading families. Her mother, Anna Hall, stood out as a beautiful woman. Her father, Elliott Roosevelt, was the dashing younger brother of the dynamic Theodore, the first Roosevelt to reach the White House.

Still, Eleanor had a very painful childhood. There seemed to be something about her own appearance that disappointed her mother. Even more disturbing, her father had a serious problem that nobody explained to her. Only after she grew up did she learn that drinking too much had caused his strange behavior.

Despite his failings, Eleanor adored him, so she felt heartbroken, at the age of seven, when he left their home "to recover his health" on a farm in Virginia. That was the first in a terrible series of tragedies.

The following year, her mother got sick and died. Eleanor knew she should feel sad, but she could not keep down a sudden surge of hope. Now she and her two little brothers could go and live with their father! However, it turned out that their mother had left strict instructions that the children were to be cared for by their Grandmother Hall.

Just a few months later, one of Eleanor's brothers died of diphtheria, and shortly before her tenth birthday, her dream of being happy again with her father finally was shattered when he, too, died.

Although her grandmother and her aunts never treated her unkindly, they were too busy with their own concerns to pay much attention to Eleanor. Very sensitive and bright, she tried hard to please them. Under her calm manner, she hated the idea that everybody pitied her—and yet how could they help it?

Not only was she an orphan, Eleanor thought she really was the ugliest girl in the private school she attended. Fully a head taller than most of her classmates, she knew she had a gawky way of walking. In addition, her front teeth stuck out so much that she did her best to avoid smiling.

But she often forgot about such worries when she was with other people. Then the eager interest she felt in what they were saying worked a sort of magic. Her blue-gray eyes would shine brightly, making her look much prettier than she imagined.

While she rarely played with other children, her grandmother sometimes let her visit her Roosevelt cousins. At Uncle Ted's summer home, Eleanor bravely joined in all the games. Clumsy or not, she impressed Uncle Ted so much by being such a good sport that he told her she was his favorite niece.

Eleanor spent much of her time trying to be a substitute mother to her brother Hall or reading aloud to her aunts. At last—in 1899, when she was fifteen—this unhappy period of her life ended when her grandmother sent her to a boarding school in England. There she blossomed forth in new surroundings, where nobody sighed over her sad history.

During the three years Eleanor spent at Allenswood, her keen mind put her at the top of her class. Her warm and sympathetic nature made her many close friends. As a result, she seemed to have a new self-confidence when she returned to America.

Approaching her eighteenth birthday, she was expected to follow the usual pattern for a proper young woman in the upper rank of New York society. That meant going to a lot of parties until she met and married a suitable young man. While Eleanor privately doubted whether any suitable young man would ask her to dance, let alone marry her, she could not even think yet of defying rules that her relatives took very seriously.

But she already had a yearning to do some sort of work that would make her feel useful, so, along with her party going, she volunteered to serve as a part-time teacher in a slum neighborhood. At least one of her relatives approved of this step.

It was her cousin—actually, her sixth cousin—Franklin. His branch of the family lived north of the city, in Hyde Park along the Hudson River. Soon after her arrival from England she had met him on a train as she was going to her grandmother's house in the country.

Franklin Delano Roosevelt, at the age of twenty, struck Eleanor as unbelievably handsome. Besides being two years older than she, he was also three inches taller. To a young woman who towered above most other females, measuring fully five feet ten inches, that seemed quite important.

Even more important, Franklin shared her interest in the world outside their narrow social circle. He was attending Harvard, and he told her he hoped to go in for politics someday—like their famous relative, Uncle Ted, who was now the President of the United States.

When Franklin kept finding reasons to visit her, Eleanor thought he was merely being kind. When he came to call for her one afternoon at the slum school where she was teaching, it occurred to her that maybe he wanted to learn about the sort of people he would not meet at Harvard. She was amazed, about a year after they had met on the train, to hear him asking her to marry him.

In her confusion, Eleanor asked a question of her own. "Why me?" she blurted out. For she was no beauty, and he could easily have found a much more attractive wife.

In 1905, following their wedding, Eleanor Roosevelt and Franklin Delano Roosevelt went to Italy. *Courtesy of the Franklin D. Roosevelt Library.*

But he wanted her, Franklin insisted. With her at his side, he could surely accomplish whatever he aimed for. Besides, he added, he happened to be very much in love. Only then did Eleanor admit that she had fallen in love, too.

Yet Franklin's strong-minded mother protested that "the dear children" were much too young to marry. Not till the following year—on March 17, 1905— did Eleanor, at the age of twenty, become Mrs. Franklin D. Roosevelt.

Their wedding in New York City attracted much more attention than other similar ceremonies. President Theodore Roosevelt himself escorted the bride to the altar. He had even offered to have the marriage at the White House, because he said he was as fond of Eleanor as if she were his own daughter.

But more than twenty years elapsed before Eleanor Roosevelt became famous. During the first ten years of her married life, she was always having a baby or just getting over having a baby. Her first child was a daughter, Anna, and then she had four sons—James, Elliott, Franklin, Jr., and John.

In this period, her husband finished law school and began his career in politics as a New York state senator. In 1913, President Wilson appointed Franklin Roosevelt as his Assistant Sec-

retary of the Navy. That meant moving to Washington.

During the First World War, which the United States entered in 1917, Eleanor Roosevelt realized for the first time what a capable person she could be. As the director of a Red Cross center where thousands of soldiers were served coffee and sandwiches, she showed an unusual gift for organizing.

After the war ended, she started writing reports about laws affecting women for the League of Women Voters. By that time they were back in New York, where her husband had resumed practicing law. Then, during the summer of 1921, when the family was vacationing at the island of Campobello, off the coast of Maine, a new crisis struck them.

Franklin, at the age of thirty-nine, came down with a dreaded disease that usually affected children. It was infantile paralysis, more commonly known as polio. Doctors said this man who had seemed to be so vigorous might never walk again—unless he kept at an intensely trying program of exercising.

In later years, Eleanor Roosevelt would shrug off any credit for helping her husband triumph over his crippling ailment. Yet everybody who knew them said she had been tireless in encouraging him. She also found the spirit to challenge Franklin's mother, who thought he ought to spend the rest of

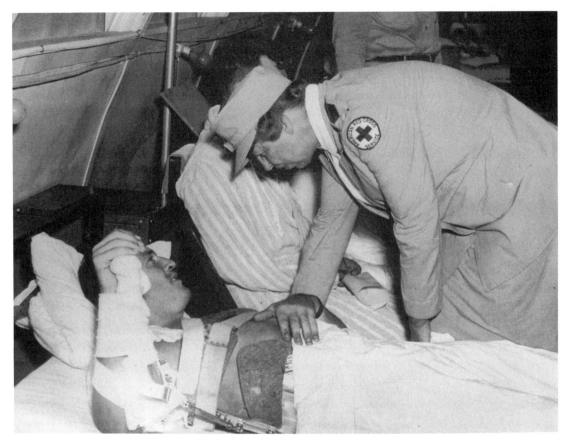

As perhaps the most active First Lady, Eleanor Roosevelt visited wounded soldiers in a military hospital in the South Pacific in 1943. *Courtesy of the Franklin D. Roosevelt Library.*

his life safely in a wheelchair at Hyde Park, puttering with his stamp collection.

No! Eleanor spoke up to her mother-in-law. What's more, to keep her husband's name from being forgotten while he was recovering, Mrs. Franklin Delano Roosevelt began making nervous little speeches at Democratic women's gatherings.

By 1929, when Franklin was elected governor of New York, his wife had be-

come an expert at organizing get-out-the-vote drives. But she had a busy life of her own, too. She was the part owner of a private school for girls, where she taught several days a week, and she also played a leading part in many women's groups.

As New York's first lady, she managed to keep up with all this work and still welcome guests at the executive mansion on weekends. Right after her husband was elected President, how-

Eleanor Roosevelt served as a delegate to the United Nations. Photograph by Clare Sipprell in 1949. *Courtesy of the National Portrait Gallery, Smithsonian Institution.*

ever, she regretfully gave up her teaching. It depressed her deeply that she would have to spend all her time just being the official hostess at the White House.

That did not happen, however. From the first week of her twelve years there, Eleanor Roosevelt kept finding new ways to be "useful." She traveled thousands of miles, inspecting all sorts of government projects, then reported what she had seen to her husband.

Even more notably, she showed her own concern about the poor and members of minority groups by organizing meetings and making countless speeches. While all of this activity brought her enormous popularity, it also made her the butt of some nasty comments from people who thought that a woman's place was in the home.

Yet the praise far outweighed the criticism. Wherever she turned up—striding out of a coal mine or riding a horse in Yellowstone Park—someone was bound to smile and cry out, "Gosh, there's Eleanor."

After her husband died in 1945, many political figures asked her to run for office herself. No, she said, she was past sixty and it was time for her to play with her grandchildren. Instead, she became even more famous when President Truman appointed her as an American delegate to the United Nations.

There Mrs. Roosevelt surprised many diplomats by her skill at negotiating with the Russians. It was largely through her efforts that the United Nations adopted an international charter on human rights.

Although she retired from the U.N. when she was nearly seventy, she still did not stop speaking and traveling in the cause of world peace. She went to Russia and Japan, to India and Israel, visiting peasants and prime ministers.

She also had an important political influence at home during these years. Many Democrats thinking about running for office sought her approval before announcing their candidacy, because a word from her was said to be worth thousands of votes. No other American woman has ever wielded any similar political power.

Eleanor Roosevelt died on November 7, 1962, at the age of seventy-eight. "She would rather light a candle than curse the darkness," one of her admirers said then. "And her glow has warmed the world."

Franklin Roosevelt

1882–1945   Governor of New York; thirty-second President of the United States.

He served as the President of the United States for longer than any other man in history, and during the years he held the office, from 1933 to 1945, he led the country through two of the worst crises it had ever faced.

But Franklin D. Roosevelt's leadership in the Great Depression and in World War II consisted of far more than merely making important decisions. Was it his beaming smile? Or the warm, sure sound of his voice? Somehow, he inspired an enormous amount of hope and confidence among his fellow citizens.

A large number of them looked up to him, even loved him, as few public officials have ever been loved. At the same time, others hated him with such intensity they could not even bring themselves to speak his name. "That man in the White House," they called him.

Clearly, F.D.R. was no ordinary person. His own life, no less than his political career, held moments of high drama. Starting with every possible advantage, he was born on January 30, 1882 into the privileged top layer of New York society.

Franklin Delano Roosevelt was his full name. His father, James Roosevelt, could trace ancestors dating back to the earliest Dutch settlers of New Amsterdam, but Franklin's mother boasted that the Delanos had an even more impressive family tree.

Thanks to her—the former Miss Sara Delano informed her only child—he was related to seven different passengers who had come from England aboard the *Mayflower* in 1620.

While the young Franklin did not see why this sort of talk interested his parents so much, it was obvious to him that they were important people. At their home overlooking the Hudson River, they had numerous servants and, when he went with them to Europe almost every year, they traveled in fine style.

Until Franklin was fourteen, he hardly ever spent more than a few hours away from his mother and father. A series of teachers who lived with the family gave him private lessons. To divert him, his fond parents provided him with his own pony or practically anything else he wanted—except freedom.

Not that Franklin ever felt seriously unhappy. His life was much too pleasant, and he had learned very early that joking with his mother would make her forget to be too strict. So he never fought with her, he just used his head to charm her into letting him have his own way.

When he was finally sent away to Groton, a select boarding school in Massachusetts, Franklin did not have an easy time getting along with boys his own age. Although his classmates came from the same sort of families, they had left home at twelve and already were so accustomed to the routine that they

made the new boy feel like an outsider. Again, though, Franklin simply joked about his problems instead of brooding about them.

Failing to make the baseball team, he cheerfully organized a new one he named the B.B.B.B., or the Bum Base Ball Boys. Then he led them to victory against another upstart group known as Carter's Little Liver Pills. In his classes, he worked just hard enough to guarantee that he would get into college.

During Franklin's first year at Harvard, his father died. Much older than his wife, he had been ailing for some time. Sara Delano Roosevelt wanted her son to aim for the same gentlemanly kind of life her husband had lived— serving on the board of directors of a few big companies, but mostly supervising his Hyde Park estate and quietly doing good as the head of the local hospital or school committee.

But Franklin showed while he was a college student that he had a much more outgoing kind of personality. He rushed around the campus, getting involved in all sorts of activities, from cheerleading at football games to editing the college newspaper.

Yet he stood out at Harvard for a reason that had nothing to do with his own talents: he had the same last name as the new President of the United

States. Theodore Roosevelt, in fact, was his fifth cousin.

This early in life Franklin had set his mind on following in his Cousin Ted's footsteps. This bold ambition may have had something to do with Franklin's first attempts to get better acquainted with another relative. She was a tall, shy young woman named Eleanor Roosevelt.

Eleanor, too, was a distant cousin of Franklin's. Her father had been Theodore Roosevelt's younger brother, so she was the President's niece—his favorite niece, he often said. Besides this close connection, her high-minded interest in more serious matters than mere party going impressed Franklin.

He could hardly help realizing he was a very handsome young man, and it would be easy for him just to enjoy life. So Franklin may have begun seeking Eleanor's company because he hoped she would prod him into accomplishing his exalted goal. But then he fell in love with her.

They were married the year after he graduated, on March 17, 1905. As soon as the ceremony was over, Eleanor's Uncle Ted shook the groom's hand vigorously. "Well, Franklin," he cried, "there's nothing like keeping the name in the family!"

Twenty-three when he and Eleanor started their life together, Franklin was studying law at Columbia University. On completing the course, he joined a New York City law firm. By the time he was twenty-eight, he had already begun carrying out his political plan.

To a remarkable extent, Franklin Roosevelt did follow in Theodore Roosevelt's footsteps. Just like his illustrious relative, he made his political debut as a member of New York State's legislature. In 1913, when Franklin was thirty-one, he went to Washington when he was appointed to a post T.R. had also held—as Assistant Secretary of the Navy.

The main difference between them, at that stage, was that T.R. had been a Republican whereas F.D.R., surprising and displeasing many of his relatives, entered public life as a Democrat. He explained that his own father had been loyal to that party, although most people in their rank of society had supported the Republicans since the Civil War.

Yet this political choice may also have been an early instance of F.D.R.'s amazingly sharp political instinct. It was no novelty for a rich young man to be a Republican. A rich young man who was a Democrat would, however, find that party leaders were more inclined to give him opportunities for advancement.

This was proved in 1920, when Roosevelt was only thirty-eight. The Democratic National Convention that year nominated him as its candidate for Vice-President. Although the Democrats lost that election, as most people expected, the tall, handsome New Yorker attracted a lot of interest around the rest of the country.

Still, most people thought he was just a likeable dabbler in politics. Those who knew him better tended to dismiss him as merely a charming man, without any strong opinions except that he himself deserved high office. In 1921, Franklin Roosevelt went through a terrible testing that changed the whole picture. At the age of thirty-nine, he was struck down by a crippling disease that usually attacked young children. Infantile paralysis, the doctors called it, but most people referred to it as polio, a shortened form of the medical name for the dreaded ailment.

For the next three years, Roosevelt

Franklin D. Roosevelt campaigned in Ohio with Governor James Fox in 1920. *Courtesy of the Franklin D. Roosevelt Library.*

doggedly refused to give up hope of walking again. "No sob stuff," he told his family. Despite the awful pain involved, he forced himself to do the exercises doctors said might possibly make his legs work again.

By 1924, he could walk a few dozen steps leaning on crutches. The Democratic National Convention met in New York that year, and Roosevelt was asked to make a speech nominating a friend of his to be President. It would be his first public appearance since he was stricken.

At Madison Square Garden, while thousands of delegates watched in tense silence, Roosevelt stood up from his wheelchair, grasped his crutches, and slowly, painfully, made his way to the speaker's stand. When he reached it, he looked out over the spellbound crowd—and he grinned triumphantly. Then all of those tough-minded political delegates rose to their feet cheering an exceptionally brave man. No matter that Roosevelt's candidate lost the election that year, Roosevelt himself had turned into a hero.

Four years later, in 1928, his recovery had progressed to the extent that he agreed to run for governor of New York. After he was elected, then re-elected in 1930 by a tremendous margin, his campaign director made a prediction. "I do not see," he said, "how Mr. Roosevelt can escape becoming the next presidential nominee of his party."

By 1932, however, the nation was deep in the most fearful economic slump it had ever experienced. Millions of workers had lost their jobs following the 1929 crash of the Wall Street stock market. The Republican President Hoover was running again, even though his main effort to combat the Great Depression had been to issue statements claiming prosperity was just around the corner. Yet Hoover always looked very solemn when photographers snapped his picture.

While Governor Roosevelt of New York offered few specific ideas for improving conditions, he waved and smiled confidently wherever he went. After the Democratic Convention did nominate him, he broke with tradition by flying out to Chicago to accept the nomination in person instead of just sending a message.

"I pledge you, I pledge myself, to a New Deal for the American people," he said in his ringing voice. Nobody really knew what this "New Deal" would bring. But the voters of America elected him that November.

By March 4, 1933, when he took the oath of office, conditions around the country had gotten much worse. Banks in many states had closed their doors, making millions of Americans fear their savings were lost. The new President, speaking into microphones that brought

Franklin D. Roosevelt was in his first term as President when H. M. Rundle made this lithograph in 1933. *Courtesy of the National Portrait Gallery, Smithsonian Institution.*

President Roosevelt met with British Prime Minister Winston Churchill and Soviet Premier Josef Stalin at Yalta in February 1945. *Courtesy of the Franklin D. Roosevelt Library.*

his words by radio all across the land, immediately reassured his fellow citizens.

"First of all," he said, "let me assert my firm belief that the only thing we have to fear is fear itself."

Then a flurry of emergency measures restored faith in the banks. Next, thousands of the jobless were set to work on government projects like fixing roads. President Roosevelt summoned bright young professors from the leading colleges to advise him on possible solutions to dozens of problems.

At first there was a huge sense of relief—but many of the New Deal programs threatened the special privileges of the rich. That was why the sort of people F.D.R. had grown up with began angrily calling him "a traitor to his class." Other solid citizens objected because it seemed to them that the

New Deal was giving the government too much power. Yet the great majority strongly approved of New Deal ideas like Social Security. They trusted F.D.R. to such an extent that, when his second term ended in 1940, they broke a custom going all the way back to George Washington and elected him for a third term.

By then, World War II had started in Europe. It seemed increasingly clear that the United States might become involved, and most people wanted F.D.R. as their commander-in-chief if the nation had to fight again.

After the Japanese bombed Pearl Harbor in Hawaii on December 7, 1941—"a date which will live in infamy," President Roosevelt gravely de-clared—he worked long hours under immense pressure, helping set the strategy that led to Allied victory in the global conflict.

The 1944 election came just as America and its Allies were at a crucial stage in their campaign against Nazi Germany. Even some of F.D.R.'s political enemies were not too upset when he sought, and won, a fourth term.

He was deprived, after all, of seeing the Allied triumph. The following spring, the sixty-three-year-old President went to Georgia for a brief vacation. It was from there, on April 12, 1945, that shocking news was flashed around the world. Then millions of people wept to hear that F.D.R. had died.

Margaret Chase Smith

1897–   U.S. Congresswoman; U.S. Senator.

When Maggie Chase was thirteen, she started working on Saturdays in a five-and-ten cent store. Sometimes she also worked evenings as a substitute telephone operator. At high school, she took courses like typing and business English—hoping to get a better job after she graduated.

Besides coming from a family with little money, Maggie lived in a small town in Maine where there were few opportunities for advancement. Summer visitors thought it was a delightful vacation spot, but the winters could be extremely harsh. Politics fascinated Maggie Chase and eventually made her famous.

As Margaret Chase Smith, she had the most successful career in Congress of any American woman. Elected re-peatedly from 1940 to 1972, she won a great deal of admiration all over the country. What's more, she was the first female who at least tried to gain a major party's backing to run for President of the United States.

"The lady from Maine," as the newspapers often called her, had been born on December 14, 1897, in the town of Skowhegan. Her father, George Emery Chase, ran a one-chair barber shop and bragged a little about being the grandson of a minister. When he did, her mother, Carrie Murray Chase, would remind him that one of her ancestors had fought in the American Revolution.

Maggie's real name was Margaret Madeline, and she was the eldest of six children. Since she understood very early that she would never be able to go to college, she made the best of her high school years. In addition to studying subjects that would help her get an office job, she enjoyed playing basketball, becoming manager of the girls' team.

Yet she was just of average height, measuring five feet four inches. Slender and trim-looking, she took special pains to dress neatly because she knew nobody considered her pretty. Again, it struck her as sensible to make the best of her appearance instead of worrying about what couldn't be changed.

In the same way, Maggie refused to be unhappy about not being popular with boys her own age. Somewhat amazing her girlfriends, she carried around the picture of a man she told them she would much rather marry. He was Clyde Smith, one of the most prominent citizens of the town.

Beyond his various business connections, Clyde Smith was the prize vote-getter of the local Republican party. He kept running for one town office or another, and he always won. It did not seem to matter to Maggie that he was twenty-one years older than she was.

After high school, she kept trying different jobs—from teaching in a one-room school, for $8.50 a week, to working in the business office of the local newspaper. Clyde Smith was part-owner of the *Independent Reporter* at that time, so she finally met him. On first-hand acquaintance, she liked him as much as she had thought she would.

However, he soon left town to become the state highway commissioner. Not until her thirty-third birthday—December 14, 1930—did she marry him and become Margaret Chase Smith. By then, she had already become a person of some importance herself. Besides working as the office manager in a woolen mill, she had become the president of the Maine Federation of Business and Professional Women's Clubs. She also was a member of the Republican State Committee.

Still, in those days a good wife was supposed to put her own interests aside to advance her husband's career. The new Mrs. Smith, therefore, kept urging her husband to take a step he had thought of before but never dared attempt. People who knew them both said it was largely because of her encouragement that at last he made up his mind to run for Congress.

Then Clyde Smith extended his long string of political victories and won this post, too. It happened in 1936, when he had already passed his sixtieth birthday.

When the Smiths went to Washington, Mrs. Smith did not stay in the background like many congressional wives. She worked full-time as her husband's secretary for the next four years. People who kept a close eye on Maine politics were much impressed by her ability, so it was not too surprising that the Republicans of the Skowhegan district began to think about having her take her husband's place when he had a heart attack in 1940. At that time, practically every woman elected to the House of Representatives had gotten her start by taking over her husband's seat.

Clyde Smith himself, realizing that he probably would not recover, urged his wife to run for his seat. As it happened, he died in April, months before the regular election. In June, Margaret Chase Smith did run—seeking the post just until that autumn—and she won easily.

In September, the month when Maine held its regular elections, Mrs. Smith ran again. This time, she was seeking a two-year term on her own— and something surprising occurred. She won by three times as many votes as her husband had received.

What was it that made people trust her so much? Political experts thought that the no-nonsense Mrs. Smith gave men as well as women a feeling of being able to rely on her judgment. While she always described herself as a good Republican, she never hesitated to sup-

port a Democratic program she approved of, such as extending the benefits of Social Security.

But she did not concentrate on welfare and similar laws affecting people's personal lives. While these were frequently described as "women's issues," Mrs. Smith put most of her effort as a lawmaker into matters that the handful of other women in Congress had been kept from dealing with until then— especially military matters.

The year after Margaret Smith began serving in the House of Representatives, the United States entered World War II. Quietly but persistently, Mrs. Smith kept telling the leaders of her party that she wanted a place on one of the important committees involved with the armed forces. As a result, she was appointed to the House Committee on Naval Affairs, becoming the first woman ever to have such a position.

She took it seriously. In the line of duty, she traveled around the country inspecting Navy bases. During the winter of 1944, she made a 25,000-mile tour of navy stations in the South Pacific.

The knowledge she gained made her one of the best-informed members of the House. Her growing influence in support of a strong navy and her independent outlook on other important issues inspired increased admiration among the voters of her district. Every two years, they kept reelecting her—and it appeared that she could remain a Congresswoman as long as she wished.

In 1948, another goal attracted her. A man who had represented Maine in the Senate for many years decided to retire. Since this upper house of Congress had more prestige and provided more opportunity to influence the course of the government, Mrs. Smith announced that she would seek election as a Senator.

However, three men—two of them former governors of Maine—also wanted the Republican nomination for the Senate seat. That meant there would have to be a primary election, in which members of the Republican party would choose their candidate. To reach voters all over the state, instead of just in one district, ordinarily cost thousands of dollars.

Mrs. Smith had no money to spend on the campaign herself, nor did she have any organized group of followers to raise money for her. In the months before the June primary, she conducted what she called a "grass-roots" drive, going with just a few aides to speak to voters in six hundred Maine communities.

One morning, she slipped on an icy pavement and broke her arm. A few hours later, with the arm newly bandaged, she appeared right on schedule at a political rally. This determination, along with her plain-spokenness, counted more than any fancy bumper stickers in a state that took pride in simple honesty.

But the rest of the country was startled by the results of that Republican primary in June of 1948. Mrs. Smith won more votes than the combined number cast for her three male opponents. Then, in September, she defeated the Democratic candidate by the greatest majority in the history of Maine politics, getting 71 percent of the total vote.

Returning to Washington after such a notable triumph, Senator Smith found herself a national celebrity. No other woman had ever moved up from the House to the Senate the way she had, and few male candidates had ever won their seats so decisively.

It was two years later—on June 1, 1950—that Senator Smith stirred the whole country by her plain speaking. In this period, Senator Joseph R. McCarthy of Wisconsin had been making headlines with his charges that a large number of people with Communist sympathies had managed to get high-ranking posts in the government.

While fair-minded citizens were disturbed deeply by these charges, because it seemed that innocent individuals had been unfairly attacked, hardly anybody dared to challenge Senator McCarthy openly. Other Senators thought he had gone much too far, yet they hesitated to say so in public.

Then Senator Smith stood up and said the Senate itself had been "debased" by letting one of its own members make unjust charges. "I don't want to see the Republican party ride to political victory on the four horsemen of calumny—fear, ignorance, bigotry, and smear," she added.

This speech struck millions of people everywhere as one of the bravest that had ever been made in Washington. It led several leading newspapers around the country to give Mrs. Smith an unusual title. The Conscience of the Senate, they called her.

It also led some forward-looking supporters of the Republican cause to suggest her as a candidate for Vice-President in 1952. Yet the long-standing prejudice against giving women any major political role prevented adoption of this idea. Senator Smith herself did not seem upset at being forgotten when Richard Nixon was nominated that year as General Eisenhower's running mate.

Two years later, her term as Senator was up and she ran again. Once more, the voters of Maine gave her a remarkable margin of victory. Altogether, she

Margaret Chase Smith of Maine called herself the "Senator-at-Large for Women." *With permission of the Margaret Chase Smith Library Center.*

won four terms of six years each, serving twenty-four years as a Senator.

During this long service, Mrs. Smith continued her Washington pioneering. Not only on the Senate Armed Services Committee, but also on other committees dealing with government spending and space exploration, she proved that a woman could make important decisions. In 1961, her sturdy support of defense programs caused a Russian leader to lose his temper. The Soviet official called her "the devil in disguise as a woman."

Senator Smith's most dramatic political experience came three years later, when she decided to run for President. By 1964, she was approaching her sixty-seventh birthday and her hair had turned white. Still as vigorous as ever, she felt strongly that the Republican party was not offering its members any middle-of-the-road leadership. Senator Barry Goldwater of Arizona represented the extreme conservative wing, whereas Governor Nelson Rockefeller of New York struck her as too liberal. Senator Smith tried for several months before her party's National Convention to win the support of delegates. Yet even if she was widely respected, her effort failed. She was not even nominated as Vice-President, which many political experts considered a more realistic goal.

Undaunted, Mrs. Smith kept on representing Maine in the Senate. In 1972, when she was nearly seventy-five, the voters of her state finally decided it was time for a change. She was defeated that year by a Democratic candidate.

She returned to Skowhegan, where she spent many peaceful years in retirement as a grand old lady.

Robert Taft

1889–1953   U.S. Senator.

At a dance, the tall and serious-looking Yale man was introduced to a young woman who asked a lot of questions. First she inquired where he came from. "My family's from Ohio," he said.

She tried again. "Do you visit there on holidays?"

"No, they're in Washington now," he said.

"What does your father do?"

"He has a government job."

Bob Taft turned away then, dreading the next question. It was 1909 and his father—William Howard Taft—was the President of the United States. This certainly made life difficult for an intensely shy but very intelligent college junior.

Years later, Bob Taft would unbend enough to confess: "I had a deathly fear that I would be accepted because of my father and not for myself." By the time he could talk about his early terrors, though, he had won his own place in American history. Mr. Republican, he was called by newspapers all over the country.

No matter that he failed three times to reach the White House himself, as Senator Taft he made a deep impression on the nation's political life. In Washington, during the 1940s when liberalism held sway, he kept up a tireless defense of the conservative cause—and thereby became a great hero among conservative-minded Americans.

Robert Alphonso Taft had been born in Cincinnati on September 8, 1889. He owed his unusual middle name to his grandfather, the first member of his family to attract much attention. Ever

233

A 1921 family photograph shows Senator Robert A. Taft standing, third from left. His father, former President William Howard Taft, holds one of his grandsons; Senator Taft's son Robert is seated on his grandmother's lap. *Courtesy of New York Times Pictures*.

since a carpenter named Robert Taft had left England to settle in Massachusetts in 1678, there had been public-spirited Tafts holding local offices in New England, then Ohio. But Alphonso Taft rose to be Attorney General in the Cabinet of President Grant, soon after the Civil War.

A strictly upright man, Alphonso Taft kept telling his sons that he expected them to excel at whatever they undertook. One of them made a fortune investing in railroads and other business ventures. That was the future Senator Taft's uncle Charley. But Alphonso's son Will, the future Senator's father, had an even more notable career.

William Howard Taft was the only President who went on to become Chief Justice of the United States. While he filled both posts creditably, future generations would remember him more for his enormous size than for any governmental achievement. He weighed over 300 pounds, so the record books cite him as the heaviest Chief Executive the nation ever had.

President Taft also possessed an enormous sense of duty, which he passed along to his own first son. What's more, the solemn-faced Bobby had an extremely ambitious mother. Helen Herron was the outspoken daughter of a prominent Cincinnati lawyer.

Besides all the family pressures that Bobby felt he had to live up to, when he was just ten he and his younger brother and sister were plucked out of their familiar, comfortable surroundings to sail halfway around the world. In 1900, their father began his political ascent by being appointed to govern the Philippine Islands, which the United States had just acquired as part of its victory in the recent Spanish-American War.

Being the sort of child who was ill at ease among strangers, Bobby grew increasingly bookish during the next three years. It did not strike him that traveling in the Far East and then in Europe, when his father's career took another turn, could be considered a grand adventure. Bright as he was, he never learned to speak any foreign language.

Yet Bob Taft, at thirteen, proved he really did have an exceptional mind. He was sent then to one of the top boarding schools in the United States—the Taft School in Connecticut, founded and directed by another of his father's brothers, his own uncle Horace. A kind but stern schoolmaster, Uncle Horace had no idea of favoring this nephew, but by Christmas of Bob's first term,

his marks had earned him the highest rank in his class.

Throughout his years there, Bob continued to lead his class. Although he tried fiercely to excel in sports, too, he never got beyond playing third-team football. But he took part in a variety of school activities, becoming president of the chess club. Gradually, he made some friends who found, once they got to know him, that he was warmer than he had seemed.

Taft followed the same pattern at Yale, where he graduated first in his class in 1910. As the son of the nation's President, his entry into Harvard Law School that autumn brought reporters bent on interviewing him. "I'm here to study," he told them tersely.

It was during his law student days that Taft met a pretty, witty young woman whose brother was one of his classmates. Martha Wheaton Bowers also had a keen mind, and she saw beneath the chilly outer shell that the President's son presented to new acquaintances. Soon he was writing to her: "I love you more than all the world."

They were married on October 17, 1914, a year after Taft began practicing law in Cincinnati. Their life together was very happy, not only because it produced four sons they both cherished. Thanks to Martha's easier way of getting along with other people, her husband advanced more smoothly than he might have otherwise.

His first taste of the excitement of being involved with major issues, beyond merely representing his uncle Charley in various business dealings, came during the First World War. Rejected as a soldier because of his weak eyesight, which caused him to wear owlish, wire-rimmed eyeglasses, Taft went to work in Washington for the agency charged with supervising wartime supplies of food.

Taft's boss in this endeavor was a former engineer named Herbert Hoover, a conservative Republican who believed in the least possible amount of government interference with free enterprise. While Hoover had not yet taken any active part in politics, his attitudes had a profound influence on the young lawyer who assisted him.

He was influenced, too, by their experience after the war ended in 1918, when they went to Europe to direct the distribution of food in war-torn areas. Taft was much distressed by the seeming selfishness of various European leaders, and he made up his mind then that the best policy for the United States must always be steering clear of any foreign quarrels.

Before Taft's emergence as a major figure on the national scene, he put in a diligent apprenticeship amid the rough-and-tumble of Ohio politics. Owing to the magic of the Taft name, he had no difficulty being elected as a member of the state legislature—and he soon joined the inner circle in the state capital of Columbus.

There his willingness to work hard, along with his quick grasp of financial problems, gave him added prestige. Besides serving as majority leader and then speaker of the state assembly, Taft continued to practice law very successfully. Representing his rich uncle Charley, he himself became wealthy during the 1920s.

But all of this, plus untiring efforts on behalf of community groups like the Cincinnati symphony, could not satisfy his high ambitions. Particularly after the Great Depression of 1929 brought the defeat of President Hoover, Taft's political idol, he felt a need to get personally involved in national politics.

His opportunity came in 1938. By then President Franklin Roosevelt's New Deal policies had so disturbed him that he determined to run for the post of United States Senator. This decision created a surprisingly bitter contest—in effect, a forecast of his whole future career.

Despite Taft's many advantages, he still lacked the easy manner that a political figure was supposed to have in order to get elected. Furthermore, he had become an uncompromising spokesman for the conservative wing of his party, and its leaders feared that his strong views would antagonize voters holding more moderate opinions.

So Taft had to fight a primary campaign to win the Republican nomination. Dry as his speeches were, his wife helped him tremendously by crisscrossing the state herself, giving more lively talks on his behalf. He triumphed in the primary, then in the November election.

In Washington, Senator Taft swiftly attained notice as a leading opponent of President Roosevelt's economic policies. If his famous name helped him, his own steady hammering away at New Deal spending was just as important. "He really *cared* about everything the Senate did," one reporter wrote about him. By 1940, Taft was openly seeking the Republican nomination to run against Roosevelt that year.

At the age of fifty-one, Taft faced daunting obstacles. His stiff and positive personality worried powerful figures in his party, who doubted whether he could run successfully against the hugely popular Roosevelt. Taft himself recognized his handicap when he wrote to his wife, "I must give the impression to people that I don't enjoy their company."

Furthermore, the Second World War had erupted in Europe, and it appeared that the United States might not be able to remain on the sidelines. But Taft's foreign views were particularly uncompromising. His hands-off attitude toward foreign dangers that alarmed many Americans convinced the convention to take a remarkable step.

Instead of nominating Robert Taft for the presidency in 1940, it chose a likeable businessman named Wendell Willkie with hardly any experience in politics. Taft swallowed his own disappointment, high-mindedly refusing to make any bitter statements even after Willkie lost the election.

For the next four years, Senator Taft kept on upholding his principles doggedly. In 1944, he was nearly defeated by Ohio's voters when he sought another six-year term representing the state in Washington. His insistence that labor unions had gained too much power had inspired a strong union campaign against him.

Still, Taft returned to Washington set on reducing the influence unions had attained under the New Deal. In 1947, he managed to secure the adoption of a law sharply restricting some of labor's practices. It was the Taft-Hartley Act, the only major piece of legislation to bear Taft's name.

For the most part, he exerted his influence indirectly. By his unswerving

Robert A. Taft sought the Republican nomination for President at that party's convention in 1952. © *Eve Arnold/Magnum.*

support of the conservative outlook on issue after issue, he gained respect even among his enemies. Even so, in 1948 he lost his second bid for the Republican presidential nomination.

In 1952, Senator Taft at the age of sixty-three made his third and most determined attempt to win the presidency. By now his status as the hero of conservative Republicans could not be doubted. Even Democrats who thought Taft's ceaseless efforts to cut government spending showed a lack of compassion for the poor had to admit that he personally was one of the most upstanding men ever to seek high office. Perhaps it was this increasing admiration that softened Taft's prickly manner and made him seem more likeable.

But luck was against him. That year, a military hero with an immensely appealing smile showed signs of being willing to run as the Republican candidate for President. General Dwight D. Eisenhower merely had to tell party leaders he would accept the nomination. Even though Taft already had won the support of around five hundred delegates, he had to give up his own quest.

Taft did so graciously. After Eisenhower's election, Taft continued to serve the new President as majority leader in the Senate. They even became good friends, and it was on a golfing vacation with Ike that Taft first noticed a strange feeling of weakness.

It turned out that he had incurable cancer. Just a few weeks later, on July 31, 1953, Senator Taft died in a New York hospital, about two months before his sixty-fourth birthday.

Harry Truman

1884–1972   U.S. Senator; thirty-third President of the United States.

"Boys, if you ever pray, pray for me now."

That was what Harry Truman said to the reporters in the White House press room right after he became the President of the United States. He had been sworn in at a hurried ceremony while he—and the whole world—still could hardly believe the tragic news about the man known everywhere as F.D.R.

Franklin Delano Roosevelt, who had served as the nation's Chief Executive longer than anybody else in American history, had just died. The sudden loss of this great leader seemed especially shocking because it came at a time when strong leadership was urgently needed.

On April 12, 1945—the date Vice-President Truman took charge in Wash-ington—the United States and its Allies clearly were close to winning the European phase of World War II. But even though Nazi Germany had almost been beaten, the Allies faced the further challenge of defeating Japan.

So Truman's humble words were not too reassuring. People everywhere shook their heads when they talked about "this little man from Missouri." How could he possibly succeed in carrying out such awesome responsibilities?

During his White House years, Harry Truman made some of the major decisions of modern history. Forty years later, a good many experts have come to think that he belongs on any list of the nation's strongest Presidents. Still, the experts hardly ever call him a great man. Instead, they say Harry

Harry S Truman took the presidential oath of office on April 12, 1945. *Abbie Rowe/National Park Services; courtesy of the Harry S. Truman Library.*

Truman proved that an ordinary, decent American can rise to greatness in an emergency.

He had been born, on May 8, 1884, in the small town of Lamar, Missouri. He had no famous ancestors, only hardworking farm folk on both sides of his family. Although his father, John Anderson Truman, tried repeatedly to make more money by becoming a cattle dealer, these efforts kept failing.

Harry and his younger brother and sister moved around a lot during their childhood. Mostly, they lived in or close to the town of Independence, about twenty miles from Kansas City. They stayed in this area because their mother, as Martha Ellen Young, had grown up on a large farm nearby, where her parents were still very active.

Grandmother Young made wonderful fried chicken for Sunday dinner. Even more than the meal, though, Harry enjoyed listening as his relatives recalled the old days when some of them had come out to Missouri by wagon train from Kentucky. Several of the men told about fighting in the Civil

War. Hearing this talk at the dinner table gave Harry a lasting interest in American history.

During these early years, there were two other ways his whole future was influenced. Though he seemed to be a bright boy—he had taught himself to read the big letters in the family Bible before he was five—Harry could not make any sense out of ordinary books. His mother, fearing he would be laughed at, would not let him start school with other children his age.

Finally, on the Fourth of July the year he was eight, she noticed something strange. During a fireworks show, he clapped excitedly each time a crackling bang sounded, but he never looked up at the exploding red and green and purple stars. Suddenly, she realized that he must have some sort of eye trouble.

The next day, Harry's mother took him to a doctor in Kansas City. He returned wearing thick eyeglasses, which were quite a rarity then for children. While Harry could see perfectly well when he had them on, they set him apart because he wasn't supposed to play ball or any rough games. As a result, he turned into a bookworm, reading about history in particular.

Once he began going to school, he caught up quickly with the work he had missed. But from the age of six, Harry

had been attending Sunday school—and there, the other important event of his childhood occurred. On his very first day, he did see the yellow curls of the girl sitting in the seat in front of him.

Her name was Elizabeth Virginia Wallace, but everybody called her Bess. Much later, Harry Truman would tell people he made up his mind to marry her right then and there. Maybe he exaggerated slightly, and yet, by the time they were in high school, he was carrying her books home for her every afternoon.

In this period, it happened that Harry's father was doing well selling mules in back of their house, so Harry looked forward to going to college, then somehow getting into politics. From all his reading of history, he had settled on a goal he kept secret because it sounded too conceited. He wanted to become a United States Senator. But when he was a senior in high school, his father had more bad luck in business and instead of college, Harry had to go to work.

For five years, he kept trying one job after another in Kansas City. The best he could find was a boring and low-paying post at a bank. As far as Harry was concerned, only one good thing came out of this dreary, disappointing time. Despite his eyeglasses, he was accepted as a part-time soldier in a Missouri unit of the National Guard. Its members took military training at night or on weekends to be prepared if the country ever went to war. Because he had missed spending much time with other boys, he especially relished the comradeship of this experience.

So Truman kept on drilling even after a drastic change in his life in 1906, when he was twenty-two. After his Grandfather Young died, he and his parents and brother and sister all moved in with Grandmother Young to help her run the farm.

Over the next eleven years, Harry's father died and his brother married, then began farming on his own. That left the would-be Senator responsible for his grandmother, mother, and unmarried sister. It seemed likely that he might spend his entire life supporting them as a plain dirt farmer.

But the First World War released Truman from endlessly plowing and planting. In 1917, when he was thirty-three, the United States became involved in this awful conflict. His National Guard training made Truman feel obliged to join the fight, and his sister Mary Jane patriotically agreed to do her best at running the farm in his absence.

Truman's two years in uniform lifted him out of the rut in which he otherwise might have spent the rest of his life. As Captain Harry, commanding a company of soldiers in France, he proved to his own satisfaction that he had what it took to be a leader.

On his return from France, at the age of thirty-five, he finally dared to ask Bess Wallace to marry him. For whatever reason, she had not accepted any other suitor; on June 28, 1919, she became Mrs. Harry Truman.

At thirty-five, Truman needed a way to earn a living. With one of his Army buddies, he opened a store selling men's shirts and ties. For a few years the business prospered, until hard times struck the country early in the 1920s. Truman & Jacobson, opposite the leading hotel in Kansas City, was forced to close.

But Truman had made many friends during his Army days. Another of them spoke a word in his favor to a powerful man known as Boss Tom Pendergast, who ruled the Democratic party in Missouri, and Truman was offered the chance to run for the job of taking care of county highways.

By 1934, Truman was chairman of the county's government. He lived with his wife and daughter in Independence in a big white house that had belonged to his wife's family. Nearing his fiftieth birthday, he received a visit from an aide to Boss Pendergast. Would he be interested in running for a much bigger job—as United States Senator?

Truman decided to seize this opportunity, even though it had one very big drawback: he understood that people might think he was only a puppet controlled by a political wire-puller widely suspected of being dishonest. But Pendergast had never asked him to do anything against his own principles, so he took the chance, and he was elected.

On January 3, 1935, Senator Harry Truman took his oath of office in Washington. Soon this friendly newcomer impressed his fellow lawmakers by working hard at learning how the government really operated. He spent long hours attending committee meetings or reading dry reports.

What a shame that he could not be reelected, other Senators said. For Boss Pendergast, at last, had been caught stealing money, so any one he had helped would surely be defeated now that his political machine had fallen apart.

Still, Senator Truman won a second term in 1940 because the voters of Missouri believed in him. The day he came back to Washington after this victory, he was greeted with enthusiastic handshaking. Nobody could call him a puppet now.

Truman returned to the capital at a time when many people felt the United States would soon be drawn into the Second World War, which had started a year earlier in Europe. Senator Truman, with his firsthand fighting experience in 1917, thought of a step that ought to be taken right away.

About ten years after World War I, a Senate inquiry had found shocking examples of waste and cheating in some of the industries that had supplied America's armed forces. Could it be that the same pattern was being repeated? On the Senate floor, Truman spoke up in his folksy style.

"It won't do any good digging up dead horses ten years from now," he warned. "The thing to do is dig this stuff up now and correct it."

Then the Senate set up a new committee to keep a close eye on money spent for defense purposes, with Truman as its chairman. The Truman Committee went to factories and shipyards and training camps, rooting out problems before they became too serious.

The success of the committee was one reason why President Roosevelt picked Truman to run for Vice-President in 1944. But the following year, when Truman suddenly succeeded to the presidency, there was widespread doubt about whether he could handle a really big job. Immedi-

Harry S Truman was elected President in 1948, the year in which Augustus Vincent Tack completed this portrait. *Courtesy of the National Portrait Gallery, Smithsonian Institution; transfer from the National Gallery of Art, Washington; gift of Mrs. Augustus Vincent Tack.*

ately, however, he began making major decisions without any weakness or shilly-shallying.

During his first month in office, the war in Europe ended. While Truman was attending a conference of Allied leaders, a message from New Mexico reached him. The most powerful weapon in human history had just been exploded in a successful test.

So it was Truman who had to decide whether an atomic bomb should be dropped on Japan. Because he believed that using the tremendously destructive weapon would save lives in the long run by shortening the war, he gave the fateful order to go ahead. On August 6, 1945, an atomic attack on the city of Hiroshima killed 80,000 people. Three days later, Nagasaki was the target.

Then Japan surrendered. The coming of peace aroused such joy that Truman was very popular—but only briefly. His idea of continuing wartime controls until industry could get back to normal angered almost everybody. As a result, his Fair Deal program aiming to help people with new measures like health insurance was practically ignored by Congress.

In 1948, nobody thought he could win a second term. Nobody, that is, except Truman himself. Crisscrossing the country aboard a special train, he kept pouring good-natured scorn on "that lazy, do-nothing Congress" for keeping his Fair Deal from taking effect. His spunky talk stirred his listeners to grin and holler, "Attaboy, Harry!"

Amazing all the experts, Truman won a narrow victory over the Republican candidate, Governor Thomas E. Dewey of New York. But foreign problems soon interrupted any Fair Deal progress. Efforts to keep the Russians from extending their influence occupied most of the President's time.

Besides this Cold War, in 1950 Truman led the country into another actual shooting war thousands of miles away in the Asian land of Korea. Here, too, his aim was to limit Communist influence but, when the conflict kept dragging on, Truman's own popularity reached its lowest ebb.

After his second term ended, he retired to his home in Independence. Fortunately, he lived long enough to enjoy reading some of the praise about his own presidency that began to be printed as the years passed. Truman died on December 26, 1972, at the ripe old age of eighty-eight.

Earl Warren

1891–1974   Governor of California; Chief Justice of the United States.

In 1969, the University of California held a ceremony to mark the opening of its new Earl Warren Legal Center. The guest of honor was a big, friendly, blue-eyed man with white hair. After many kind words had been spoken about him, he made a brief speech himself.

With a broad smile, Earl Warren started out: "You don't have to be a great success in law school to have a building named after you."

Still, he had certainly proved that getting just a C average in law school did not prevent "great success" later on. As the Chief Justice of the United States Supreme Court for sixteen years, Warren had more impact on the country than many presidents have had. He aroused much bitter controversy as well.

The Judge Who Changed America was the title of one book about him. People who favored the changes—including broadening the civil rights of black citizens and increasing the legal protections for individuals accused of crimes—admired him deeply. Others, however, hated him. Their slogan, on billboards and bumper stickers, was IMPEACH EARL WARREN.

The object of such differing feelings had been born on March 19, 1891, in a dingy little house a block from the railroad station of Los Angeles, then a small city with only about 50,000 residents. Earl's father, Methias Warren, worked as a skilled mechanic in the repair shop of the Southern Pacific Railroad.

Methias Warren had been born in Norway, where the family name was

247

spelled Varren. Soon after he came to America with his parents, relatives told them Americans would find it easier to pronounce Warren than Varren, so the change was made.

In Minneapolis, Methias married a shy, pretty young woman with a similar background—Chrystal Hernlund, who had come from Sweden. A year later, they had a daughter Ethel. But the cold winters of Minnesota brought on health problems, so they decided to move to California.

An ambitious man, Methias Warren was not happy with his railroad job. His son Earl would always remember how he shook his head over the way the powerful railroad corporation controlled the lives of everybody who worked for it. He kept saying that Earl must have a good education, which would open up opportunities for a better life.

Earl himself did not much enjoy studying. A tall, good-natured boy with a knack for getting along with all kinds of people, he tried hard, though, to avoid disappointing his father. Because his parents were saving money to send him to college, while he was in high school he found a summer job so he could save some money, too. He became a "call boy" for the railroad. Twelve hours a day, six days a week, he rode around on his bicycle looking for men whose names were listed as members of train crews. Sometimes he had to search barrooms or other places he ordinarily wouldn't have been allowed into, in order to tell men they were needed.

For all this adventuring, Earl was paid the grand sum of 22 cents an hour. Yet his earnings helped make it possible, late in August of 1908, when he was seventeen, for him to enter the University of California at Berkeley.

There Warren made friends with students from a variety of backgrounds. In the gym, he practiced boxing with an outstanding athlete who was one of the few blacks on the campus. He also mingled easily in a fraternity where most of the members came from well-off San Francisco families.

"The greatest thing I got out of college was companionship," Warren admitted years later. "It was probably more important than anything I ever learned in my classes."

Yet he also heard a speech that influenced his whole future. The speaker was an outstanding member of the United States Senate, "Fighting Bob" LaFollette of Wisconsin, a leader in the Progressive movement. Warren recalled long afterward that LaFollette's stirring talk had turned his own mind toward a career in politics.

First, though, Warren knew he

would have to earn a living and also show that he deserved to be elected to public office. As a means of accomplishing both of these ends, he enrolled in 1912 in the first class at the University of California's new law school. Two years later, ranking nearer the bottom than the top of his class, he received his law degree.

Warren's gift for making friends led him—slowly and gradually, at first—toward national fame. After a few minor law jobs, he enlisted in the Army during World War I. Before his unit could be shipped to France, an armistice agreement ended the fighting. But one of the friends he made while in uniform became a member of California's legislature the following year, in 1919, and as a result, Warren himself got his first taste of politics. He was appointed clerk for one of the legislature's committees, and he relished the experience. From then on, he had not the slightest doubt about how he wanted to spend his life.

During the next several years, two things happened that had a major effect on his future course. At a swimming party, he met a beautiful young widow named Nina Palmquist. And, thanks to another friend, he was appointed as an assistant district attorney of Alameda County, taking in the city of Oakland and its environs right across the bay from San Francisco.

In 1925, both of these circumstances came together to create a big milestone. At the age of thirty-four, Warren was chosen for the top job in his office, becoming the district attorney in charge of a large staff of assistants. This promotion led him to decide it was high time he and the lovely Nina got married.

The marriage would prove to be a very happy one, producing six appealing blonde and blue-eyed children— three girls and three boys. Politically, too, Warren's family would turn into a tremendous asset. Although he believed in keeping his wife and children out of the public eye, pictures of them did appear as he became more prominent. Having such an attractive family helped to make him a very popular candidate.

Yet his own record undoubtedly helped even more. After thirteen years as the notably fair and firm district attorney of an area that attracted attention all over the country, Earl Warren himself was widely admired. One writer called him "the most intelligent and politically independent district attorney in the United States."

In 1938, Warren decided to run for attorney general of California. Suddenly, the matter of his political party allegiance assumed much importance. While he had always considered himself a good Republican, most local elections in his state were contested without any party labels.

Trying for his first statewide office, Warren had to run on a party ticket for the first time. But he chose to try a tactic that California law then allowed. He cross-filed—that is, he filed petitions to run in the primaries of both the Republicans and the Democrats. He won the endorsement of both parties. Even though the Democrats had a majority in California then, the Republican Warren easily managed to become the state's attorney general that autumn.

Four years later, in 1942, Warren tried the same system for a much more important race. Running for governor this time, he won the Republican endorsement by a large margin. However, he could not manage the coup of winning the Democratic primary, too.

Still, he won election that November. His record as the chief executive of one of the nation's largest states attracted interest all over the country. While he reassured Republicans that his basic ideas were "safely" conservative, he also earned wide approval among Democrats by building more new schools and hospitals than any governor in American history.

As a result, in 1946 when he ran for a second term, he achieved the astonishing feat of being endorsed by both the Republican and Democratic parties. This popularity, of course, made him a leading candidate for national office.

In 1944, Warren had quietly turned down an offer to run as the Republican vice-presidential candidate. He neither liked nor trusted New York's Governor Dewey, the party's nominee for President. Without ever saying so in public, Warren indicated that he really thought the Democratic President Franklin Roosevelt deserved reelection.

However, in 1948, to show his party loyalty, Warren did accept the vice-presidential nomination Dewey offered him again. Then Democratic President Harry Truman surprised almost everybody by winning his bid to remain in the White House. Warren made no secret of his own relief at the election results. "It feels as if a hundred-pound sack had been taken off my back," he said.

So the independent-minded and extremely popular Governor Warren of California posed quite a problem for the Republican party leadership. How could he be kept from aiming for the presidency himself? If he ran, he would surely split the party.

In 1953, President Dwight Eisenhower chose a remarkable way to end Earl Warren's political career: He appointed him to be the Chief Justice of the United States. By long tradition,

Miriam Troop sketched Earl Warren in 1957, four years after he had been appointed Chief Justice of the Supreme Court. *Courtesy of the National Portrait Gallery, Smithsonian Institution.*

the holders of this high post stayed above the pushing and pulling of party politics. The appointment raised many eyebrows, though, because Warren did not seem qualified to hold the nation's highest judgeship.

Yet, within a year, the country began seeing that Chief Justice Warren was not going to disappear from the head-lines when one of the most important legal cases in the history of the United States came before the Supreme Court. Its title, *Brown v. Board of Education*, did not sound revolutionary, but it brought great changes in the nation's schools.

The case had started because Oliver Brown, a black citizen of Topeka, Kansas, thought that his eleven-year-old daughter, Linda, was not getting as good an education as white children. He filed a lawsuit to get her admitted to a better school.

At that time, public schools in twenty-one states were segregated by race. Brown and his lawyers claimed that the separate black school system in Topeka was unfair to Linda and a violation of the United States Constitution. Since it was a question of interpreting the Constitution, the Brown case could be decided only by the highest court in the land.

On the morning of May 17, 1954, nine dignified men, dressed formally in black robes, sat in the chamber of the Supreme Court. Chief Justice Warren was ready to deliver their unanimous verdict.

"We conclude," he said, "that in the field of public education the doctrine of 'separate but equal' has no place."

Warren paused, for he was well aware of the significance of the words he had just spoken. Ever since 1896, when the Supreme Court of that era had decided an earlier case, the phrase "separate but equal" had stood as the legal grounds for having segregated schools. Reversing this old decision, Warren added: "Separate educational facilities are inherently unequal."

That victory for Oliver Brown started a new stage in the struggle of black Americans to gain fair treatment. It opened the door for more lawsuits by blacks to gain equal rights in buses, restaurants, and movie theaters as well as in schools. Yet the Brown case and similar ones that followed aroused wide opposition, too. In the center of that storm, Earl Warren calmly kept following his conscience.

He continued to increase his fame as a champion of liberty and justice for all. In other major cases, the court under his leadership supported the idea of "one man, one vote," forcing local officials everywhere to make sure every election district had roughly the same number of voters. The court also ruled, in the *Miranda* case, that policemen must notify criminal suspects of their right to keep silent under police questioning.

While this decision infuriated some upholders of law and order—they accused the Warren court of "coddling" criminals—among the general public it increased Warren's reputation for fairness. Because so many Americans trusted him, in 1963 President Johnson appointed the Chief Justice to head a commission charged with investigating the assassination of President John F. Kennedy. The Warren Commission report did much to quiet the nation's worry about the background and causes of that awful event.

Warren remained on the court until his retirement in 1969, at the age of seventy-eight. After leaving the court, he received many honors and he spoke out energetically in support of liberal causes until his death five years later, on July 9, 1974.

Chronology

	WORLD EVENTS	U.S. EVENTS
1765		Stamp Act and Quartering Act passed; Stamp Act Congress convened in New York
1766		Stamp Act repealed; Benjamin Franklin goes to London as agent for colonies
1767		Townshend Acts passed
1770		Boston Massacre; Townshend Acts repealed
1773		Boston Tea Party
1774	Louis XVI crowned King of France	"Intolerable Acts" passed; First Continental Congress convened in Philadelphia
1775		The American Revolution; Second Continental Congress names George Washington commander-in-chief of Continental Army

	WORLD EVENTS	U.S. EVENTS
1776		Thomas Jefferson drafts the Declaration of Independence
1777		Washington establishes winter quarters at Valley Forge
1779	Spain declares war on Britain	
1780	Holland and Britain are at war; Joseph II made Holy Roman Emperor	Alexander Hamilton proposes a constitutional convention
1781		British General Cornwallis surrenders to Washington
1782	Spain gains control of Florida	John Adams, Benjamin Franklin, John Jay negotiate peace treaty with Britain
1783		Washington resigns as commander-in-chief
1786		Shays' Rebellion
1787	Turkey declares war on Russia	Constitution drafted and signed; Hamilton writes first of Federalist Papers
1789	French Revolution	Washington becomes President, Adams Vice-President
1791		The Bill of Rights is ratified
1792	War between Turkey and Russia ends	Political parties formed: Jefferson leads Republicans; Hamilton, Adams lead Federalists
1793	Reign of Terror in France	Washington, Adams reelected; Neutrality Proclamation
1794		Whiskey Rebellion; Eleventh Amendment ratified
1795		U.S. and Spain agree on Florida borders
1796	Napoleon assumes command in Italy, wars with Austria Spain declares war on Britain	John Adams elected President, Jefferson Vice-President

	WORLD EVENTS	U.S. EVENTS
1798	France captures Rome, occupies Egypt	Alien and Sedition Acts
1799	Austria declares war on France; Britain forms alliance with Russia and Turkey	John Adams' negotiations keep America out of war with France
1800	France conquers Italy; Britain conquers Malta	Washington, D.C., becomes national capital; Jefferson and Aaron Burr tie in presidential election
1801	Peace of Luneville between Austria and France ends Holy Roman Empire; Act of Union between Ireland and Great Britain	Jefferson is chosen President; Adams appoints John Marshall Chief Justice of the Supreme Court; Tripoli declares war on U.S.
1803		James Monroe and Robert Livingston negotiate purchase of Louisiana Territory from France
1804	Napoleon crowns himself emperor	Jefferson reelected President; Burr kills Hamilton in a duel; Twelfth Amendment ratified
1805		Tripolitan War ends
1806	Prussia declares war on France	
1807	France invades Portugal	Embargo Act
1808	France invades Spain	James Madison defeats Monroe in presidential election; importation of African slaves prohibited
1810	Napoleon annexes Holland	
1812	Napoleon invades Russia	Congress declares war on Britain; Madison reelected President
1814	Napoleon banished to Elba	The burning of Washington; Francis Scott Key writes "The Star-Spangled Banner" after Fort McHenry is bombarded; Treaty of Ghent ends War of 1812

	WORLD EVENTS	U.S. EVENTS
1815	Napoleon returns to France but is defeated at Waterloo Brazil declares its independence	Andrew Jackson defeats British at Battle of New Orleans
1816	Argentina declares its independence	Monroe is elected President
1818	Chile declares its independence	U.S. and Canada agree on their border
1819		John Quincy Adams negotiates acquisition of Florida from Spain
1820	Revolution in Spain and Portugal	Monroe reelected President; the Missouri Compromise is achieved
1821	Peru, Guatemala, Panama, and Santo Domingo become independent	
1823	Mexico becomes a republic	The Monroe Doctrine is promulgated
1824		House of Representatives elects John Quincy Adams President; John Calhoun is Vice-President
1825	Bolivia and Uruguay achieve independence	
1826	Pan American Conference in Panama	
1828	Liberal revolt in Mexico	"Tariff of Abominations"; Jackson defeats John Quincy Adams in Presidential election; Calhoun remains Vice-President
1830	Ecuador achieves independence; revolution in Paris	
1831	Separation of Belgium and the Netherlands	Nat Turner's revolt
1832		Calhoun resigns as Vice-President in support of states' rights; Jackson reelected President
1833	Santa Anna becomes President of Mexico	Jackson removes deposits from Bank of the U.S.; formation of Whig Party
1835	Texas declares its right to secede from Mexico	

	WORLD EVENTS	U.S. EVENTS
1836	Battles of the Alamo and of San Jacinto result in Texas' independence from Mex-Mexico	Sam Houston elected president of Texas
1842		Daniel Webster, Secretary of State, negotiates Webster-Ashburton Treaty
1844		James K. Polk elected President
1845		Texas and Florida become U.S. states
1846	Revolts in Poland	U.S. enters into war with Mexico; northern border of U.S. established at 49th parallel
1847		U.S. captures Mexico City
1848	Revolution in Paris, Vienna, Venice, Berlin, Milan, Parma, Rome	End of Mexican war brings Texas, New Mexico, California, Utah, Nevada, Arizona, and parts of Colorado and Wyoming into U.S.
1850		Henry Clay introduces compromise slavery resolutions in Congress
1854	Britain, France, Turkey declare war on Russia	Elgin Treaty with Britain on Canadian trade
1856	Anglo-Chinese War begins	James Buchanan is elected President; Abraham Lincoln joins newly formed, antislavery Republican party
1860	Garibaldi and Victor Emmanuel proclaim Italy a kingdom	Lincoln is elected President; South Carolina secedes from the Union
1861	Emancipation of Russian serfs; Victor Emmanuel becomes King of Italy	Southern states secede from the Union; Confederate Congress elects Jefferson Davis President; Confederates fire on Fort Sumter, and Civil War begins
1862	Military revolt in Greece	Emancipation Proclamation issued (to become effective January 1, 1863)
1863	France captures Mexico City and proclaims Austrian ruler its Emperor	Union wins Battle of Gettysburg; Lincoln delivers Gettysburg Address

	WORLD EVENTS	U.S. EVENTS
1864	Austria and Prussia invade Denmark	Ulysses S. Grant made commander-in-chief of Union Army; Lincoln reelected President
1865		Confederates surrender to Union; Lincoln is assassinated; Thirteenth Amendment abolishes slavery
1868	Revolution in Spain	President Andrew Johnson impeached and acquitted
1870	Queen Isabella of Spain abdicates; Franco-Prussian War; revolt in Paris	Fifteenth Amendment guarantees right to vote despite color or race
1881		President James Garfield assassinated
1884		Grover Cleveland elected President
1896		William McKinley elected President
1898		Congress declares war on Spain, and U.S. is victorious
1900	Creation of Commonwealth of Australia	McKinley reelected President with Theodore Roosevelt as Vice-President
1901	Social Revolutionary Party founded in Russia	Theodore Roosevelt becomes President after McKinley is assassinated
1902		U.S. acquires perpetual control of Panama Canal
1903		Theodore Roosevelt settles Alaska boundary dispute
1904	Russo-Japanese War	Theodore Roosevelt elected President
1905	Norway separates from Sweden	Theodore Roosevelt wins Nobel Peace Prize for negotiating treaty between Russia and Japan
1912	Balkan wars	Woodrow Wilson elected President

	WORLD EVENTS	U.S. EVENTS
1913	Suffragettes become active in London	Federal Reserve System is established
1914	Beginning of World War I in Europe	Wilson issues proclamation of neutrality in response to European wars; establishment of Federal Trade Commission
1915	German submarine sinks British passenger ship *Lusitania*	Wilson sends strong protest to Germany after Americans are killed on *Lusitania*
1917	China enters World War I	Congress, under President Wilson's leadership, declares war on Germany
1918	Germany surrenders; armistice between Allies and Germany; execution of Russian royal family	Wilson proposes Fourteen Points for world peace
1919	Treaty of Versailles signed at Paris Peace Conference; Red Army begins to overtake White Army in Russian Revolution	Wilson leads American delegation to Paris Peace Conference and campaigns unsuccessfully for American membership in League of Nations; Wilson receives Nobel Peace Prize
1920	The Hague is seat of new International Court of Justice; end of Russian Revolution	Nineteenth Amendment gives women the right to vote
1928	Sixty-five nations sign Kellogg-Briand Pact to outlaw war	
1929		Stock market collapses and ushers in the Great Depression
1932		Franklin Delano Roosevelt wins his first presidential election
1933	Adolf Hitler becomes Chancellor of Germany	Roosevelt formulates New Deal for economic recovery
1936	Spanish Civil War; Hitler and Mussolini form alliance; China declares war on Japan	Roosevelt reelected
1938	Germany occupies Sudetenland	Roosevelt calls on Hitler and Mussolini to settle problems peacefully

WORLD EVENTS	U.S. EVENTS
1939 Germany invades Poland, and World War II begins	
1940	Roosevelt is first to serve third term as President
1941 Japan bombs Pearl Harbor	U.S. enters World War II
1943	Dwight D. Eisenhower named Supreme Commander of Allied Expeditionary Force to invade Western Europe
1944	Roosevelt reelected President with Harry S Truman as Vice-President; Eisenhower commands Allied invasion of France on June 6 (D-Day)
1945 Germany surrenders; Japan surrenders after atomic bombings	President Roosevelt dies, and Truman assumes office; Truman authorizes first use of atom bomb to be dropped on Japan
1947	George C. Marshall, Secretary of State, develops European Recovery Program (Marshall Plan); Congress passes Taft-Hartley Act
1948 Creation of Israel	Truman wins presidential election
1949	Formation of North Atlantic Treaty Organization (NATO)
1950 Korean War	Eisenhower named Supreme Commander of NATO
1952 Elizabeth II becomes Queen of England	Eisenhower elected President with Richard M. Nixon as Vice-President
1953 Korean armistice	Earl Warren becomes Chief Justice of Supreme Court; George C. Marshall wins Nobel Peace Prize
1956 U.S.S.R. occupies Hungary	Eisenhower and Nixon reelected
1960	John F. Kennedy defeats Nixon in presidential election

	WORLD EVENTS	U.S. EVENTS
1962		U.S. establishes military council in South Vietnam
1963		Assassination of President Kennedy; Lyndon B. Johnson becomes President
1964		Intensification of U.S. military involvement in South Vietnam
1967	Six-Day War between Israel and Arab nations	Thurgood Marshall becomes first black Supreme Court Justice
1968	U.S.S.R. invades Czechoslovakia	Nixon elected President
1971		Twenty-sixth Amendment lowers voting age to eighteen
1972		Nixon visits China, is reelected President
1973	Cease-fire agreement reached in Vietnam	Watergate scandals compromise Nixon; Congressional investigations uncover criminal acts by Nixon administration
1974		Impending impeachment proceedings prompt Nixon to resign as President

Bibliography

The basic tool for any research into the lives of important figures from this country's past is the great *Dictionary of American Biography,* published by Charles Scribner's Sons starting in 1928. Its twenty-seven volumes provide full and reliable summaries of the careers of thousands of individuals—the longest article, fittingly on George Washington, fills eighteen large pages. So the DAB's entries, written by outstanding scholars, were our starting point in assembling facts for most of the profiles included in this book.

But the DAB, composed mainly in the days before the contributions of women were much heeded by male authorities, does not give females sufficient attention. The newer biographical dictionary *Notable American Women,* issued by the Belknap Press of Harvard University Press beginning in 1971 was, therefore, very helpful to us, too.

Similarly, for our chapters on contemporary men and women or figures from the recent past whose careers have not yet been covered in the supplements that the DAB and *Notable American Women* put out periodically, we sought birth dates and the like from such publications as *The New York Times* and *Current Biography,* issued regularly by the H. W. Wilson Company of New York.

Beyond mere factual details, though, to distill the special flavor of the lives we wanted to write about we consulted so many memoirs and other biographical works that it would be unwieldy to list them all. Instead, here are just those we found most useful for each of our chapters:

Part I: The Founding Fathers

JOHN ADAMS

Adams, James Truslow. *The Adams Family.* Boston: Little, Brown & Co., 1930.

Bowen, Catherine Drinker. *John Adams and the American Revolution.* Boston: Little, Brown & Co., 1950.

Shepard, Jack. *The Adams Chronicles.* Boston: Little, Brown & Co., 1975.

BENJAMIN FRANKLIN

Franklin, Benjamin. *The Autobiography of Benjamin Franklin*. New York: Modern Library, 1944.

Lopez, Claude-Anne, and Eugenia Herbert. *The Private Franklin*. New York: W.W. Norton & Co., 1975.

Van Doren, Carl. *Benjamin Franklin*. New York: Viking Press, 1938.

ALBERT GALLATIN

Adams, Henry. *The Life of Albert Gallatin*. Philadelphia: J.B. Lippincott & Co., 1880.

ALEXANDER HAMILTON

Flexner, James Thomas. *The Young Hamilton*. Boston: Little, Brown & Co., 1978.

Loth, David. *Alexander Hamilton: Portrait of a Prodigy*. New York: Carrick & Evans, 1939.

McDonald, Forrest. *Alexander Hamilton*. New York: W.W. Norton & Co., 1979.

THOMAS JEFFERSON

Bowers, Claude G. *The Young Jefferson*. Boston: Houghton Mifflin Co., 1945.

Schachner, Nathan. *Thomas Jefferson*. New York: Thomas Yoseloff, 1957.

Smith, Page. *Jefferson*. New York: American Heritage Publishing Co., 1976.

JAMES MADISON

Anthony, Katharine. *Dolley Madison*. Garden City: Doubleday & Co., 1949.

Gay, Sydney Howard. *James Madison*. Boston: Houghton Mifflin Co., 1889.

Moore, Virginia. *The Madisons*. New York: McGraw-Hill Book Co., 1979.

JOHN MARSHALL

Magruder, Allan B. *John Marshall*. Boston: Houghton Mifflin Co., 1885.

JAMES MONROE

Styron, Arthur. *The Last of the Cocked Hats*. Norman: University of Oklahoma Press, 1945.

GEORGE WASHINGTON

Alden, John R. *George Washington*. Baton Rouge: Louisiana State University Press, 1984.

Flexner, James Thomas. *George Washington: The Forge of Experience*. Boston: Little, Brown & Co., 1965.

———. *Washington: The Indispensable Man*. Boston: Little Brown & Co., 1984.

Freeman, Douglas Southall. *George Washington*. 7 vols. New York: Charles Scribner's Sons, 1948–1957.

Part II: The Early Days of the Republic

JOHN QUINCY ADAMS

Adams, James Truslow. *The Adams Family*. Boston: Little, Brown & Co., 1930.

Shepard, Jack. *The Adams Chronicles*. Boston: Little, Brown & Co., 1975.

JOHN CALHOUN

Coit, Margaret L. *John C. Calhoun*. Boston: Houghton Mifflin Co., 1950.

Wiltse, Charles M. *John C. Calhoun*. 3 vols. New York: Russell & Russell, 1944–1951.

HENRY CLAY

Schurz, Carl. *The Life of Henry Clay*. 2 vols. Boston: Houghton Mifflin Co., 1887.

SAM HOUSTON

Houston, Sam. *The Autobiography of Sam Houston*. Edited by Donald Day and Harry H. Ullom. Norman: University of Oklahoma Press, 1954.

James, Marquis. *The Raven*. Indianapolis, Ind.: Bobbs-Merrill Co., 1929.

ANDREW JACKSON

James, Marquis. *Andrew Jackson: The Border Captain*. New York: Literary Guild, 1933.

———. *Andrew Jackson: Portrait of a President*. Indianapolis, Ind.: Bobbs-Merrill Co., 1937.

JAMES POLK

McCormac, Eugene Irving. *James K. Polk: A Political Biography*. New York: Russell & Russell, 1922.

DANIEL WEBSTER

Bartlett, Irving H. *Daniel Webster*. New York: W.W. Norton & Co., 1978.

Part III: The Civil War through the First World War

WILLIAM JENNINGS BRYAN

Cherny, Robert W. *A Righteous Cause: The Life of William Jennings Bryan*. Boston: Little, Brown & Co., 1985.

JEFFERSON DAVIS

Strode, Hudson. *Jefferson Davis*. 3 vols. New York: Harcourt, Brace & Co., 1955.

ROBERT LAFOLLETTE

Greenbaum, Fred. *Robert Marion LaFollette*. Boston: Twayne Publishers, 1975.

ABRAHAM LINCOLN

Hertz, Emanuel. *The Hidden Lincoln*. New York: Viking Press, 1938.

Sandburg, Carl. *Abraham Lincoln*. 4 vols. New York: Harcourt, Brace & Co., 1939.

Thomas, Benjamin. *Abraham Lincoln*. New York: Alfred A. Knopf, 1939.

JUSTIN MORRILL

Parker, William Belmont. *The Life and Public Services of Justin Smith Morrill*. Boston: Houghton Mifflin Co., 1924.

JEANNETTE RANKIN

Jeannette Rankin: Activist of World Peace, Women's Rights and Democratic Government. Oral History Project, Bancroft Library. Berkeley: University of California, 1974.

THEODORE ROOSEVELT

Hagedorn, Hermann. *The Roosevelt Family of Sagamore Hill*. New York: Macmillan Co., 1954.

Morris, Edmund. *The Rise of Theodore Roosevelt*. New York: Coward, McCann & Geoghegan, 1979.

Putnam, Carleton. *Theodore Roosevelt*. New York: Charles Scribner's Sons, 1958.

WOODROW WILSON

Daniels, Josephus. *The Wilson Era*. Chapel Hill: University of North Carolina Press, 1944.

Link, Arthur S. *Woodrow Wilson*. Chicago: Quadrangle Books, 1963.

Smith, Gene. *When the Cheering Stopped*. New York: William Morrow & Co., 1964.

Part IV: Modern Times

DWIGHT EISENHOWER

Davis, Kenneth S. *Soldier of Democracy*. Garden City: Doubleday, Doran, 1945.

Eisenhower, Dwight D. *The White House Years*. Garden City: Doubleday & Co., 1963.

———. *At Ease: Stories I Tell to Friends*. Garden City: Doubleday & Co., 1967.

OLIVER WENDELL HOLMES

Bowen, Catherine Drinker. *Yankee from Olympus: Justice Holmes and His Family*. Boston: Little, Brown & Co., 1944.

GEORGE MARSHALL

Faber, Harold. *Soldier and Statesman*. New York: Farrar, Straus & Co., 1964.

Pogue, Forrest C. *George C. Marshall*. 4 vols. New York: Viking Press, 1963–1987.

THURGOOD MARSHALL

"High Court Appointee." *The New York Times*, June 14, 1967.

"Mr. Justice Marshall." *Newsweek*, June 26, 1967.

RICHARD NIXON

Mazo, Earl. *Richard Nixon: A Personal and Political Portrait*. New York: Harper & Brothers, 1959.

Nixon, Richard M. *Six Crises*. Garden City: Doubleday & Co., 1962.

_____. *Memoirs of Richard M. Nixon*. New York: Grosset & Dunlap, 1978.

GEORGE NORRIS

Neuberger, Richard L., and Stephen B. Kahn. *Integrity: The Life of George W. Norris*. New York: Vanguard Press, 1937.

Norris, George W. *Fighting Liberal: The Autobiography of George W. Norris*. New York: Macmillan Co., 1945.

ELEANOR ROOSEVELT

Lash, Joseph P. *Eleanor and Franklin*. New York: W.W. Norton & Co., 1971.

_____. *Eleanor: The Years Alone*. New York: W.W. Norton & Co., 1972.

Roosevelt, Eleanor. *This Is My Story*. New York: Harper & Brothers, 1937.

_____. *This I Remember*. New York: Harper & Brothers, 1949.

FRANKLIN ROOSEVELT

Burns, James MacGregor. *Roosevelt: The Soldier of Freedom*. New York: Harcourt Brace Jovanovich, 1970.

Schlesinger, Arthur M., Jr. *The Age of Roosevelt: The Crisis of the Old Order*. Boston: Houghton Mifflin Co., 1957.

_____. *The Age of Roosevelt: The Coming of the New Deal*. Boston: Houghton Mifflin Co., 1959.

MARGARET CHASE SMITH

Cheshire, Maxine. "What Is Maggie Smith Up To?" *Saturday Evening Post*, April 18, 1964.

Rice, Berkeley. "Is the Great Lady from Maine Out of Touch?" *The New York Times Magazine*, June 11, 1972.

ROBERT TAFT

Patterson, James T. *Mr. Republican: A Biography of Robert A. Taft*. Boston: Houghton Mifflin Co., 1972.

HARRY TRUMAN

Truman, Harry. *Memoirs*. 2 vols. Garden City: Doubleday & Co., 1955–1956.

Truman, Margaret. *Harry Truman*. New York: William Morrow & Co., 1973.

EARL WARREN

Pollack, Jack. *Earl Warren: The Judge Who Changed America*. Englewood Cliffs, N.J.: Prentice-Hall, 1979.

Schwartz, Bernard. *Super Chief: Earl Warren and His Supreme Court*. New York: New York University Press, 1983.

Index